Temptation at Twilight

LORDS OF PLEASURE

JO CARLISLE

HEAT

HEAT

Published by New American Library,
a division of Penguin Group (USA) Inc.,
375 Hudson Street, New York, New York 10014, USA
Penguin Group (Canada), 90 Eglinton Avenue East, Suite 700, Toronto,
Ontario M4P 2Y3, Canada (a division of Pearson Penguin Canada Inc.)
Penguin Books Ltd., 80 Strand, London WC2R 0RL, England
Penguin Ireland, 25 St. Stephen's Green, Dublin 2,
Ireland (a division of Penguin Books Ltd.)
Penguin Group (Australia), 250 Camberwell Road, Camberwell,
Victoria 3124, Australia (a division of Pearson Australia Group Pty. Ltd.)
Penguin Books India Pvt. Ltd., 11 Community Centre,
Panchsheel Park, New Delhi - 110 017, India
Penguin Group (NZ), 67 Apollo Drive, Rosedale, Auckland 0632,
New Zealand (a division of Pearson New Zealand Ltd.)
Penguin Books (South Africa) (Pty.) Ltd., 24 Sturdee Avenue,
Rosebank, Johannesburg 2196, South Africa

Penguin Books Ltd., Registered Offices:
80 Strand, London WC2R 0RL, England

First published by Heat, an imprint of New American Library,
a division of Penguin Group (USA) Inc.

First Printing, November 2011
1   3   5   7   9   10   8   6   4   2

Copyright © Jo Carlisle, 2011
All rights reserved

HEAT is a trademark of Penguin Group (USA) Inc.

LIBRARY OF CONGRESS CATALOGING-IN-PUBLICATION DATA:
Carlisle, Jo.
Temptation at twilight: lords of pleasure/Jo Carlisle.
p. cm.
ISBN 978-0-451-23482-7 (pbk.)
1. Vampires—Fiction.   2. Brothers—Fiction.   3. New Orleans (La.)—Fiction.   I. Title.
PS3603. A7526T46 2011
813'.6—dc22   2011026919

Printed in the United States of America

To my family and dear friends,
who got me through a really rough year.
You know who you are, and I cherish you all.

ACKNOWLEDGMENTS

As always, my special thanks to:

My family, for putting up with my mad deadlines and takeout for dinner.

My agent and friend, Roberta Brown, for your unwavering support.

My editor, Tracy Bernstein, for making my work shine and my job easier.

My publicist, the art department, and the rest of the team at NAL for being the finest people to work with anywhere.

And the readers, for making what I do such a joy. You inspire me.

Temptation at Twilight

1

Above nearly all else, Soren Fontaine loved playing with his food.

This particular feast rode his cock with enthusiasm, a fall of blond hair framing full, bouncing breasts tipped with pert, rosy nipples. His fingers dug into the soft globes of the woman's ass, and he hissed with pleasure as she sank onto his slick rod again and again, her cries getting louder with every thrust.

Snug heat surrounded him, massaged his length as his breaths shortened. Too soon the wonderful bliss became fire that spread through his belly, balls, and thighs. So close.

Along with the impending orgasm, hunger rose swiftly, demanding the ultimate completion to assuage the predator within. Sitting up, he pushed her hair aside, exposing the pale skin of her neck, where he immediately fixated on the pulse of life flowing there. His tongue flicked out, tasting salt and desire, a hint of the nectar too sweet to resist.

He struck, sinking his fangs deep into her throat. Hot blood splashed over his tongue, more potent than his most expensive liquor and ten times as satisfying. *Gods.* He was lost in ecstasy, barely aware of her pussy spasming around his cock, fingers clutching, pulling his long hair, urging him on. To take more.

Take it all.

Shit, he longed to do just that. Tear into the delicate throat, drink until her heartbeat faded to silence and both his body and thirst were sated. Until he'd taken every drop, was drenched in sweat, blood, and cum.

Vampires were killers by nature. Creatures of seduction and death. Perfect predators.

But he'd learned restraint since those early blood-and-sex-soaked days nearly three centuries past.

Now he unleashed the full deadly nature of his beast only on those who deserved it.

"Oh, fuck, yes!" Trisha cried, gyrating on his lap. "Master!"

Master. That word sent him over the edge, his release exploding in a blinding flash of white. He filled her, gradually coming down from the incredible high that never got old, the haze of passion lifting. Carefully, he removed his fangs and licked her neck to seal the small wounds. The tiny scars would join the others, marking her as one of the coven's Chosen—a willing human selected to live permanently at La Petite Mort, serving Soren and his brothers exclusively, tending to their bodies' needs.

"Thank you, *ma chère,*" he said softly, kissing the top of Trisha's shiny head. Exhausted, she slumped against his chest, head on his shoulder.

"My pleasure as always, Lord Soren." Her voice was barely a whisper.

Lips curving in fondness, he eased her off his lap and

situated her in the center of his huge bed, then tucked the covers around her shapely form. "Sleep, *petite*. You've earned the rest."

"Yes, master." She was asleep almost instantly.

Moving quietly, he retrieved fresh clothing from the walk-in closet and stepped into the bathroom, closing the door so as not to disturb the slumbering Chosen. Trisha was one of his favorites. As he turned on the shower, he thought once again of how much she resembled Helena lying there, tired out from his attentions.

Helena, his one true mate, human and therefore fragile. Dead and gone. But perhaps not lost forever.

The warm glow of great sex and good feeding dissipated like the steam rising from the shower. How simple it would be if he could take Trisha, or another of the Chosen, as his mate. Any one of them would make a fine companion to change into one of his kind and ease the loneliness of existing forever without someone special to share his burdens and joys.

If only he could accept someone other than his gentle, beautiful Helena.

But he couldn't bring himself to mate with another. If it meant a bargain with the devil himself, he'd bring his love back to his side. No matter the price. He *would*.

The pain of Helena's loss hit him fresh, and he shoved down the debilitating sorrow with effort. Tonight, after more than a century of fruitless searching, he'd have an answer to the question of how to bring her back. *Sure, you've said that many times before.*

But the thought of defeat was unacceptable.

Dressed in a pair of jeans and a black T-shirt, he slipped out of his quarters and went in search of his brothers. Aldric was nowhere to be seen, but in the library, Soren found Luc. The resort's resident golden boy was sprawled on the sofa with his nose stuck in a book, no doubt the latest crime thriller. Soren was always amazed that his hyperactive sibling could settle long enough to get into the story.

"Don't you have anything better to do?" Soren asked, leaning against the doorframe.

"Not really." Luc didn't look up.

"Where's Aldric?"

A shrug. "How should I know?"

"You haven't seen him at all?"

"Hmm . . ." He shifted to get more comfortable and flipped a page. "Nope."

Soren fielded a surge of annoyance. Little brothers never changed, whether they were twenty-three years old or four hundred. And this one existed to drive him and Aldric out of their minds on a regular basis.

"He *did* return from the meeting with the Council, didn't he?"

"Got no idea."

"Satan's balls, Luc! Put that down while I'm talking to you." Pushing away from the door, Soren walked into the room and stood glaring at his brother.

"Right at the good part," Luc grumbled. With a false put-upon scowl, he lowered the book and laid it on his chest. "Happy?"

"I'll be happy when—"

"Yes, I know. You're going out to stir up the priestesses again, right?" Soren's silence was answer enough. His brother was no longer faking his irritation as he sat up, swung his feet to the floor, and set his book on the coffee table. "You won't be satisfied until you've run us all into the ground, looking for a solution that doesn't exist, and pissed off every witch in the Southern

Coalition on top of that. Helena is *dead*, brother, has been for a long time, and nothing is going to bring her back."

Pain stabbed his gut, the words more agonizing than his earlier recollections of the woman he loved. Even more so than her loss. He stared at Luc, unwilling to examine why. A tiny inner voice spoke up anyway, whispering that perhaps the quest itself had become more of an obsession than the reason for it, and he ruthlessly quashed the idea.

"I've never forced either of you to tag along," he snapped. "Stay here if you want. I really don't care."

Spinning around, Soren stalked out, ignoring his brother's muttered curse. Whether Luc agreed with his actions or not, the kid would follow. He always did, if for no reason other than not wanting to be left out of any adventures—even the useless ones. When he heard Luc's boots thudding on the tile behind him, Soren stifled a grim smile.

His brother remained silent until they were in the back of their limo. "Who's on your list tonight?"

Luc's curiosity was spurred in spite of himself, just as Soren thought. Soren took his time in answering, knowing part of this night's agenda would meet with even more disapproval than the seemingly futile endeavor itself.

"Two priestesses who live in New Orleans proper. They are both descendants of powerful witches I consulted when Helena . . . was killed." Such an understatement for the brutality of his mate's death. He swallowed the lump that threatened to strangle him.

"If neither of them was able to help you bring back Helena," Luc pointed out reasonably, "I doubt their descendants have the power, abilities being passed down as they are."

He restrained a surge of temper. Barely. "True. But I have to try. And if they can't . . ."

Soren paused a couple of beats too long. Luc arched a blond brow, waiting. "There is another. She lives deep in the swamp. I have a boat ready to take us there."

"She who?"

Soren held his gaze, unflinching. "Leila Doucet."

Luc's mouth fell open and his eyes widened in disbelief. "God's blood! What the fuck is going on in your head to even think of putting yourself—all of us—on the radar of that hell-spawn? Do you know how much trouble Aldric's had in blocking that bitch from grabbing a seat on the Council?"

"Yes, but—"

"And you know she'd do anything to obtain that seat, right?"

"I know, but—"

"And you also know that if you give a venomous snake like her any opening at all, she'll slither right inside and wait for the opportune moment to deliver her deadly bite in order to gain what she wants! The things she's done—"

"Been *accused* of doing," Soren corrected. "None have been proven."

Luc snorted. "Tell that to the poor bastard she fucked to death. The man was Fae, brother. She left him a dried husk, drained of his magic and his life! No normal witch should've been able to do that!"

"Normal witch? Isn't that an oxymoron?"

"Don't mock me." Cool blue eyes narrowed.

"Sorry. I didn't mean to. Just trying to infuse some levity." *And failing.* "Anyway, the Council hasn't proved she's the one who drained him," he repeated. "She freely admitted they had sex and claimed he was fine, not to mention thoroughly satisfied, when she left him that night."

"What else was she going to say when facing swift execution?" his brother parried incredulously.

"I'm not blind to her questionable character, all right? But if neither of the two in the city can help me, Doucet's my last resort." In this century or any other, because he didn't know whether he could take the disappointment any longer. Yet the thought of giving up twisted his guts once again.

"She's wicked, Soren. You'd place us all in danger for the merest hint of hope from a user like her," Luc said softly. It wasn't a question.

Impasse. Despite Luc's adventurous spirit, he and Soren would never agree on this point. Falling silent, Soren looked out the tinted window of the car at the night. Absently, he noted an old truck parked on the opposite side of the road as the limo approached, obviously broken down. He didn't see a driver inside, but it was difficult to tell from his position in the car, not to mention in the blackness that cloaked the swamp at this hour. Then the limo passed, and he brushed aside a tinge of guilt for not ordering their driver to stop. Immediately, he was again immersed in his own misery.

Never had he felt so isolated. So lonely. When even Luc argued against the wisdom of his actions, perhaps it *was* time to quit. No matter how much it hurt.

After tonight, I will.

But I have to try just once more.

Harley Vaughn waited until the sleek black limo had passed, traveling in the direction from which she'd come—what the hell was a fancy car like that doing out here in the boonies, anyway?—then got out of her ancient pickup truck, slammed the driver's door, and stalked to the front.

"Thanks for the assistance," she muttered, giving the retreating taillights a glare. Huffing in annoyance, she crouched, turning the evil eye to the flat tire as though her anger alone would be enough to reinflate the damned thing.

"Shit!"

Just great. Stuck in Creepsville at night with a broken-down piece of crap and no spare tire. Snakes and gators would be the least of her worries if she didn't get moving, quick, and find someone to help with the tire. Maybe there would be a house or a gas station down the road. Standing, she wiped her hands on her worn jeans and listened intently. Soft peeps, croaks, and blurps drifted in the heat, and some of the tension eased from her shoulders. Those were good, normal sounds. It was the absence of them that counted, when all went deathly still and the smaller, more vulnerable creatures cowered in fear. Then a body had better be on alert.

Not that she was helpless and quivering in terror. Simply cautious. Humans had occupied the bottom of society's hierarchy since the Great War had decimated the planet, making way for the global rise of vampires, demons, Fae, and shifters, and the formation of the Ruling Council, which was now divided into several territorial coalitions. The fallout was a history lesson older than time—the weaker beings succumbed to the more powerful and existed to serve their desires.

Slavery had become commonplace in the decades that followed, mostly due to the economy, and was largely voluntary. In recent years, there had been no shortage of humans and other creatures who were down on their luck and in need of work.

A place to belong. To survive. That meant signing over their lives and security in exchange for the pleasure of their masters.

Others sought the auction block to fulfill their fantasy of being owned and used by an insatiable, immortal master. A vampire or demon lord or a Fae royal were the masters of choice, though one wasn't guaranteed his or her preference. Uncertainty, of course, was part of the thrill. Several people whom Harley had known, both friends and mere acquaintances, had fallen prey to their own dark desires, had freely given their bodies and souls to experience the ultimate erotic highs—providing blood and sex to their masters in a variety of kinky and sometimes lethal ways.

A select few even died while screaming in ecstasy as they came.

So she'd heard.

Despite the sweltering night, Harley shivered, rubbed her arms, and began to walk. Her nipples had stiffened to poke at her thin blouse, and she told herself it was just the illicit direction of her thoughts. A natural reaction, that was all. She absolutely was not titillated, not the *least* bit interested, in becoming a predator's plaything, the mouse to his hungry cat.

Was *not*. Especially after the dismal outcome of her first attempt.

Warmth chased away the chill, especially between her thighs, and she sighed. Okay, so she was a lousy liar. There was a certain erotic mystique to the idea of granting an immortal complete control over her body, knowing that once she did, she was his to do with whatever he wished. But that didn't mean she'd ever be stupid enough to follow through again, no matter that *she* was one of those folks fallen upon hard times.

The darkness pressed in around her and she picked up her pace, scanning the impenetrable gloom on either side of the road. She was still much too far from New Orleans proper. She'd be lucky to make the outskirts of the city before nightfall. *Damn that limo driver for not stopping to help!* Again she wondered why the car had been heading away from the city rather than into it.

Suddenly, she became aware of the total, complete stillness. A heaviness in the air that had nothing to do with the temperature. Her steps faltered and stopped, and she listened. Her heart jack-hammered in her chest and the blood rushed in her ears. The night creatures were hiding, and not because of Harley's unthreatening presence. Which meant she'd better do the same, and fast. Whirling, she looked behind her, trying in vain to see how far she'd walked from the broken-down truck. She'd run back, lock the doors, and take refuge there until morning.

What I should've done in the first place. Idiot!

The sense of something out there, stalking, prickled her skin, and she ran—

Straight into a solid black wall. She bounced back with a screech, head snapping up as two hands grabbed her shoulders, long, cold fingers digging in painfully. Gasping, she peered into her captor's face and her stomach lurched at the glowing red eyes set in a sharply angled face, brutally beautiful as only his kind could be.

"Let go of me, demon," she cried, jerking futilely in his hold.

A deep rumble of amusement sounded in his broad chest. "A spitting cat. Why, those are the best kind. So much more fun than the ones that simply die of fright. Wouldn't you say, Zenon?"

Harley froze. *Two of them!*

"Great Hades, Valafar! You always snare the best ones, you bastard," the second demon declared in admiration, sidling close. "Tell me we're not selling this one right away."

Blinking, she cleared her throat and interrupted, trying a friendly approach. "Um, it's great to meet you both, especially now, since my stupid truck has a flat. If you'd just give me a lift into the city, I'd be grateful."

The pair exchanged a glance before the second one, Zenon, spoke up. "Did you hear that, Val? She'll be *grateful*."

"*How* grateful is the question," Val mused, pulling her flush against his hard body. And, boy, was every inch of him solid as a rock, including the ten inches or so pressing against her tummy. The demons exchanged a knowing glance.

Harley looked between them but couldn't see the nuances in their expressions very well in the dark. But it didn't take a genius to figure out she'd landed right in the frying pan.

She just hoped that didn't mean literally.

The few demons of her acquaintance rarely did favors, and never without expecting the moon in return. She had nothing to bargain with except herself, and she'd be damned lucky if they ever let her go. They weren't to be trusted, but what choice did she have? It wasn't like she could escape.

And that shouldn't give her the tiniest of perverse thrills—but it did.

Licking her lips, she said, "I'm sure we can reach an understanding."

Val dipped a claw into the V of her blouse and sliced downward, neatly shearing the material in half all the way to the hem. "I'm positive you're correct."

"Hey! That's my last good shirt!"

"Where you're going, sweet, you won't need clothing," he said softly.

Her pulse quickened and she found herself leaning toward him. *Mmm, they both smell so good.* Earthy and masculine. Totally the opposite of what she would've thought, but then again, their kind were masters of seduction.

"Let's go before someone else gets wind of her and makes a challenge for our prize," Zenon urged.

"As if they could best us."

"Of course not. But who needs the trouble?"

"Good point. Hold on, gorgeous." Turning Harley so that her back was against his front, Val wrapped an arm around her middle. She had about a half second to realize what he was going to do. And then the demon launched into the air with a great flap of his wings.

Her scream was cut short by the pressure of his muscular arm holding her tight, squeezing her diaphragm like a vise as he ascended rapidly. As the earth fell away, she could do nothing but hang there and cling to his arm, praying he didn't lose his grip. In this dizzying position, she could see lights clustered in a spectacular display in the center of the city, fanning out to become sparser in the outlying areas.

It was a bird's-eye view she never wanted to have again.

More terrified of heights than of the demons themselves, she screwed her eyes shut and desperately hoped they'd soon reach their destination. Whatever lay in store couldn't be nearly as awful as the thought of falling thousands of feet to splatter on the ground.

Or so she told herself, right up until Val descended a few minutes later, bringing them to an easy landing in the middle of several buildings. *Homes,* she corrected herself, looking around. Modest and sort of plain but nice, they were laid out in a neat circular pattern with interconnecting sidewalks and a larger home in the center of the arrangement.

"You guys live here, in this . . ." She faltered, not knowing what to call the place.

"Clan compound," Zenon supplied. "You were expecting a dirty cave or a hovel in the swamp?"

"Well, no," she lied, and then blushed at Val's arch look. "Okay, maybe. But only because the demons in St. Louis, where I'm from, live in the cave system and aren't exactly winning awards for neighbor of the year."

"Didn't one of them go on a rampage and eat a bunch of innocent people a few months back?" Zenon frowned. "Uncivilized bastards."

"Yeah. I've never eaten anyone who didn't deserve it," Val quipped with a wink at her.

Harley stifled a shaky laugh, hoping he was kidding. In spite of her earlier fear, she was starting to like these two. They seemed okay for demons. "So, which house is yours? Do you two live together? I'm your captive, right? The deal was for you to take me into the city, you know."

Val grinned, his teeth white and sharp in the darkness. "Satan's balls, you ask a lot of questions. This house is mine." He gestured, indicating the front porch of the dwelling closest to them. "No, we don't live together, because Zenon and I are not mates, and only the mates of our kind cohabitate well. Yes, you're my captive, and I will take you into the city. But I never said *when*. After you."

Val waved a hand at the front door and it swung open,

manipulated by his magic. Harley mounted the steps and entered the foyer, squashing a spurt of self-recrimination at her predicament. After all, it wasn't her fault she'd lost her job and her apartment, forcing her to throw her meager belongings in the truck and hit the road, only to have the piece of crap break down in the middle of Bumfuck—where she was accosted by two demons.

Sexy demons. She turned as they trailed her inside, getting her first clear look at them in the lit interior of the house. Neither was wearing a shirt—not surprising because of the wings—but both wore snug jeans. Val was tall, broad shouldered, and ripped with muscles. Black hair brushed his shoulders and framed an angular face dominated by dark eyes that no longer glowed red and a grin that showed off a set of large fangs. A huge pair of black wings were settled against his back, the beautiful, shiny feathers just grazing the floor.

Beside him, Zenon wasn't as tall or broad, but was still every bit as impressive, with similar wings and sharp fangs. His dark blond hair was shaggy and layered and just shy of touching his shoulders, and his almost-pretty face was accented by lovely blue eyes that held a glint of good humor. If it weren't for the feathers and canines, she'd think him an angel rather than a demon.

"See something you like?" Zenon asked her, smirking.

"I know *I* do." His friend's hungry gaze was fixed on her ruined blouse.

Belatedly, she remembered he'd reduced it to little more than a scrap. Glancing down at herself, she hastily grabbed the torn halves and pulled them together, not that it made any difference. They'd already seen the goods up top, and from their expressions, they were eager to unveil a whole lot more.

"So, what happens now?" she demanded with false bravado. "If you think I'm going to make it easy for—Mmmph!"

Okay, never mind. Why bother to protest when domination was what she craved?

Faster than she could blink, Val's mouth was eating hers, his hot tongue slipping inside to lick and explore. Her hands came up to skim over his smooth chest and brushed a nipple, which instantly perked under her touch. He groaned and broke the kiss, dragging her into a spacious sitting area and seating her on the sofa. Standing over her, he spread his legs and gazed down, and his lips quirked upward as though he could read her thoughts. Maybe he could.

This dominant position thrilled her more than was wise, as did the big bulge behind his zipper that was inches from her nose. Tentatively, she reached out for the button at his waist, then hesitated.

"Go ahead," he said in a low, sensuous voice. "Release me."

Trying not to appear too eager, she worked at the button and lowered the zipper, but her hands shook, giving away her nerves. She parted the denim and eased him out, noting that she'd guessed right—his cock was at least ten mouthwatering inches, thick and blue-veined, heavy balls hanging resplendent underneath. She couldn't wait to get a taste.

Wrapping her fingers around the base, she stroked upward, relishing the silky feel of him. Hard yet smooth. Hot, almost feverish. Slowly she pumped him, smiling a little as he pushed his hips forward with a curse, seeking more.

A pearly drop oozed through the slit in the bulbous head, and she flicked it with her tongue. *So good.* Both salty and sweet, his essence could become addictive. She deep-throated him, taking in as much of his huge rod as possible, barely aware of Zenon nearby, hurriedly stripping off his jeans. His friend could wait. At the moment, she wanted all she could get of this yummy treat. One of his hands fisted in her hair firmly but not enough to hurt as he fucked her mouth with long strokes, groaning in pleasure. When she began to manipulate his balls, he sucked in a sharp breath and pulled back.

"Enough, or this will be over much too soon. Undress for us, pretty one."

As Harley shimmied out of her ruined top and bra, she thought about his compliment. She was a practical woman when it came to her appeal, and while she wasn't hideous, neither was she anything special in a world that still valued stick-thin, blond, and waifish. Standing at five feet, eight inches tall and with a voluptuous figure, full lips, high cheekbones, long auburn hair, and green eyes, she wasn't anywhere near petite. And her looks, coupled with a matching outlook on life, were as bold as the vintage motorcycles her great-grandfather had favored.

She figured there wasn't any changing those things about herself, so why waste an opportunity with a pair of virile males who didn't find her lacking?

Wiggling out of her jeans, she ogled her captors, and her heart quickened. Because what was about to happen was more than the slaking of a thirst. No, it was *much* more. Somehow, she knew in her soul that tonight signaled a life change. Whether the change was for the better remained to be seen.

Once her jeans had been kicked aside, Val knelt between her knees and pushed her thighs wide. "My turn. Scoot to the edge."

She did, and he draped her legs over his shoulders, lowering his mouth to her sex. His tongue tickled her clit with exquisite torture, sending tiny sparks of delight to every nerve ending. She shivered as he laved her pussy and cupped her breasts to thumb the pert nipples, giving her every ounce of attention she'd lacked for so long. Moaning, she arched into him and buried her fingers in his long, dark hair. He drove her crazy with want, but when he lifted her ass and his wet tongue sought the rosebud of her back passage, she gasped.

She'd heard of rimming, but no one had ever done it to her before. Once the initial surprise had passed, she relaxed and gave herself over to the odd sensation that rapidly spread fire from her pussy to her limbs. She melted into a puddle of bliss. His to devour.

"Oh, gods . . ." Her fingers tightened in his hair, and she wanted to say more, to beg, but she couldn't find the words.

He knew what she wanted and laughed darkly. He licked and suckled, eating her ass like the seasoned pro he undoubtedly was. By the time he lifted his head and wiped his mouth, she writhed helplessly under him, almost insane with need.

"We're going to fuck you, pretty. Get on your hands and knees."

Doing as he ordered, she slid off the sofa onto the carpeted floor. Never had she felt so slutty—or so wonderful. Yeah, she should probably be more afraid of what a couple of demons would do with her after this, given the tainted reputation of their race, but caution succumbed to her adventurous spirit. Her desire to be owned.

"Look at her," Zenon praised. "What a gorgeous piece, ours for the taking."

Val's eyes flashed red. "Mmm. And we're going to ream her from both ends. Feed this hungry slave your cock, Zen."

"With pleasure."

The blond demon brought the head to her lips, and she opened like a baby bird. Suckled the spongy head and then swallowed him down, the length and girth every bit as daunting as Val's meat. Still, she managed a great deal of him, tonguing and sucking the interesting ridges in time with his slow thrusts.

From behind, Val moved in, knelt, and parted her folds. The head of his cock eased inside, worked in and out for a moment to spread her cream. Then he speared her in one forceful glide, making her cry out around Zen's length.

Gods, it was so fantastically naughty, being filled by two cocks. A pair of sexy males owning her body. Using her for their desires.

If she'd had any remaining doubts, now she fully understood why people sold themselves as sex slaves.

The demons established a rhythm, using her as their fuck hole. Sliding deep and withdrawing to pump her again and again, so wild and hot. How much more of this heaven could she take? Not much. Any second she'd explode.

They powered into her without mercy, her muffled squeals of delight exciting them. Their raw, musky scent of sex teased her nose and her pussy caught fire, her womb quickened—

And she went over the edge with a cry, senses shattering.

Her orgasm triggered the demons' and they stuffed themselves as deep as possible, gripping her tight. Hot cum spurted, filling her mouth and cunt. She swallowed as fast as she could, but some of Zen's jizz dribbled down her chin. When they were spent, each of them pulled out, petting her hair and sweaty back with such care that it surprised and pleased her. Replete, she wiped her chin and waited to see what came next.

"You did well, pretty," Val praised as he joined his friend in front of her. He stroked his rigid length, which showed no sign of tiring. "We're going to have such fun together . . . before we sell you on the auction block."

Stunned, she sat back on her heels and stared at the grinning duo.

And acknowledged the rush in her veins for what it was.

Dark, decadent excitement.

2

"Slumming, vampire lord?" a husky voice inquired in amusement. "I can't imagine what could possibly bring a fine man like you to my door."

If Soren possessed one shred of common sense, he'd have listened to his brother and steered clear of Leila Doucet. A touch of sarcasm in her tone hinted that she'd been expecting him. *Not good.* Beside him, Luc adopted a deceptively loose-limbed stance as Soren greeted the priestess.

"Miss Doucet," he said smoothly, taking her hand and briefly pressing his lips to the back of it. An old-fashioned gesture, but one that typically disarmed even the most jaded of women.

This was not a typical woman.

"Why do I get the feeling you already *know* the reason?"

The witch leaned against the doorjamb, a catlike smile curving her full lips as she eyed him from head to toe. She had alluring pale skin and long, dark hair flowing around her shoulders.

With her willowy body hugged by low-slung, slashed jeans and a minuscule halter top with no bra underneath to hide her pert breasts, she looked like she belonged in a biker bar. Or in his bed, wearing nothing but that naughty smile while his cock was buried in her pussy.

Unfortunately, if the rumors and accusations were true, the book didn't match the cover. He'd seen her in the city, hanging around the Council meetings that were open to the public, but studying her up close, actually speaking with her, provided a deeper perspective. There was no denying she was beautiful, but her lovely face was a cool mask, dark eyes flat and calculating, devoid of warmth. Absent of a soul.

Soren wondered if she had a dalmatian coat hidden in her closet.

"Come in if you want my help. Makes no difference to me."

With a smirk, she turned and disappeared into the modest cabin, leaving them to stare after her.

"Soren," Luc hissed, grabbing his upper arm. "Forget this and let's just get the fuck out of here."

"You know I can't do that." Firmly, he removed Luc's hand from his arm and shook his head. "Not if there's a chance."

"Priestess Benoit said getting Helena back wasn't *possible*," his brother reminded him, worry clouding his blue eyes. He ran a hand through his short, spiky blond hair in frustration. "Not the way you remember her, and not without paying a terrible price. You should heed the woman's warning. Dammit, I've got a bad feeling about this."

So did Soren. Still, if there was any way at all . . .

"Wait at the boat if you want. I'll be fine." Ducking inside, he left Luc to follow him—or not. A few strides took him directly into a modest living area that boasted a battered green sofa, worn chair, and tatty rugs. The room was dimly lit by a multitude of candles cluttering every available surface. Beaded curtains hung over the two entryways on either side of the room, and Soren headed toward the one that was still swinging, the small, colored orbs clattering together.

Footsteps thudded behind him, and he glanced over his shoulder to see Luc on his heels. Ever Soren's shadow. His staunchest ally, save Aldric, despite their differences. Suddenly Soren wished they'd waited for their big, badass older brother to accompany them.

A short hallway led to two rooms. One door was open and he picked that one, halting just inside to study their surroundings. This dark workroom was much the same as the others they'd seen, packed with bottles of unknown liquids, bowls, beads, dolls, cloth, large straight pins, and an assortment of various items he couldn't name. The priestess moved about a long table, comfortable in her element, placing a wide wooden bowl full of liquid in the center.

A rich, familiar scent touched Soren's nose, and a pang of hunger cramped his stomach as his mouth watered. *Blood.* Not human, and not his first choice. What the hell was she doing with a bowl of animal blood? And how had she acquired it? Whatever the answers, need pooled in his gut, throbbed in his groin.

Perching on a stool, she looked up and gestured to a pair of seats across the table. "Most people see me for love potions or spells. Occasionally a client will have me scry the future or spy on someone, or will even buy a spell or talisman that will allow him a tiny bit of revenge against the one who has it coming."

Frustration coupled with the rising need for food and sex made for poor companions at the bargaining table, and he fought to control them. "I'm not most people, as you know," he said shortly, taking his seat. "I'm not here for your cheap parlor tricks."

Her eyes flared and she laughed. "Oh yes. Nothing simple for you, I've heard. Bringing back the dead is difficult and costly business—if you can afford to pay."

So the bitch *did* know the exact reason for his visit. He gave a quiet, humorless laugh. "I can handle your price, whatever it might be. That is of no importance to me." Glancing at Luc, he caught his brother's grim expression and barely perceptible shake of his head. Thankfully, his sibling kept a lid on voicing more disapproval. For now.

Leaning forward, she rested her arms on the table, giving him a perfect view down her top to the swell of her small breasts. "*Any* price?"

"Name it."

The witch fell silent for a moment, studying him thought-fully. A long red fingernail tap-tapping on the surface of the table was the only sound in the room. Annoying, as well, which she probably knew. They regarded each other openly, two players across a macabre chessboard. Winner take all. "First, tell me about the one you wish to return."

"My mate's name was Helena," he said quietly. "She died more than one hundred years ago from wounds sustained in a demon attack. She passed before I could turn her. I want you to bring her back to me."

Saints, the pain of her loss was just as excruciating now as it was a century ago. He and his brothers had returned home to La

Petite Mort from a long Council session to find their lands ravaged, the servants and Chosen dead, and Helena lying helpless in his bed, weak from blood loss and consumed with sickness from the demon's bite. Crazed with grief upon her passing, he had almost fallen on his sword. Aldric had stopped him. Kept him in silver chains for days while Soren raged like a lunatic.

"A demon attack," she mused. "Unfortunate." Another lengthy silence as the witch stared at him. Then, "I don't know if I can help you."

And so the game begins.

"I thought you might possess the skills necessary to assist me." He started to rise. "Since I'm wasting my time—"

"I didn't say for certain that I couldn't," she countered. "Do you really want to throw away your last chance so easily?"

She was toying with him, and he couldn't fucking stand it. He longed to reach across the table and throttle her, but didn't dare. Slowly, he lowered his ass onto the stool again and willed himself to settle down. She had the advantage, and they all knew it.

"Name. Your. Price."

Pinning him with those fathomless eyes, the witch continued in a silky voice. "You said I could have anything at all. Remember?"

"Yes, but . . ." Dread squeezed his heart, and he fought to keep the emotion off his face. "That wasn't an open-ended offer of payment. Tell me what you want specifically."

Her smile was predatory. "Only what you promised— anything at all. So we'll *start* with you acquiring me a seat on the Council."

Mercenary bitch! He should have known it wouldn't be as simple as opening his wallet.

"Done."

"Soren," Luc said sharply. "You can't promise that. Only Aldric can, and he'll never agree."

"I can and I did," he replied grimly. "What else?"

"You'll take me back with you to live at La Petite Mort, where I'll reside in complete comfort, and you'll see that my every need or desire is satisfied." The heat in her gaze, the spicy scent of her arousal, left no doubt as to what those needs and desires entailed.

His cock hardened and he bit back a groan. That was a simple promise to make; Soren would enjoy fucking the witch. For all her gentleness, Helena had understood the dark needs of vampires, Soren and his brothers in particular. While she hadn't participated in the resort's debauchery and had no desire to do so, neither had she objected. She'd loved him just as the gods—or, rather, fate—had made him, had accepted the Chosen warming his bed during feedings, not to mention his duties as a host, which included making their guests' sexual fantasies come true.

Soren could enjoy the witch's luscious body *and* keep an eye on her more dubious activities—while having his heart's desire. It was a perfect solution.

"Also done," he said. "You'll return with us tonight."

"As your mate."

The softly spoken words froze the blood in his veins. Stunned, he stared at Leila as the implications washed over him. "What? You're fucking crazy!" he shouted, bolting to his feet. "No way in hell am I going to take you as my mate!"

"You did say you would give anything to have your Helena back." She shrugged. "But if you don't wish for her to be returned to the loving family fold, you may leave. No harm done."

Helpless fury nearly stole his speech. "The whole purpose of the bargain is to have my mate returned to me," he managed, fists clenched. "My *true* mate."

But as she smirked at him, he understood. Leila had her reasons, and she wasn't going to share them until it suited her.

"Brother," Luc cut in, laying a hand on Soren's shoulder. "No one can force a mating bond on a vampire, not even the most powerful witch or sorcerer, who are only humans with special abilities. Humans can't affect us that way. She knows this." He sent a glare in her direction for emphasis.

Again, the schemer didn't appear fazed in the least. "So? The only two parties who can sense the bond are the vampire in question and his 'mate.' When Soren introduces me as his mate, who's to say differently?"

Was she insane? "My *true mate* will know," Soren pointed out. "She might not recognize it at first, but eventually she'll figure out the truth and— Wait. You don't care. You just want to hurt her by flaunting our relationship in her face, right? If that's your game, I'm not playing."

"How shortsighted of you to believe I'd care about your lady love's feelings one way or the other. That's not what this is about."

No, it was about a power play for some higher purpose he'd learn in time. But he wasn't fooled into thinking she wouldn't enjoy every second of the havoc she'd cause along the way.

A realization hit him: backing out of their bargain wasn't an option. He had to pretend to be Leila's mate, find out what the witch was after—beyond gaining a Council seat and a cushy life at the resort as his mate—and stop her cold.

"How long would this arrangement between us be in effect? A few weeks? Months?"

Dark eyes glittered. "Why, as long as I wish—until I tire of you, of course."

His heart sank. That could be decades.

But wait—not forever, because Leila was human. Eventually, she'd grow old and die. So would his true love, of course, unless he turned her, which he would be sure to do this time. One day, he'd be free of Leila, their arrangement ended.

But waiting for the natural end of Leila's mortal life was a worst-case scenario. With any luck, he'd quickly learn what she was up to and bring it to the Council's attention. Then he wouldn't be bound to honor their bargain.

"I will not turn you," he stipulated. "Nor will you seek another vampire to do the deed in order to make yourself immortal."

"Agreed."

Far too easy. *What's your game, you bitch?*

Swallowing his anger, trepidation, and a great deal of pride, he nodded. "We have a bargain, then. You'll have your Council seat. While you live, you'll do so as my mate and enjoy every comfort I can provide."

"You will do my bidding."

"Yes," he rasped.

Luc cursed and pushed from the table. "I'll be outside." Shooting Soren a pissed-off glare, he stalked out.

Gods, how that grated. Soren bowed to no one, male or female. Ever. And he'd just sold his body and soul to the witch for the duration of her human lifetime.

For Helena. You can't forget that.

"Come here, my sexy vampire. You *did* just agree to give me whatever I wanted, and I want you. Now." Rising, she stepped away from the table and grasped the hem of her halter top. Slowly, she pulled the material up over her head and dropped it negligently to the floor. Her eyes locked with his. She cupped her breasts and rolled the dusky nipples between her fingers, teasing them to points.

Against his will he stood, skirted the table, and went to her. He didn't want any part of the witch, but his traitorous body disagreed. His nerve endings began to hum, and the familiar heat spread through his veins. His cock began to fill and his fangs lengthened in anticipation of the feast being unveiled before him.

Her hands moved downward, sliding over her taut belly to the button on her jeans. Deftly, she parted the denim and pushed it past her hips, revealing smooth, pale skin and a triangle of dark hair between toned thighs. She stepped out of the jeans and kicked them aside.

"Hungry?" Amusement colored her husky voice. "I've got what you crave, vampire lord. Come here."

Fear wasn't a companion he was used to, and hadn't been for as long as he could recall. But since he'd walked into the witch's lair, he'd felt a growing sense of doom mixed with an unhealthy dose of lust. Was it merely Luc's trepidation affecting him? Or was this how she had lured the Fae male to his death? With the dark allure of her sweet body, promising heaven and delivering hell?

He walked to her, chafing at following orders from her or anyone yet helpless to do otherwise. A deal was a deal, and he was a vampire of his word, even if he couldn't say the same of the priestess. As he stopped in front of her, she reached up and ran her fingers through the fall of his long hair. The witch's touch both attracted and repulsed him, leaving him confused.

"On your knees," she commanded.

One part of him wasn't the least bit hesitant, and it stiffened between his legs, eager and leaking pre-cum. Stifling a growl of irritation, he knelt at her feet, supplicating himself like one of his own damned servants. *But I agreed to this,* he reminded himself. Whatever it took to achieve his goal.

Her fingers slid to his face, caressed his cheek, and he was surprised at the coldness of her skin. He couldn't help but shiver as she raked a nail down his cheek and underneath his jaw . . . and then mimicked the action of slicing his jugular. *What the fuck have I gotten myself into?*

"Pleasure me."

Her mocking tone spoke volumes. She sensed his distaste but knew he couldn't help but obey, and she reveled in her power over him. The decades ahead of him loomed like a vast ocean, and he knew that in time, he'd hate the witch. Balls, he resented her already.

Still, the pungent fragrance of her sex called to him, and he skimmed her thighs with his palms. Leaned in to nuzzle the moist mound between her legs. Probed the protective folds with his tongue to taste her essence. The rest of her skin was ice, but her cunt was silken fire, like hot chocolate and cherries, delicious and creamy. And something else almost masked by the dual flavors, a spicy hint of something he couldn't name. It didn't have a certain taste so much as a zing that went straight to his head, rushed through his veins just like he imagined a designer drug would. Alcohol was the only substance that gave him the slightest buzz, and that limited effect was nothing like this.

His favored whiskey could never pack such a sinister punch.

Unease skittered through him, quickly overtaken by his body's baser urges. The predator in him wanted satisfaction now. He ate her slit hungrily, hardly aware of her fingers tightening in his hair, pulling just enough to sting. He relished the slight pain and lapped at the juices teasing his tongue, fucking her channel until she moaned. She melted a bit, relaxing against him, urging him on.

The change in her was subtle, but the tide was gradually turning in his favor. She was putty in his hands now, trembling with need. This, at least, was familiar territory—Soren taking control and his lovers becoming slaves to their own desires, giving him everything they'd intended to take.

Confidence restored, he stood and turned her to face the table. "Brace your hands on the surface and spread those pretty legs for me, witch. There you go. Bend over a bit."

She maneuvered into position, ass poking out, pouty sex slick from his attentions and begging for more. Quickly, he freed his aching cock from his jeans and gave the hard length a few strokes, knowing he wouldn't last long despite his earlier session with the Chosen. Vampires were insatiable and had quick recovery periods between bouts of sex, which was either a blessing or a curse, depending on his mood and the situation.

At the moment, he was leaning toward curse.

He brought the head of his cock to her opening and pushed inside, hissing at the glorious feeling of her pussy clasping his rod, squeezing like a tight glove. When he was fully seated, he had to pause for a few seconds or risk spilling too soon.

And immediately he berated himself for wanting to draw out their intimate contact. He had to keep his bargain, but the cunning manipulator didn't deserve his tenderness.

"Fuck me hard, damn you!" she shouted, reaching around to grab his ass.

Neither did she require sweet nothings, it seemed. Fine.

Pumping fast, he pounded into her cunt without mercy, smiling a little at her fierce swearing. Obviously she liked it rough, which suited him.

"Bite me!" she cried. "Drink me! Do it now!"

The predator in him rejoiced, and he struck without a second thought. Dark delight flowed over his tongue, the same rich flavor as her pussy juices but a thousand times more intoxicating. The release that had been boiling in his balls exploded and he came deep inside her, cock spasming again and again. Leila screamed with the force of her own orgasm as he drank, her channel milking him of every drop.

When the waves subsided, he withdrew his fangs and collapsed onto her back, panting with exertion. His vision was doubled, his brain fuzzy with an incredible high. A very real high, not a metaphorical one. His mind felt weird. Altered. Already he craved more of her blood.

It was then that he realized a black thread was making its way through his veins, slowly connecting him to the witch. A tangible bond that pulsed with sickening life, demanding that he feed again. *Mother of all the gods, what's happening?*

"What have you done to me?" he rasped.

She chuckled, low and satisfied. "I merely took what you offered."

The chill of her skin penetrated his awareness once more and this time bled into his very being, as well. Slipping out of her, he spun her to face him and dug his fingers into her shoulders. "What are you?"

"Why, I'm just the lowly priestess who can give you what you desire," she said, blinking, the picture of false innocence. "Just as you can give the same to me."

The bitch lied. Somehow she'd done the impossible and created a bond with him. Not a mating bond, but something similar. How? The female was more than she seemed, just as her bargain was much more than it appeared on the surface.

Smirking, she ran a fingernail down his cheek in a gesture he already hated. "Get dressed, my mate, and we'll get to the first part of our deal—bringing your love back to you."

Suddenly, he recalled an old short story called "The Monkey's Paw," in which the grisly severed paw granted the wishes of its owner, but did so in an evil way guaranteed to bring untold horror upon the unsuspecting fool.

Reaching for his jeans, Soren shivered, fearing that the consequences of what he'd just done might be a matter of life imitating art. Once they were dressed and seated again, she waved a hand at him.

"I'll need something that belonged to Helena. A cherished item. A piece of jewelry or clothing. Something that was a gift from you is even better. I assume you came prepared?"

"Of course." Hoping Leila didn't detect the slight tremble of his hand, Soren, now fully dressed, reached into the inside pocket of his leather coat and withdrew a small, yellowed envelope. He handed it to her, and she opened the flap to peer inside.

"A cameo brooch?"

"My mating gift to her."

"How cliché," she purred.

"It fits your criteria," he snapped. Damn, her snide tone grated.

"So it does."

He leaned his elbows on the table, striving to look casual. It wasn't easy with the anxious ball of hope and misery at war in his churning gut. With no little unease, he observed as she palmed the brooch and closed it in her hand, holding it suspended above the bowl of blood. Surely she didn't intend to—

She let go of the brooch, and it fell into the bowl with a plop. Ignoring his muttered oath, she closed her eyes and held her hands palms down over the liquid and began a soft chant. After a few moments this ritual ended and she rose from the table, heading for a shelf filled with small dolls that all looked alike save for yarn hair of varying lengths and colors. Curious, he watched as the priestess selected a doll with long yellow hair and then proceeded to rummage through a chest, examining and discarding what appeared to be doll clothes, until she apparently found something that met with her satisfaction.

With unhurried movements, she worked a scrap of blue material onto the doll. *A dress?* Yes, a blue dress. Much like the one Helena had been wearing the night they'd met at a Council ball. A shiver ran through Soren. The long blond hair, the dress. How could the witch have known?

Stupid. Plenty of immortals knew what Helena had looked like, and it was clear the priestess made it her business to know things. And blue was a common color. He was being paranoid, letting his imagination run wild, thinking she had the talent to conjure those sorts of physical details in an instant. Wasn't he?

She returned to the table and sat, laying the doll in the center of the table, and he put the matter from his mind. More pressing was what she would do next, how she'd make good on her end of the bargain. Reaching for a jar at her right hand, she unscrewed the lid, took a pinch of what appeared to be dark green herbs, and sprinkled them into the bowl. Next, she took a long-handled silver spoon and stirred the curious mixture, then lifted the brooch from the bowl with the spoon. The once-beautiful piece of jewelry looked gruesome floating in the puddle of crimson, but when she laid it on the doll's throat, he had to swallow hard to keep from gagging.

Yarn became bloodied golden tresses. Cloth became flesh. Torn, mottled flesh where ivory skin used to be, dangling meat bisecting his mate's delicate throat. Ripped out by the demon as she lay fighting for breath, poisoned by the bite. The cameo resting sadly there was a horrible reminder of love lost.

Soren bolted to his feet, sending the stool skittering backward to tip over with a noisy clatter. "What the fuck are you doing to me?" he shouted.

Desperately, he scrubbed at his eyes to clear them of the terrible image burning his retinas. When he focused on the doll . . . it was just an inanimate object again, presented in a gruesome parody of murder.

"I did nothing but what you asked," she claimed with a shrug. "I called Helena's soul back from beyond and back to you. How long until she arrives, time will tell."

Another mistake on his part, not insisting she be specific on when his love would return. "If you're fucking with me—"

"I'm not, vampire." She smiled. "At least not yet."

"Leila," he began, his tone low with warning. "I'm serious. If you're thinking of double-crossing me, I'll make certain you regret it."

"Threats before the honeymoon? How disappointing." She didn't appear concerned. "I'll just pack a bag for now. Tomorrow you can send a few of your slaves to box the rest of my belongings and close the cabin."

"We don't own slaves," Soren said shortly. "Though it's

perfectly legal and even economical, Aldric doesn't believe in the caste system, and, frankly, neither do I."

"Really?" She arched a brow. "That will soon change."

With that cryptic statement, she went to gather her things, leaving him to scowl after her and wonder exactly what he'd gotten himself into. Already, he felt . . . different. The blood he'd drawn from her still tingled on his tongue, coursed through his veins like an illicit drug.

He craved more of it. Of her. And that need within him frightened him more than any dangerous enemy he'd ever faced. He couldn't let it overwhelm him, couldn't allow dark desire to obliterate his purpose.

Somewhere his true love waited. Soon he'd have her back.

Even if the price was far higher than he'd dreamed.

3

"*You* did *what?*"

Soren's head throbbed as Aldric paced their large office at the resort, working himself up to an explosion of epic proportions. Luc caught his eye, mouthing, *I told you so*, and Soren shot him a glare in return.

Ever the peacemaker, Luc came to his defense, despite the fact that he'd tried to dissuade Soren from his course of action. "Hey, it won't be so bad. So what if he has to fuck the witch's brains out for the next sixty years? He'll get Helena back, and all's well that ends well. Right?" He tried an engaging smile on the fuming Aldric.

Which failed miserably. "Do either of you think I give two shits if Soren has to screw that vile woman until his dick falls off? He deserves it!" their older brother shouted. Whirling, he shook his finger in Soren's face. "What I *do* care about is that you've played right into that scheming cunt's plans and handed her on a *silver fucking platter* the very thing I've worked for the past four years to keep her from snatching!"

"The Council seat?" Luc ventured unwisely.

"Yes, the gods-damned Council seat! Where Leila will waste not one second lobbying—read: *manipulating* with every dirty trick she knows—to gain supporters until she has enough votes to pass whatever laws she sees fit for who knows *what* evil purpose!" He grabbed Soren's shirt and yanked him close, so that they were nose to nose. "All so you can be reunited with that weak little mouse of a human."

Soren had been fielding the abuse pretty well until then. His brother had very valid points and had every right to be angry, but throwing down insults on his dead mate crossed the line.

Rage descended in a crimson veil, and Soren lunged with a snarl. The suddenness and momentum of the attack took Aldric completely by surprise and propelled them both across the antique mahogany desk. Papers and pens scattered, and a lamp crashed to the floor alongside them. Soren's strength, while great, was normally no match for his brother's, but Aldric couldn't shove him off. He tried bucking his hips, pushing Soren's chest with both hands, but couldn't budge him.

Finally, an inner voice hissed. *It's about time I got the better of you, showed you who's stronger! I'll make you pay for what you said.*

On the floor, Soren spied something glinting in the morning sunlight filtering through the window. A letter opener from the desktop, the slender silver blade ready. Deadly.

Kill him. Do it and be free of his constant criticism, his unbending rules!

In an instant, the handle was in his grasp, the blade raised high as his older brother's eyes widened in shock.

"Soren, no!" Luc yelled.

His younger brother slammed him from the side in a flying

tackle, sending them down in a tangle. Luc grunted and slumped to his side, where he lay unmoving. Pushing to a sitting position, Soren reached for his brother, intending to throttle him. . . .

And then he spotted the handle of the letter opener protruding from Luc's chest. The haze of rage vanished, releasing him from its foul grip. He stared in horror at what he'd done. His brother impaled on a silver blade. "Oh, gods! Luc!"

Scrambling forward, he gently rolled his brother to his back and gasped at the sight of blood oozing from around the wound. "Luc?" he whispered, gripping his shirt and shaking him. "Luc, please."

Beside him, Aldric cursed and shoved Soren out of the way. Gathering Luc in his arms, their eldest brother stood and rushed from the office while shouting for help, leaving Soren to follow. He trailed after them in shock, unable to believe what just happened. They'd all lost their tempers with one another before, but never anything like the choking rage that had overcome Soren moments ago.

Upstairs, Trisha spread towels on Luc's bed while another Chosen sprinted into the adjoining bathroom for washcloths and a basin of water.

Trisha wrung her hands, face scrunched in worry. "Should I get the healer? Or the priestess? Maybe she can—"

"No," Aldric interrupted, voice and expression hard. "The witch has already done quite enough, and I don't want anyone else to know what's happened, especially the guests. Make sure the staff understands."

"Yes, Lord Aldric." Ducking her head, she hurried to obey him.

Leila? Had she somehow caused this? Again he felt that black thread running between them, strangling his heart, and wondered. . . . Guilt stabbed him in the chest, every bit as painfully as the blade in Luc's. What disaster had he wreaked on his family by bringing that woman here? The bargain had seemed so simple. Surely a mere human wasn't so powerful!

"Aldric—"

"Not now. Hold this, and press hard when I pull out the blade."

Aldric passed him a towel and ripped open Luc's shirt. Soren swallowed with difficulty and held the cloth ready as his brother took the handle of the letter opener and pulled. The instrument slid free easily, blood gushing forth, and Soren mashed the towel to the wound. A groan escaped Luc's lips and he stirred a bit. His face was pale, too much so. Aldric smoothed a lock of blond hair off their younger brother's forehead, his expression softening momentarily. Then he sat on the bed next to Luc and sliced his wrist open with one fang.

Using his free hand, he parted Luc's lips and placed his wrist above the younger vampire's mouth to allow a few crimson drops to fall inside. "Luc? Come on, kid. Here's a taste, and there's more where that came from."

For all Aldric's gruff exterior, Soren could hear the worry in his voice. Long seconds stretched out unbearably. A sliver of real fear began to writhe in his gut like a deadly snake, making him sick. If Luc died, Soren would follow him. Knowing that his bargain had caused his beloved brother's death would leave no chance for him to ever be happy with his mate again.

Blood trickled from one corner of Luc's mouth, and the towel in Soren's hands became soaked with red. *Gods, this can't be happening! Please, no!*

At last, Luc's tongue flicked out to catch the droplets. Then he reached up and yanked Aldric's wrist to his mouth, latching on and suckling like a newly made vamp starving for his first sustenance. Soren nearly fell over in relief, but the feeling was quickly tempered. The blackness inside him was a real presence, an unknown entity with barbed talons that had latched on to his core and had no intention of letting go.

What if next time he lost control and there was no one to break the spell?

There couldn't be a next time. He had to speak with Leila soon. If he had to, he'd kill that conniving—

"Soren."

Snapping back to himself, he gazed down at Luc, who was looking at him in concern. His throat tightened, because he didn't deserve anyone's worry, especially now. "How are you feeling?"

"Better," he said hoarsely. "Stop blaming yourself. I can see the misery written on your face."

He gave a bitter laugh. "Who am I supposed to blame? You tried to stop me from bargaining with that devil, and I wouldn't listen. If you hadn't stopped me, I might have murdered Aldric, and I almost murdered you instead."

His older brother snorted. "You wouldn't have killed me. You got the drop on me, but I was about to punch your lights out."

"And I'm fine. See?" Luc mustered a weak smile.

Love for his brothers swelled, clogged in his throat. Even after near catastrophe, they protected him. He pushed from the bed, unable to look either of them in the eyes any longer. "Rest, all right? I'll check on you later."

He strode for the door and made the hallway before Aldric caught him by the arm and forced him to turn around. "Forgive me for what I said earlier. I understand that you did what you felt you had to do. I don't blame you."

"I blame me enough for all of us," Soren said, shamed. He shook his head. "I'll figure a way out of this, even if it costs me the chance to find Helena."

Giving up would end him. He had not a single doubt. But for his brothers, he'd do it without hesitation.

"We'll do it together. We're going to learn what Leila's game is besides acquiring the Council seat, because I suspect there's something more she's after. Then perhaps we can get rid of the priestess *and* bring back your mate. If there is any loophole, we'll find it." One of his big hands clamped down on Soren's shoulder.

"And if there isn't?"

"We'll deal with that when we have to. And, brother?"

"Yes?"

"I'm ashamed that I disparaged Helena's memory," he said sincerely. "I never thought she was suited to our lifestyle, but I was fond of her."

"I know you didn't mean it." He took a deep breath. "I'm not myself. Ever since I bit Leila, took her blood, there's something terrible inside me, and that's what drove me to attack you when I never would have done such a thing before. The violence roiling inside me is like a storm waiting to explode. . . ."

"We'll fix it." His older brother's gaze was intense, his tone allowing for no other outcome.

"Thank you." Soren nodded toward Luc's room. "I'll be back later to see about him."

Aldric nodded and Soren took his leave, striking out in search of the priestess. The resort was rather large and spread out. But this early in the morning, the guests were still in bed, snoozing off their partying from the night before, so that should cut down the number of places she might be found. Unless she was off snooping somewhere, or was occupying someone else's bed already. One could hope.

Exhaustion dragged at his limbs. He needed sleep, badly. But that wasn't happening until he had it out with Leila.

After taking a look in her suite—he drew the line at allowing her to share his—he moved outside. A few minutes of wandering one of the many footpaths brought him to the pretty gazebo by the pond. Inside was the priestess.

Inside the priestess was Nikki, the cute kitchen boy who helped the cook by doing all the menial prep work. Well, he'd gotten an early start on his day and had certainly done some prep, but not in the kitchen. The twenty-two-year-old was waxing her pussy, driving several inches home, causing her to moan loudly while she clung to the back of the bench he'd bent her over—proving he wasn't such a *boy*, after all.

Soren mounted the steps and stopped in the archway. Normally, it took more than the sight of an attractive couple fucking to arouse him, but his damned cock had other ideas. The pungent scent of their sex reached him, and he steeled himself against the onslaught of lust that threatened to overtake his common sense.

Sexual creature though he was, pleasure was his *business*. He always had the ability to rise above his desires when the situation warranted caution. Yet he found himself a puppet dancing to Leila's tune. He hated it.

"Harder, damn you! Fuck me harder. . . . Oh yes! Yes!"

"Gods, you feel so good on my cock! So tight!"

"I'm coming. . . ."

"Fuck, yeah!"

They reached a noisy climax, yelling their completion loud enough to awaken half the resort. When they were done, the young man slipped out of her and accepted her heated kiss as she turned and cupped the back of his head. There was a lot of tongue involved, and Soren wondered if one of them would swallow the other.

And as he watched with growing impatience, he noticed something strange. Where the priestess's hands rested on Nikki, at the back of his head and on his bare arm, there appeared to be a faint bluish glow around her fingers. He squinted, thinking it must be his imagination, but no. The glow was there, so dim that a creature with lesser vision, such as a human, wouldn't have noticed at all. What was more, the young man paled and began to sway on his feet.

Alarmed, Soren finally made his presence known. "What in blazing hell do you think you're doing?" he practically shouted.

Nikki, misinterpreting the reprimand as meant for him, sprang back from Leila, his wide-eyed gaze finding his boss bearing down on them. In his fright, he missed the venomous glare the witch shot between them. But Soren didn't.

"I-I'm sorry, Lord Soren!" he stammered. "I'm not on duty yet and I didn't think you'd mind if I . . . well . . ."

"Don't worry, sweetness. Lord Soren doesn't mind if you fuck his mate." The witch delivered that in a seductive purr, raking one nail down Nikki's cheek. Then she gave Soren a poisonous grin. "Do you, darling?"

The younger man looked panicked. "Your mate? Oh, shit." He started to backpedal, holding out his hands. "I didn't know—I swear!"

Choosing to ignore Leila for the moment, Soren anxiously closed the distance between himself and Nikki, touching his shoulder. "Relax, kid. You okay?"

"I guess," he began. For a couple of seconds, he seemed relieved that his boss wasn't about to gut him. But then he swayed in place again and had to be steadied. "I'm not sure. I don't feel so good. I'm sorta dizzy and sick to my stomach."

Soren shot a scowl at Leila, who shrugged in indifference. He was going to find out what she was about, sooner or later. "Nikki, get dressed and go to the main house. Tell Lord Aldric you need to get checked by the healer."

"Yes, sir."

Eager to make tracks, the young man dressed, but not without a little help. Soren let him hold on to an arm to stay steady, but by the time Nikki had on his jeans and T-shirt, he wasn't as wobbly. Muttering another apology, the kid quickly split.

Soren rounded on his phony mate, barely keeping his temper in check. "What did you do to that kid?"

"Nothing he didn't beg for."

Slowly, he stalked forward. "What was that blue light when you touched him? What were you doing to him?"

"I don't know what you mean." From her tone, she knew very well and didn't care that he wasn't fooled. She obviously had no worries that he would be able to learn her secrets, whatever they were.

"You were doing to him what you did to that Fae male," he snapped, getting in her personal space. "The one you left a dead husk. Why? What do you get out of it?"

"I was cleared of that charge, and I wouldn't go making accusations if I were you. Attacking your own brother, a worthy

Council elder? What would the Council have to say about one of the community's finest going off the deep end?" She slanted him a sly look. "I hope I'm not forced to tell them. Feral vampires are executed, you know."

He gaped at her, anger and a dose of fear snaking through his veins. "Are you *threatening* me?" Blazing Hades, how had she known what had happened in the office when she was out here screwing the help?

"Of course not! You're my mate." She winked at him. "I would never speak against you . . . unless you left me no choice."

The awful rage boiled within him, and he willed it down with an effort. So this was how she wanted to play? Then he'd have to make sure he was better at the game. Not easy when she already had him at a disadvantage.

He tried a different approach. "I have no choice but to presume you're innocent, and I have no proof you were harming Nikki." *But I will.* "Now that you're ensconced at the resort and have everything you could possibly want, including a cushy life and the Council seat, I fail to see why you need me. You and I can simply go our separate ways. The resort's big enough that we'd rarely have to see each other."

"We *could* do our own thing," she allowed, then shot him down. "Except that doesn't suit me at all. The Council is a tight-assed bunch of bastards, and I'll be the only woman currently sitting on the panel. I'll need to be seen as your mate, and Aldric's sister-in-law, if I'm to make any headway with them."

"Right." He gave a derisive laugh. "It's all to further your mysterious agenda. Do I get to know what it entails?"

"In time. For now, you'll play your part and look pretty at my side in public."

Somehow, he managed not to curl his lip at her. *Pretty, my ass.* "I don't have to put up with this. I'm tempted to call off this arrangement and forget the whole deal."

She tsked. "Sorry, but you can't. It's much too late."

"Why? Because of this dark *thing* inside me?" His hands clenched. "What have you done to me? I want an answer this time."

"Just a bit of insurance."

"Obviously, but that doesn't tell me what it *is.*"

"No, it doesn't. You'll know when you need to and not before." She smiled. "Be glad you can't undo our bargain. . . . If you did, you'd miss out on finding your long-lost lover."

"Mate," he corrected, and felt hope flaring despite everything. "My *real* mate. Does that mean you have an idea where she is?"

"Better—I know where she'll be three nights from now." Reaching up, she caressed his face. "You and I are going out that night, and you'll wear your best clothes suitable for Club Lash. Oh, and take plenty of credits. You're going to need them."

A barrage of emotions—hope, sick fear, and confusion— weakened his knees, but he didn't dare show them to the viper. Why was his genteel Helena going to be at a down and dirty sex club like Lash?

A club known for one very hot commodity. Beautiful slaves, trussed and ready to do their masters' bidding.

And why would Leila follow through at all with bringing home his mate? To torture him, most likely. The witch would enjoy that.

Soren had no choice right now but see this through.

· · ·

Harley had to admit, Val and Zenon were pretty fucking awesome. Not to mention pretty awesome at fucking. The two of them were unlike any demons she'd ever met, not that she'd met many, and certainly none so civilized. Well, for demons.

Even their clan at the compound seemed all right, if a little loud and scary sometimes. Though she hadn't seen too many of them up close, because her new friends-slash-captors kept her mostly hidden and safe from scrutiny. The pair claimed it was to make sure their investment wasn't harmed before the auction, but she caught the softening of their expressions when they thought she wasn't paying attention. They liked her, but at the end of the day, they were demons, with all of their mischievousness and faults.

"It's time to go, pretty," Val said, strolling into his bedroom. She'd been staying with him, and she had to admit she'd miss his solid warmth.

"Why don't you just keep me? I like this arrangement," she admitted, then dropped her gaze to the floor.

Valafar tilted her chin up, forcing her to look at him. "Why?"

Anxiety fluttered in her stomach, and she cursed herself for speaking up. "Why should you keep me?"

"No. Why do you like being here with us?"

"I . . ." Why did she? Was it Val and Zen she wanted, or . . .

"Be honest with yourself, Harley. Drop the pretense," he demanded.

"What do you mean?" Her attempt at being obtuse failed.

"In the few days you've been here, I've seen you behave like a young woman stumbling your way through life without a clue, as when we found you on the road. But unlike most of the clan, Zen and I have seen through your act."

Her mouth fell open. "What act? I have no idea what you're talking about!"

The demon studied her for a moment. "Perhaps you really don't," he said thoughtfully. "Tell me, why were you traveling in that broken-down heap through this part of the country, especially a sultry place like New Orleans?"

"I lost my job and—"

"That's not what I'm getting at," he said patiently. "Why here?"

"I don't know." But a picture began to form. Of herself, packing and running away.

"I think you do. Of all the places you could've run to, you chose the most debauched city on the continent. You arrived with practically nothing to your name. Why?" he pressed.

She swallowed. "Because I want something . . . more."

"Yes? What are you lacking? Go on." His intense gaze bore into her, prying out her intimate secrets.

Where to start? "What am I lacking? I've never had anything." Sadness rose in her breast, the pain crushing her all over again. "I was raised in the orphan sector of St. Louis, and turned loose to fend for myself at age eighteen. I had a series of jobs that didn't pan out, but finally landed a good one that I liked, writing up local events for the newspaper. Gallery showings, black-tie dinners—things like that."

"Sounds boring as hell."

"It paid the bills," she defended. Then slumped in her seat. "I actually liked keeping up with the Who's Who. And I even managed to snag a wealthy businessman of my own."

"Obviously, things didn't end well between you."

"No." The memories, the bitter disappointment, rose to try to drag her under. "He was a regular human male, a handsome patron of the arts. We met at one of the showings I covered, and the attraction was instant. For a while, I thought I'd found my prince. He was attentive and loving, and bought me expensive stuff."

"But?"

She hunched her shoulders. "The sex was . . . nice. Missionary. And not real frequent."

"Ah," Val said knowingly. "You became bored."

"Yeah," she whispered, shame clogging her throat. "I was restless, and I tried to get him to be more adventurous in the bedroom. He wasn't comfortable stepping out of the sexual box, though. I really tried to be happy, but I felt like something was missing. Then one night Jason threw a cocktail party, invited some of his rich friends. One of them was a wolf shifter, sexy as sin and ready to find a playmate for the night."

"And he found you, a flower ripe for plucking," Val guessed, smoothing her hair. His voice was quiet, without censure.

"More like a slut ripe for a good hard fucking." She laughed, but the sound was sad. "He kept cornering me, and he wasn't shy about getting across what he wanted. He radiated bad boy from every pore, and he smelled so damned good. He said I deserved more than what his staid friend could give me, and he'd show me what I'd been missing."

She paused, but Val waited for her to continue.

"He finally took my elbow and steered me toward a guest bedroom. The party was going strong, and no one would notice. The excitement, the thrill of doing something naughty, was too hard to resist. I told myself maybe Jason would like us being more open with our sex lives, more daring, if only he knew. After that, I didn't think at all."

"Was the wolf good?"

Despite her shame, heat flooded her limbs at the memory. "Better than. He treated me like I was there for his pleasure, ordered me around. Finally, he flipped me over, got me up on my hands and knees, and gave me the hard fucking I'd been craving. And he did it in half-wolf, half-man form."

"Kinky," Val praised in admiration.

"It was such a turn-on. I can still feel his fur brushing my thighs and my back. His long, thick cock pounding deep as his claws dug into my hips. I'd never come more violently in my life." Gods, she'd loved it. Every second.

"The two of you must've made quite a sight."

"Especially to Jason, who walked in during our incredible orgasm. He was shocked at first, hurt, and then . . ." She shuddered. "I've never seen any man so angry. He started screaming at me, calling me a whore. In less than half an hour, I was out on the curb beside my truck with a bag and nothing else to my name."

"You had your job, though."

"Not for long. First thing the next morning, my boss called me in to his office. He was very up-front about the fact that Jason had wielded his substantial influence to get me fired."

Val's eyes glowed. "Those bastards! They forced you out of St. Louis? Left you with nothing?"

"Not exactly. The shifter felt bad about what happened and how Jason had reacted, so he offered me a place to stay. But I left after only a week."

"Why? Wasn't there chemistry between you?"

"Oh, I really liked him. But I still longed for something more, something he couldn't give me."

Valafar laid his hand over hers. "And now I believe you can answer my question. Why New Orleans?"

Val was right. She let out a deep breath. "Because New Orleans is a place of old magic and even older sin. It called to me, and I knew I could find what I'm looking for here."

"Which is?" Though he already knew.

"A male who'll own me completely, who won't hold back. Who's used to taking what he wants and will make me his."

"That wasn't so hard, was it?" His lips curved up and his eyes danced with mischief.

"Just the part about hurting Jason," she admitted. "I still feel guilty about that."

Val snorted. "To hell with Jason! The spineless twerp couldn't keep his woman satisfied and ignored her needs. Then he tossed that woman onto the street and cost her a good job! No real man would've done those things. Instead, he would've learned what made her happy and fixed the problem. No, don't waste another second feeling guilty over the likes of him."

"You make it sound so easy."

"Easy, no. But the solution is closer than you think."

"And that means I can't stay here?" Another pang hit her at the idea of being parted from them. Seemed like she was destined never to stay in one place for long and would always have to endure the pain of people slipping through her grasp.

"Not if you hope to find where you truly belong," Zen said, stepping into the room.

It was inevitable—she couldn't stay. It was time to admit that.

She glanced between the two demons. "Will you come to me if I need you?"

"You bet," Zen said.

Val agreed. "Call or send word. Not only will we come—we'll personally tear apart the slimeball who's hurting you. I promise." Demons didn't make oaths lightly.

She nodded. "Okay. I guess that will have to do."

He laughed. "Cheer up. You're going to be fine. Ready?"

"Do I really have to wear this? I feel ridiculous." She frowned down at her attire, if a skimpy see-through wrap of black lace that barely covered her naked ass could be called that.

"You're going to be auctioned, and then you'll be wearing nothing at all, so why does it matter?" He sighed, gazing at her fondly for a moment before straightening and schooling his features. "For what it's worth, I wish you were my mate. Then I wouldn't ever let you go and I would reward your devotion by spoiling you rotten and fulfilling your every sexual desire. Though I suspect you'll soon have your new master eating from your hand. Shall we?"

They led her outside to a big black Hummer with tinted windows. There was a driver, a demon she'd never met, and as they slid into the back, he merely waited in silence until they were settled before pulling away.

This trip with her captors was much smoother than the previous one, preferable by far to flying without her own set of wings. The interior of the car was dark and quiet, and the demons provided a sense of security, for which she was grateful. But she had to wonder how safe she'd really be tonight.

"Is there some sort of screening process at this club, or do they just let any potential owner in to bid on slaves?" Her hands were clenched in her lap, nearly bloodless from having been squeezed together. She found it hard to believe anyone there would be as potently male as Val and Zen.

Zen shrugged. "They have to be rich to even darken the door of Club Lash."

"Just because my owner has money doesn't mean he won't be cruel," she pointed out.

"Or she."

Harley's eyes widened. That was a possibility she hadn't considered, and her pulse quickened in dread. Women could be unbearably mean to one another in all sorts of creative ways. More so than men, sometimes. What if her owner was a mated female and wanted Harley only for menial work? Like cleaning house or cooking.

Well, she hated cleaning with a passion, but that would be safe. And, yeah, she'd be bored to tears within a week.

A big finger tilted up her chin, and she looked into Val's eyes. "Don't worry, sweet. I happen to know several prominent citizens who're attending tonight's auction, and once the crowd gets a look at you, no worthy male in his right mind would allow such a beautiful slave to be purchased by anyone who's not going to savor your lush body."

She flushed at his words. "Flatterer," she muttered.

"No. Flattery is insincere, and I'm very serious. You are gorgeous, and your master will know he's a lucky bastard."

"Thanks." She wasn't so sure. But showing fear would gain her nothing but the wrong kind of attention.

All too soon, the limo arrived at the back entrance to the club, and she was ushered inside under the watchful eyes of her companions. *Captors.* A hysterical giggle bubbled up and she somehow stifled it. Val and Zen might be demons, but they weren't nearly as ruthless as they'd have most folks believe. More than likely they'd let her out of this if she *begged*—and she hadn't done that. They knew her most secret desire and were allowing her to play it through, with the promise they'd come to her rescue if things went south.

She must be crazy to actually want to go through with this.

Val whispered a warning in her ear. "Don't speak unless you're asked a direct question. There's a fine line between showing spirit and displaying insubordination that could get you punished, and it's best not to test unknown waters."

Heart fluttering in her throat, she nodded.

The club staff was waiting for them, and a slim young man with long purple hair ushered them into a small dressing room. Or, in her case, an *un*dressing room. The boy, who couldn't have been a day over twenty-one, directed her to stand in the center of the room.

He gave her an impish smile. "My name is Kai. My, aren't you a looker? The bouncers will have to beat the bidders off you." Waving a hand at the wrap, he said, "Drop it so we can polish the goods, honey. And don't look so worried—you don't have anything I haven't seen a zillion times before, and I prefer guys anyway."

Following Val's advice, she remained quiet, though she suspected this young staff member wouldn't mind if she spoke. Maybe asked a few questions. However, she had no idea whether he'd get in trouble for being too friendly to the slaves, so she buttoned her lip.

She let the wrap fall to the floor in a puddle at her feet and gave a shiver. Soon her audience would consist of a whole room full of horny men.

"Cold?" Kai inquired, grabbing a jar of something off a nearby shelf.

"Yes, a little."

"You won't be for long. My job is to warm you up." He punctuated the statement with a cheeky wink.

She wanted to ask how, but figured that would be pointless when he'd show her soon enough. Opening the jar, Kai scooped out a generous amount of a pale, shiny substance. Not lotion, but what, she wasn't sure. A sweet scent, a hint of almond and honey that was quite pleasant, teased her nose. Smearing some on her arm, he began to spread and work in the stuff as he talked.

"This is slave oil. It's a natural compound designed to make the skin take on a healthy-looking glow without the heavy presentation of regular body oil. It's totally edible, which means your master can lick your sweet body to his heart's content. Or you can lick him. It contains an aphrodisiac that absorbs into the skin, though, so treat it like alcohol and never ingest too much of it in one session. It's expensive, but no master worth his salt will be without a supply."

He looked up as he rubbed the cream onto her other arm, as if awaiting a response. She nodded in understanding, and he happily kept up his task. She noted that, indeed, her skin began to tingle, and soon became comfortably warm. True to Kai's word, the properties of the paste chased away the chill, and strange things began to happen.

As she inhaled the yummy scent of the almond-honey paste, the buzzing warmth started to fan out, creeping with clever little fingers, making her hyperaware of her nakedness. Suddenly she felt so very wicked and wanted to wallow in it. She longed to be seen and touched, her body spread for delight.

"That's it, sweetie," Kai crooned softly, his voice hypnotic. His capable hands smoothed the cream over the length of each of her legs, then moved to her back and down, lightly over the curve of her ass. "Just let go and enjoy."

Vaguely, she heard Kai tell the demons to move her to the stage for the final preparations. She guessed other slaves had been sold tonight in similar fashion, and now it was her turn.

They helped her to stand between two poles, and then Kai directed the demons to cuff each of her wrists to the top of them while he did her ankles. She was spread in a human X, completely at the mercy of fate.

Her pussy heated, and she whimpered. She made another helpless noise when Kai again took up his jar and began to rub the cream on a nipple, making it instantly harden under his expert touch. Then the other.

The real torture came when he applied the same care to her exposed, pouting pussy lips, getting them nice and slick. She groaned, tilting her hips as he rubbed her slit and teased her clit, creating whorls of unbearable delight that spiraled from her cunt outward to every nerve. Then he stopped, leaving her right on the edge and ready to scream.

"No coming, honey," he said. "Not yet."

Not yet? Did he mean . . . ? Her eyes widened and she stared at him.

"That's right. You will come, but you'll do it for the audience, before the bidding starts. Gets the prospective buyers all excited so they'll drop more credits."

This time, she broke the rule and stammered, "I-I'm going to orgasm in front of an entire club packed with people?"

"That's right. It's part of the show. Gets the audience riled up. And now my part is done. The handler has volunteered to master your body for the crowd."

"What?" Oh, gods, she burned. Her pussy was on fire.

Kai smiled. "Relax and enjoy the ride. It'll be a high like nothing else you've experienced, and before this night is over, you'll be the perfect, dirty little slut your master is going to devour with a spoon."

She moaned, writhing in her restraints, helpless against the burning need consuming her.

Dirty little slut. Devoured.

Oh, please, yes!

"Curtain time!"

The velvet slowly parted, and the crowd no longer mattered. She needed to be fucked. Owned.

She finally knew—this was Harley Vaughn. All those lonely years of searching ended here tonight.

At last, she would have a place to belong. And with any luck, a master who'd appreciate and cherish his slave.

4

"We have your table waiting, Lord Soren!" a blond twink chirped. "Right this way."

Soren eyed the interior of the club as he and Leila followed, wishing he hadn't let the witch talk him into coming here. His Helena would never have been caught dead—or undead—in a place like Lash, with its sleek decadence, lust heavy in the air. That she was an innocent in such a depraved world was a big part of what he'd loved about her; she'd been his refuge from the excesses of indulgence.

There would be no refuge here.

The club itself was living, breathing sex. The waitstaff wore little, were young and beautiful down to the last male and female alike. They existed to tempt, to fuel lurid fantasies and drive customers insane with the thought of what treasures were for the taking, if they cared to reach out and grab them.

His fangs throbbed and his groin tightened in black pants that were suddenly much too small in the crotch. There was no use pretending he wasn't affected, so he didn't try. Here he was just one aroused male among many, and acting differently would make him obvious in a place where standing out wasn't good.

The twink showed them to one of the best tables: near the stage, yet off to the side in a private alcove. Soren didn't like sitting in the middle of a crowd or having people at his back in the dark. The Fontaine name alone ensured the brothers had enemies, and he had no desire to entice one of them to bury a knife between his shoulder blades. It wouldn't be the first attempt.

Leila scooted into the booth beside him, flicking her black hair over one shoulder with a toss of her head, a calculated move he loathed. There was nothing more unattractive to him than a female who knew she was physically perfect and wanted to make certain everyone else noticed, as well. One night, he'd take a pair of shears to the gleaming tresses while she slept. Butch her up a bit and then watch the fireworks.

Better yet, he'd help her *really* toss her head—by using his sword to cleave it from her neck. Too bad he wasn't carrying. But he'd been ordered never to use it again, a mandate he'd followed to the letter.

Leila stroked his arm, gaining his attention. "You're so tense. I would've thought our quickie before we left had fixed that."

He shot her a look of annoyance. "Sex doesn't fix everything."

"Right." She snorted. "Says the man who owns a sex resort."

"Our guests are seeking the unusual, an escape from their troubles," he pointed out shortly. "For most, it's not everyday life."

"Yet you and your brothers, former Warriors of Exodus, decided to make pleasure your business," she mused. "Why is that, I wonder? What made you stop fighting monsters, especially when you have those wonderful, magical swords that can supposedly slay any supernatural creature, no matter how ancient its powers?"

A nasty jolt of surprise went through him as he stared at her. "Where did you hear that?" he hissed, glancing around even though they were shielded from most conversation. "Our tenure with Exodus was more than a century ago. It's not common knowledge outside the Council."

"From the same place I heard you were dismissed from Exodus, and all three of you were forbidden to use the swords ever again."

Surprise gave way to a chill that slithered down his spine. "Ancient history. I can't imagine why it would interest you."

"A few decades isn't so long ago. And you're my mate! I'm interested in knowing everything about you." Leaning in, she kissed his cheek and then looked toward the stage. "Oh, look! The show is starting."

Thank the gods. Sex might not be a fix, but it *was* a refuge at times, especially from nosy questions. How the hell had the priestess learned about their banishment from Exodus? Did she know why? And how had she known of the swords' existence when he and his brothers had done their best to let them fade into a distant memory? She'd been fishing; he was certain of it. He'd have to find out what she was after.

Turning his attention to the stage, he forced himself to uncoil and try to appreciate the display of beauty being paraded for their pleasure. Some were to be auctioned for household duties or factory work, but the prime stock destined to be used for sexual purposes was presented with a bit more fanfare. This was the case with a human male who was escorted forward and placed on a torture rack, blue eyes wide with fear. Not all of him was afraid, though, as evidenced by the rock-solid hard-on jutting from between his slender thighs.

The crowd gave a collective cheer, then began to murmur among themselves as his oiled body was stretched, his nipples clamped, and his round little ass filled with the biggest dildo Soren had ever seen. The handler worked the dildo in and out of his channel, claiming loudly that the boy was extremely sensitive and loved pain. He would come without his cock and balls ever being touched.

Minutes later, after being whipped, pinched, and ass-fucked with the toy, the boy gave a loud cry and shot ropes of pearly white cream all over the stage before slumping in exhaustion. The delighted crowd cheered again, and the bidding was opened at twenty thousand credits, which quickly soared as determined would-be masters attempted to outdo one another.

Soren had to admit that the sight caused his already aching erection a great deal of misery. Though he preferred the soft curves of a woman, beautiful bodies were meant to be enjoyed, and there wasn't much he hadn't done with either sex. The boy would've made an entertaining addition to the resort if he and his brothers believed in keeping slaves. Which they didn't.

Thinking of Aldric's reaction when he learned where Soren would be tonight deflated his erection more than a little. Their argument, three days ago was fresh in his mind, and he didn't fancy a repeat should his fear turn out to be true. Maybe the witch was wrong and Helena wouldn't be here.

As the auction went on, he kept an eye on the club's staff, searching in vain for a familiar, petite blonde, though he knew deep down she wouldn't look exactly the same. But similar, perhaps? At least a resemblance in her expressions, the way she walked, her gestures. Or maybe—

His train of thought was arrested when the dark velvet curtains slid open to reveal the next subject. A woman standing between two poles, wrists and ankles cuffed so that she was stretched wide. Like the others, she was gloriously naked. But none so far were as beautiful as this female.

She was rather tall, her skin glowing and supple, graceful limbs tanned and toned. Her figure was lush, with full breasts and a tapered waist that flared into hips and a nice round ass that he could picture being more than a delightful double handful when he plowed into it. Auburn hair swept past her shoulders and framed a face he could only describe as bold. She possessed high cheekbones, large green eyes laced with long, dark lashes, and pouty lips that would look fabulous wrapped around his cock.

In a word, she was stunning.

Sitting up, he felt his rod thicken again as he studied her. Dazzling and dramatic, she looked nothing at all like his small, pale Helena. Immediately, he felt disloyal making those comparisons, but he couldn't help but notice.

What was he thinking? Did he actually believe this was the one he'd been waiting for?

He did feel drawn to her, and it wasn't just her beauty. Despite the crowd, the proximity of too many bodies carrying a variety of odors, one sweet scent made its way to him, almost masked by the almond-and-honey cream the club's assistants smeared on the slaves. Something warm that reminded him of tropical flowers growing wild, of sunny beaches and naked bodies writhing in the sand.

Gods, he must be nuts. But he stared in rapt attention as the handler began to put her through her paces. He removed a string of graduated anal beads from his pants pocket.

Soren couldn't have moved at this point if a horde of bloodthirsty ogres charged into the room. He couldn't tear his eyes from the spectacle as the handler spun the platform around so that her backside faced the audience. Smiling, he pried her ass cheeks apart so everyone could get a good view of the pink rosette of her back passage. A young man with purple hair quickly came onto the stage, holding a jar of what Soren figured was the aphrodisiac paste, and the handler took a scoop before the boy disappeared again.

With two fingers, he began to work the paste into his captive's tight little asshole. She made the loveliest sounds, little whimpers that betrayed how much she craved this sweet torture. Her rear shoved back into his hand, encouraging more. The handler stretched and worked her, no doubt driving her insane with need.

Then he took the end of the string of anal beads and began pushing them in, using the smallest one, slowly. One and another. The beads got larger, and her little hole ate them as she groaned, pushing against his hand, begging with her body.

A hand worked at his belt, and Soren became aware of Leila unfastening his pants and lowering the zipper. He didn't have the will to protest as she fished out his rigid cock, began stroking the heated length.

"Didn't I tell you that your love would be found here?" she murmured into his ear. Her tongue traced his lobe and her hand felt so good.

"You did," he said, sucking in a breath. The beads continued to be sucked into the woman's plump ass. "But this female doesn't resemble Helena at all."

"Don't you feel a connection?"

"I feel something," he admitted in confusion. He shouldn't, though. Not for this wanton creature who looked and acted nothing like his mate. "How do I know for sure it's really her before I bid?"

"I think you know. Can't you scent her? Doesn't she smell irresistible?"

"Yes."

The stroking was delicious, her fingers diving down to caress and squeeze his balls before she stroked again. He pumped his hips into her touch. The priestess's voice was husky, seductive.

"Look at her, the hungry little slut. Imagine what you will do to her once she is yours."

He could. His mind didn't need much suggestion to go down that dark, dangerous road. Leila's thumb brushed his slit, smeared pre-cum around the sensitive head. Onstage, the beauty was full, and the handler took a paddle to her ass, delivering loud smacks. Her cries were so needy as the paddle did its job, jostling the beads inside her passage and driving her insane with lust.

Soren imagined he could almost feel what she felt with every hit of the paddle. He burned, so hot, wanting to be the one with the right to use her.

"You will have her, and my bargain will be fulfilled," the witch promised, as though reading his mind. "Just think how you'll make her writhe and whimper, bend her to your will, make her scream. She'll be your slave, your fuck toy, and you can do anything you want to her. Isn't that right?"

"Yes," he groaned. "Anything."

The handler slowly pulled the beads from the woman's ass, and she was nearly insensate now. Leila's wicked siren song called to the dark thing inside him that had been patiently lying in wait all evening. The beast unfurled, stretched its claws, and awakened, smirking evilly inside him.

I am you, it told him in his head. *And you are me. Together, we can have anything we want.*

The handler tossed the beads aside, freed himself from his pants. Pressed the head of his big, dripping rod into her anus and pushed inside, inch by inch. The slave cried out for more.

Listen to the priestess and to me! Leila is our true mate, our salvation! Only she can free us to enjoy our most secret desires, the ones that even your brothers would forbid us.

"Ahh, gods!" Freed, the beast exulted. *We will have ultimate power and we all will rule as one.* A rush poured through Soren's veins, both icy and hot, as his new companion settled into his very bones, his soul. His beast craved the combination of sex and death, something that as a vampire he'd always struggled to keep leashed. And now . . .

The handler was reaming the woman's pretty ass now, splitting it with that huge cock just as *he* would do when she belonged to him. Pounding her hard.

Leila worked Soren's cock faster. "She looks so right bound like that, at his mercy, being fucked. She'll spread so wonderfully when you torture her, darling. When *we* torture her."

"Fuck, yes," he rasped. "We're going to do all sorts of nasty things to her sweet body, my love." The thought filled his balls to the point of bursting, and a laugh he didn't recognize escaped him, low and hungry, joined by hers.

"That's right, darling. I knew you'd start to come around. You're a strong-willed one, but the magic of our bond is stronger."

Oh, gods! Had he really said that and meant it? *What's wrong with me?*

Shh, the beast soothed. *Don't fight us. Just give in and you'll love how it feels, the power. Can't you feel it deep in your balls? Let us free you.*

Onstage, the handler plunged to the root with a shout, ass clenched, and pumped his cum into her channel. The slave screamed with the force of her orgasm, spasming under him, on and on. The audience went wild, shouting appreciatively. Many were getting off on the scene, in front of anyone who wanted to see.

Soren's release exploded as Leila captured his mouth with hers. She kissed him deeply and he opened to her, letting her have him. When she broke the kiss, her lips curved into a cruel smile, and his beast purred.

"Now I know our bonding has been completed. You are my mate, in the way of *my* kind, not yours as a vampire."

No!

Yesss, his beast purred.

"And what *is* your kind? What are you?"

"I've told you—you'll find out more when you're ready. As of yet, all that matters is that you're mine, and together we'll be unstoppable."

Reaching onto the table, he grabbed a couple of napkins and cleaned himself off. He tossed the napkins onto the table again, and a server quickly whisked them away. Returning his attention to the stage, he saw that the handler had tucked himself away and was just finishing with cleaning the woman. He spun the platform around so she faced the audience again. She was slumped, expression sated but weary.

His heart tugged, but the beast intervened. *Do not feel sorry for her, and do not soften. She will be yours to fuck and let others fuck, as is your right. Even the law is on your side, and your brothers cannot refute that.*

He shook his head, trying with minimal success to clear the seductive voice. Beside him, Leila placed a possessive hand on his thigh, and he let it stay. He was more interested in the auctioneer, who had stepped up to the podium that was positioned off to the side and was ready to start the bidding. Soren didn't want to miss his chance.

The portly man began his pitch. "That was quite a show, wasn't it? Nowhere else are you going to find a slave of such fine quality to warm your bed! What a lovely creature, and so responsive. Let's start the bidding at fifty thousand credits!"

And so it began. But no bastard in this room was going to outbid Soren, no matter how hard he tried. One black-haired, black-winged demon across the room did try, though Soren could swear by the twinkle in the demon's eyes that he was driving up the price on purpose, with no intention of winning. Why the hell would he do that?

In the end, it didn't matter. Soren finally placed a bid the demon wouldn't top.

"Sold! To the gentleman in the booth there for one hundred fifty thousand credits! Sir, if you'll come see my assistant about settling up."

With a nod, Soren slid from the booth and went to do business. Honest elation warred with that darker side of him that was quickly taking over, merging with his old self. How long until the Soren he and everyone else knew and loved disappeared? The idea scared him to death, as did the idea of his hurting the woman, his brothers, or anyone else. He'd have to talk to Aldric tomorrow. And, luckily, the beast didn't respond to that last thought or attempt to dissuade him. Hopefully, it hadn't heard.

While Leila waited in the club, the assistant led Soren to his office, where the credits were paid. For the first time, he wondered what had landed this woman in circumstances dire enough to be sold on the block. Yes, she was incredibly responsive, but was she happy about her new circumstances? Or afraid? He was ashamed he hadn't considered her feelings before now.

Transaction completed, the assistant pointed. "You can take possession of your slave now. Just go right and continue down the hall to the second-to-last door on the left. That's where she's being held for transport."

"Thank you."

With every step down the hall, he felt as dirty as if he'd rolled on the ground. People shouldn't be possessions. He and his brothers had always believed that, and the only reason he was doing this was to rescue his mate, if Leila was telling the truth and that's who she turned out to be. Except the witch called *herself* his mate, and the other woman a toy.

Leila is your mate, and the woman our toy, the beast reminded him.

"Shut up," he muttered.

Somehow, he wasn't surprised to see the big demon that had participated in the bidding war standing outside the door to where the woman was being held. He halted a few feet from the other male and held out a hand, cautious.

"I'm Soren Fontaine," he said in greeting. Now that the demon was close, he believed the male looked vaguely familiar, but he couldn't place him.

The demon shook hands with him. "I've heard of you and your brothers and I've seen you around. But, then, who hasn't?

Your eldest brother sits on the Council, and the three of you run the infamous resort."

The demon's tone was cordial, allowing him to relax some. "That's right. And you are?"

"Valafar. My clan lives just outside the city limits."

Valafar. He stared at the demon as the name formed meaning. *By the gods, it can't be.* But it was, and from the wry curve of the male's lips, he saw the exact moment when Soren figured it out.

"Prince Valafar," he said, giving a slight bow. "It's good to meet you. You certainly keep to yourself and your clan these days, refusing to reclaim your seat on the Council."

A flash of sadness darkened his eyes, then vanished behind a mask of indifference. "Obscurity is often a necessity and a relief in a world like ours. There is nothing public life has to offer that I want any part of, and there hasn't been for many eons."

"To the disappointment of many in the Southern Coalition," Soren informed him seriously. Prince Valafar was an anomaly among demons, a worthy male who ruled his clan with strength and fairness. And if the long-standing rumors were true, his magic was extremely powerful, making him the most sought after of allies.

"They seemed to have managed just fine in my absence."

That tone said *closed subject* in no uncertain terms, but Soren had a different question. "Does the woman know who you really are?"

"Her name is Harley, and I saw no reason why she should. My friend Zenon and I found her stranded on the road a few nights ago. We took her home, and naturally had some fun together before bringing her here."

"Naturally," he replied, his tone stiff. It burned that the

demons had enjoyed her first, but there was not a damned thing he could do about it. Knowing demons, especially that particular clan, the woman had no doubt been more than willing and had the time of her life. And, yeah, Valafar had deftly changed the subject.

"Just yanking your chain. Though I'm not involved in politics any longer, I pay attention and recognized you when you began bidding. Couldn't resist a bit of fun there at the end, after the others had given up." His eyes twinkled with mirth.

"Yeah, thanks for that," he drawled sarcastically. He was starting to like the prince, though he didn't want to. "You cost me a bundle."

Valafar looked unperturbed. "You can afford it, Lord Soren."

"I can." He paused, curious. "So, you and your friend are what? Her captors?"

"That's the way things began, yes. But the female burrowed under our skin, and before we knew it, we'd become . . . fond of her."

Soren took notice. Forming any sort of emotional attachment wasn't something a demon admitted lightly. "Then why not keep her? Though I'm glad you didn't."

"She's not my destiny or Zen's. She's not our mate, nor is she the mate of anyone in our clan, and although we could have kept her for our pleasure, I had the strong sense that she belonged somewhere else. That if I brought her here and cast her fate to the winds, her destiny would be fulfilled. Perhaps it has been." He eyed Soren in speculation.

"Maybe it has," he allowed. "I scented her, and she called to me. I believe she might be my mate."

No! Lies! Leila is our mate!

With an effort, he forced down his unwelcome hitchhiker. But what if his beast was right? How did he know this stranger was his true love? It seemed he was surrounded by lies, and picking through them would take some time.

"From your reaction to her, I suspect as much, also." Frowning, Valafar leaned closer and peered into the depths of Soren's eyes for a long moment. Slowly, he straightened, and when he spoke, his voice was quiet enough that it couldn't be heard by anyone else. "What sickens you, vampire?"

Shit. "What do you mean?"

The demon hesitated, then shook his head. "I think you know. There is something wrong inside you. A presence that is something . . . other than vampire."

"So what if there is? I can't imagine how that's your business."

"Normally I would agree, but Harley makes it my business," the demon prince said, his tone cool.

His fists clenched at his sides. "She's bought and paid for, and therefore no longer your concern. Why this interest in a slave?" That sounded so horrible, so unfeeling, he cringed inwardly.

"Is that what you think?" Valafar looked upon Soren as though he were a particularly disgusting bug. "That the purchase of this human makes her less?"

"Isn't that what demons believe?" he snapped. "You sold her."

"Ah, but it isn't a question of what *my* kind believes, is it?" Valafar said quietly. "And *I'm* not the one who bought her."

Touché. Soren felt about an inch tall. Who was the monster here?

He looked away, fighting the sudden urge to lunge and rip out the demon's throat and show him. Not his urge, but that of the interloper that had taken up residence in his soul. "The woman, Harley. What is she to you?"

"In truth? A capture that turned into more of a rescue. I can't say that I've ever had a mere human affect me the way she has." Valafar took a step closer. "If something terrible were to happen to Harley, I'd take it personally."

"She's under my protection now, and I'll do my best to make sure she's safe."

"But?"

After glancing behind him to ensure they were still alone, he returned his attention to Valafar. "I can't put a name to the darkness inside me," he admitted. "It appeared shortly after I made a bargain with a priestess, then fed from her."

Valafar flinched at this news. "What was the bargain?"

"To return my dead mate to me."

"And you think this deceased mate is Harley?"

Did he, really? Their physical differences were great, and so was their scent. "I don't know," he said in frustration.

"Who is this priestess? Was she the one in the booth with you?"

Soren carefully watched his reaction. "Yes. Her name is Leila Doucet."

"Satan's balls," the demon muttered with disgust. "Even my clan won't fuck with that rank whore. Stupid vampire, what were you thinking? That witch is a pestilence, always hanging around the Council and draining her opponents of their lives."

"Wait. What do you mean, *their lives?* I've heard only of the one Fae she was accused of killing."

Valafar gave a dark laugh and shook his head. "He wasn't the first, nor will he be the last." He dropped his voice to a whisper. "Don't you know she is not what she seems?"

Anxiety tightened his gut. "Tell me what you know. Please."

The demon opened his mouth but then flicked a glance over Soren's shoulder. "Not now. Your black widow crouches at the end of the hallway like the venomous thing she is. Wouldn't do for her to overhear."

"Later, then?" *Dammit!*

"You can count on it. I'll pay you a call in the next few days to check on Harley." He grinned. "And perhaps partake of your resort's infamous offerings, since I've never had the pleasure."

"Consider yourself invited. Your friend, too."

"Until then."

The big demon prince strode away with a brush of raven wings, but in the opposite direction of the club's main room, and disappeared around the corner. Soren guessed there was a back entrance. If so, that was the route he'd be taking.

Steeling himself, he walked to the door of the room containing the woman who would no doubt change him completely. Pushed it open.

And stepped inside to meet his destiny.

5

*H*arley stood shaking in her shoes. Well, her bare feet, since she was still as naked as the day she'd entered the world.

She was cold, but that wasn't the only reason for the attack of shivers. All she'd been through in the past few days had finally caught up with her. And out there tonight . . .

Blazing Hades, she'd been a total slut in front of all those people. Creatures. Whatever. They'd reacted in kind, hurling all sorts of lewd comments and suggestions, and she couldn't even blame them. Part of her had been freaked out. But the other part had loved the attention and the control the handler possessed over her body. He'd played her like a master does a fine instrument, making her sing.

The trembling was a culmination of everything. Her old life gone in the blink of an eye. And good riddance, anyway, because it had mostly been for shit. But would the future that lay in wait be any better?

The door to the dressing room opened, and she jumped.

Beside her, she was vaguely aware of Kai doing the same with a gasp. All her focus was on the male filling the doorway.

Oh. My. She stared, and he returned her regard with a heated look.

He wasn't as big in muscle mass as Valafar, but he commanded the room all the same. He was tall and broad shouldered, with just the right amount of muscle on his lean frame, from what she could tell with him fully clothed. His legs, hugged by black dress pants, went on forever and showed off a nice package at the front. Long, straight, silky, dark brown hair brushed the shoulders of his tailored blue shirt and contrasted with his piercing amber eyes fringed with dark lashes. *Eagle's eyes,* she thought. And his *face.*

Beautiful. Whereas the demons were sexy in their brutal, primitive way, this man was simply the most gorgeous creature she'd ever seen. Bar none. Full lips, high, arched brows, cheekbones to die for. He could have been the signature model for one of those art exhibits she used to write about. What artist wouldn't long to immortalize that face?

His eyes flicked from hers momentarily to pin the assistant to the floor. "What's your name, boy?"

The kid swallowed. "Kai, sir."

"Where are her clothes, Kai? She can't leave like that," he said, gesturing to her nakedness.

"She didn't arrive with anything but this wrap." Quickly, the boy fetched the lacy scrap and held it up.

"That won't do. Get her something decent to wear, and make it fast."

"Right away, sir!" He fled.

Which left her alone with this man she had no idea how to address. She opted for keeping it simple. "Thank you."

He nodded. "You're welcome, Harley. But there's no reason for thanks. Clothing is a simple, basic need."

"Some wouldn't think so where a slave is concerned." She wondered how he'd known her name, but decided one of the club's workers must've told him.

"True. But I have no intention of keeping you as my slave."

"Oh." That news should've given her vast relief. But it didn't. All she felt was sharp disappointment. "So you bought me for someone else? Where will I go?"

Stepping up to her, he reached out and ran his fingers down her cheek. "Oh, you're going home with me, just not as my slave. My brothers and I don't believe in that practice. We're much more into . . . *willing* captives."

Her drooping spirits lifted again. "Really? That sounds rather tempting," she said, her voice husky. *Am I let down? Do I actually need to be an official slave in order to be dominated? No,* she decided. A strong male wouldn't need that distinction between them. "How does it work for me, then? Legally, I mean."

"Easy. You go home with me and we light a bonfire with your papers before my oldest brother shoves them up my ass."

She laughed softly. "Well, we can't have that. Can I ask . . . I don't know what I should call you."

"How rude of me. I'm Lord Soren Fontaine."

A vampire lord! *Soren.* The name sent a skitter through her, and her pulse fluttered. For a moment she couldn't catch her breath, and he took her arm.

"Are you all right?" he asked in concern.

"I think so. Just felt a little strange for a second. I'm okay now."

"You're sure?" He didn't sound convinced.

"Positive. Your name sounded familiar," she said, changing the subject. "I could swear I've seen or heard it before."

A flash of very real pain was there in his golden eyes, gone in an instant to be replaced by a neutral expression. "We're in the society pages quite a bit. My brothers and I run La Petite Mort, an adult pleasure resort outside the city. Aldric is the oldest, then me, and then Luc. You might have seen any of our names in the paper, recounting our legendary carousing." He winked. "Or, more likely, you've read about Aldric and his battles on the Council. He's the leader of all the vampires in the Southern Coalition. The ancient ones would call him king, but he hates that term and refuses to be addressed as such."

"I might have read of you all. I'm from St. Louis and I wrote society articles at the paper there. Sometimes we'd catch news from the south, so it's possible."

Just then, Kai returned with a pair of sweat pants and a T-shirt, and handed them over to her with an apologetic smile. "Sorry there's no underwear. These aren't the greatest, but you'll be covered."

"A little late for that," she said wryly. Still, she took them gratefully, yanking on the sweats and then the shirt with relief. Nothing stranger than being naked among clothed people.

"Here's your slave's papers, sir." Kai handed them over. "The manager sends his regards."

Soren took the documents, a faint look of distaste crossing his face. "Thanks."

"Good-bye, Kai," she added.

"Take care," the assistant said cheerfully. Satisfied with his night's work, he left.

She eyed Soren curiously as he tucked away the papers. "Tell me something."

"If I can."

"Why go to the trouble of coming here, going against your

own policy to buy me, only to free me five minutes later? Especially when I'm sure you have willing captives, as you put it, at your beck and call."

The vampire hesitated, appearing unsettled. "I'm not sure I have a good answer for you just yet, other than 'I have my reasons.' But in the meantime, I plan to keep you busy."

"Doing what, exactly?" At least she'd have a purpose.

"Do you know what it means to be a vampire's Chosen?"

A jolt of excitement went through her every cell, but she tried to contain it. He might be leading up to something else for her rather than an offer that many men and women would give their souls to obtain. "It means being available to the vampire any time of day for feedings and sex. It's a symbiotic relationship, because while the Chosen provides those two essential things to the vampires of his or her coven, the Chosen's life is naturally extended by the contact."

"Extended by a few decades, but it doesn't make the Chosen immortal or keep them from aging," he clarified.

"Right. But it's still good job security," she said.

Soren laughed, and she liked the deep rumble. "That's one way to look at it. Anyway, you will be one of my Chosen, for my exclusive use."

Oh yes! Inside she did the victory dance, but common sense demanded more answers. Outwardly, she remained collected. "How is that any different from being a vampire's slave?"

"Very. Acting as my Chosen is a job offer. Yes, I'm requiring you to try it out for a few weeks before I grant your freedom. But should you find that you dislike the duties, or me in particular, you have the option to leave and seek other employment. Unlike a slave."

A thrill went through her body at the prospect of belonging to this man—in every way. Staring at him, taking in the determined set of his jaw, the heat in his eyes, she knew that no piece of paper, or lack thereof, would stand in his way when it came to owning her.

He stepped close, reached out to brush a strand of hair from her face. That golden gaze mesmerized her, drawing her into the flames. Her skin burned from the mere graze of his fingers, and she wanted more. "Is this acceptable to you?"

"Yes," she breathed. "I want to know what it's like to be Chosen."

He gave her a sexy half smile. "It's pure pleasure, like nothing you've felt before." Cupping the back of her head, he brought his lips to hers, whispering against them. "It's addictive, a little dangerous. Complete ecstasy. I'll show you."

"Please."

He captured her mouth and thrust his tongue inside, exploring. The vampire tasted so good, and felt even better with his hard chest pressed against her, holding her close. He surrounded her totally, and while she knew the very real dangers of succumbing to such a cunning predator, she'd never had the sense of peace that swamped her now. There was freedom in allowing him to have his way, a sense of rightness. She wanted him to take everything.

As he ate her mouth, one big hand slipped under her T-shirt to palm a breast, and he squeezed firmly but not hard enough to hurt. Two fingers pinched a taut nipple, then the other, sending wonderful little shocks through her nerve endings. Then his palm skimmed down her stomach, his hand dipping inside the waistband of the sweats to brush through the curls between her thighs, and on to rub the moist folds of her sex.

"Spread for me, sweetheart," he murmured.

Widening her stance, she locked her arms around his neck, breath hitching. "I need . . ." She didn't know how to verbalize it. She'd never been with a vampire.

"I know what you need. Trust me."

His fingers caressed her pussy, parted the slick flesh to enter her channel. He pumped them in and out, slowly finger-fucking her, taking care to rub against her throbbing clit.

"Ohh, it's so good," she rasped.

"It gets better, baby. Much better."

The hand at the back of her head burrowed in her hair, pulled back her head to expose her neck.

His voice was low, hypnotic. "You're mine. I'm going to feast on you, do whatever I want, and there's nothing you can do to stop me. And you're so fucking hot and ready for me, I think you love that idea."

She couldn't deny it. At the moment she was helpless against his power, and that knowledge was such a huge turn-on, she could hardly stand the anticipation of what he'd do next. Her pussy was wet, his fingers gliding, spreading her arousal. But when he bent and grazed her vulnerable neck with his fangs, she almost came.

So this was what it meant to be under a vampire's thrall! Every cell in her body screamed to be claimed. Used.

"Do it, please," she begged.

He nibbled kisses along her neck, teased with lips and tongue. Then he lingered at a spot near her jugular, hesitated—

And struck. The pain was indescribable, a jolt of agony that shot straight to her heart and limbs as she cried out. But it was over just as quickly as it began, and in its wake was a slow pulse.

It started like ripples in a pond, deep in her womb, flowing to her aching sex, to her toes and fingertips. The pleasure grew with every draw he took of her life's blood, became so big it couldn't be contained.

"Oh, gods, yes. Yes! Please don't stop."

She plastered herself to his front, clinging desperately, babbling. So close.

Her orgasm exploded and she cried out again, riding the waves crashing into her over and over. Just as she thought her body would shake apart from the sheer intensity, the pleasure began to ebb, gradually bringing her down from the awesome high to leave her sated. And so tired.

She slumped against his chest, and he withdrew his fangs, licking the wounds to close them. "Thank you, Harley." He kissed her temple. "You taste like the sweetest wine. I didn't want to stop."

"I've never felt anything like that. It's incredible."

Pulling back, he held her cheeks in his hands. "How are you feeling?"

"A bit tired, but good." She paused. "It was painful at first, and then . . . wow. What a high."

He nodded. "That's what you can expect as my Chosen, and the initial pain of my bite will become less with every feeding, until it has faded to mere discomfort. Or so the other Chosen tell me."

Others? she wanted to ask, but the details could wait.

"I'm taking you home. Are you ready?"

"I am." The word *home* chimed in her head, and she tried to imagine what having an actual *home*, not simply a place to sleep, would be like. Obviously Soren wanted her there. But it was much too early to pin her hopes on this new relationship, whatever his motivation.

Soren took her hand and led her out into the hallway, where Harley was met with another surprise—and this one nowhere near as pleasant as the introduction to Soren had been.

"Finally fetch our little slut, darling? Took you long enough."

Harley stopped in her tracks, processing what the woman in front of her had said as she assessed what was clearly an opponent. The woman was pale and slender, with long black hair and pointy features. Like an elf. Or a witch. She had on a gauzy black tank top with no bra underneath. But, then, why bother when all you had were two little bumps?

One corner of Harley's mouth quirked at the uncharitable thought.

"Find something funny, slave?"

Ooh, the bitch is displeased. "I'm not a slave," she declared, hoping Soren had her back on this. She hitched a thumb at the man. "Soren said so."

"Did he?" The woman shot a glare at him that was full of venom, promising a not-so-fun conversation later on.

"Yes, I did," he said, his tone uncompromising. "We don't keep slaves, and you know it. We don't need to and never have, and procuring one wasn't part of our bargain."

Looked like the sexy vamp could handle her, though. But what was this about a bargain? She had a feeling any deal the vampire had made with this unpleasant woman couldn't be good.

"Are you sure?" The witch leaned closer to Soren and looked intently into his eyes.

Something flashed across his expression before he steeled his gaze. "Yes, and I won't have any argument from you. It's her choice whether to come with us or not." He looked at Harley.

Harley realized what he was doing, and her opinion of him rose a notch. Despite his earlier firm resolve that she *would* leave with him and would try out her position as his Chosen, he was establishing Harley's place as an equal in his household, and she liked that. A choice and a place to be. It was more than she'd had to her name in a very long time.

"I'd like to go with you," she replied in a strong, sure voice. "I have nowhere else to stay, no living family, and I'm intrigued by what you've told me about your resort."

And I can't wait to serve you again, next time with you fucking me. Best to leave that unsaid for now.

"Then let's get out of here. Shall we?" He smiled and gestured toward the back entrance, where she'd come in.

Outside, the vampire waved, and a limo pulled up. She couldn't help but notice that he was solicitous and helped her into the car before climbing in after her, leaving the other woman to fend for herself. She fought back the urge to gloat in the bitch's face. Barely.

The woman sat across from her and Soren, glaring hard. Harley gave it right back to her, not willing to cower. She'd faced meaner, nastier people and survived. She didn't intimidate easily.

"Harley, this is Leila Doucet," the vampire lord told her. He glanced between them. "And this is Harley . . . I'm sorry, I didn't get your last name."

"Oh, it's Vaughn."

The vampire paled to the color of ash. "Vaughn?" he repeated in a tight voice.

"Yes. Why?"

After staring at her for a moment, he sort of shook himself and pasted on a strained smile. "I used to know someone with that last name, that's all."

"Oh." Obviously, there was more to it, but she let it go. For now. She shouldn't nose into his business at all, but once her curiosity was piqued, she couldn't rest until it was satisfied. Must be the journalist in her.

"Indulge me by telling us how you ended up in your predicament, captured by Valafar and Zenon, and placed on the auction block?" he prodded.

"That's a short, sad tale. Things ended badly between me and my last boyfriend. He got me fired, I hit the road, and here I am. The end."

Soren chuckled. "I have a feeling there's a lot more to the story. Like how your demon, Valafar, seems to have developed quite a soft spot for you and then gave you up anyway."

They both ignored Leila's rude snort.

"He's not *my* demon, and I'm not their mate. I guess that's reason enough."

Intrigued, he studied her thoughtfully. "So he told me. Still, two virile demons giving up such a lovely prize? I'm sure that almost never happens."

"I wouldn't know." She flushed at the compliment and cast about for another subject. "From what you've told me, La Petite Mort sounds wonderful. What do you do there, specifically?"

"Very little, from what I can see," Leila interrupted in a snotty tone. "Besides lie about and sex up the guests when he's not out spending Aldric's money."

Soren's expression darkened and he glanced at the other woman, clearly annoyed. "It's my job to make certain the guests receive the good time they've paid for and leave relaxed and happy at the end of their stay, but I don't 'lie about,' as you put it. And the income we make from the resort is one-third mine. I do not, and never would, sponge off either of my brothers."

The tension between the vampire and the woman was a trip wire pulled taut and ready to set off an explosion. Again, Harley wondered what the connection was between these two. Why did the vampire tolerate her?

Harley decided to continue as if Leila hadn't spoken. "You and your brothers are *hands-on* hosts, then?" she teased.

He eyed her, the slow burn returning to his gaze. "We take our clients' needs very seriously. And, yes, sometimes that means seeing to their desires personally. I hope that doesn't bother you."

"No, not at all," she said, not quite disguising the tiny thrill of intrigue in her voice. Then she remembered that he was her master. "Of course, what I think about it doesn't matter." In truth, the image of this delicious man *pleasing* his guests conjured all sorts of images that made her pussy tingle.

"It's about to become your home, too. I want you to be comfortable there."

"Do you treat all your captives so well?" The question burst out before she could stop it.

Instead of taking offense at her bluntness, he smiled. "Remember, you're not really my captive and can leave after you've given your new position a shot. I'm not a complete bastard, in spite of the fact that I'm a vampire who gets to have my cake and eat it, too. Besides . . . I have reason to believe my path and yours were destined to cross."

At this, he exchanged a quick, indecipherable look with Leila, who sat across from them, gloating like a cat with a mouthful of feathers. Harley felt the silent current running between the two and shivered a little. Was it her imagination, or was there a cold, dark presence that had suddenly manifested in the small confines of the limo? The drop in temperature in the vehicle was real enough, and she crossed her arms, rubbing at the chill bumps.

"And you have reason to think that why?"

The vampire returned his attention to Harley. "The details aren't important right now. What matters is that you're going home with me, where you'll spend a day or so getting your bearings before assuming your new duties."

She liked this prospect a lot. Not that she envisioned wanting to leave so soon, but that once again, she's been given a choice. "Okay, this sounds good. I just want to get a few more things straight. Before, you said I'd belong to you exclusively. Does that mean that I won't serve your brothers as a Chosen?"

He frowned, his expression darkening. An internal struggle seemed to rage in his golden eyes before he said, "Never. I may ask that you participate in entertaining our guests with me, but you'll not service Aldric or Luc. Even *my* proclivities don't extend to the incestuous, and I forbid it."

"Fine by me," she affirmed. "I suppose I could've dealt with that particular kink, though I'm glad I don't have to." She paused. "You said I'll be *one of* your Chosen. . . ."

"Yes. I must have sustenance every day, same as any other creature, and my appetites are great. That means using several Chosen per week," he said, almost apologetically. "It's much too dangerous and, in fact, would eventually be fatal for a single human to serve a vampire every day. We value our Chosen too highly to tax their bodies to the point of complete exhaustion.

Unfortunately, not every coven believes as we do, and some Chosen are discarded like broken toys once they're drained."

"That's horrible!"

"Yes, it is," he replied gravely.

"So, I'll get days off?"

"Same as any other employee at the resort," he assured her. "Our Chosen are the highest in rank of any employee, and each one works only three days per week—though some occasionally volunteer to work four, which is the absolute limit. One of Aldric's no-bullshit rules."

"Sounds smart and more than fair. What's the pay?"

"Other than room and board?" He named a number of credits per month that made her eyes widen in amazement.

"Wow. Sign me up!"

"Just be sure you read the contract first," Leila drawled.

Damn, she'd almost managed to forget the skinny ghoul parked across from her and the vampire. She managed to affect an innocent look. "Oh? Is that how Lord Soren got stuck with you? By not reading the fine print?"

The woman's eyes flashed, and for a split second Harley saw something truly frightening in her gaze. Something not quite . . . human. Or thought she did, because the vision passed so quickly, she might have imagined that the other woman's irises had totally disappeared into a pool of inky black. She could not possibly have seen her raven hair crawling, writhing like a nest of snakes.

And for a mere second, Leila's teeth appeared razor sharp when she smiled. "My mate and I have no need of paper. Our deal is sealed in blood."

Mates? Soren and that horrible woman? Proof that men were

truly ruled by their dicks. Why did that knowledge hurt far more than picturing the vampire feeding from and fucking all of his Chosen?

Harley turned her attention back to the vampire, who was looking away from both of them, his eyes a reflection of pure misery. Ah, so this was no love match, but indeed some kind of business deal. That lifted a weight from her heart, though she couldn't say why. Maybe it was simply that Soren didn't seem to deserve to be unhappy.

After that downer, conversation lagged, and the drive seemed endless. Finally, the limo turned down a long driveway and crawled at a sedate pace toward the most beautiful, sprawling mansion she'd ever laid eyes on. Illuminated by floodlights, the house seemed like a palace out of a childhood fairy tale, with nothing missing but the tower and moat.

This house, however, wasn't a castle but a white, plantation-style home with black shutters, three stories high, with soaring columns supporting a covered front driveway and a multitude of steps leading up to the front veranda. She couldn't see the guest cottages from here, but guessed they could be spotted by wandering the paths behind the main house and peering among the tall trees. Tomorrow she'd do some exploring.

The limo pulled to a stop in front of the mansion. Soren got out first and again gave Harley a hand out of the vehicle, leaving his *mate* to her own devices. Harley knew it was wrong of her to feel good about that, but Leila didn't exactly inspire waves of sympathy. There was something really off about the woman's relationship with Soren, but she'd have to be patient to learn what was going on.

Harley let the vampire guide her up the steps, grateful for

the warmth of his hand at the small of her back. This adventure suddenly seemed scarier than it had an hour ago, but perhaps her attack of nerves had been brought on by being tired.

A handsome young blond-haired man wearing brown leather pants and a snug black shirt met them at the door and ushered them inside, exclaiming at their arrival with enthusiasm, despite the lateness of the hour.

"Lord Soren, you're back! Super! And I see you've brought us a guest? Hello," he greeted her with an infectious smile. "I'm Jordan. And you are?"

"I'm Harley Vaughn," she answered, returning his friendliness. "Nice to meet you."

"The pleasure is mine, Harley. My, you must be dead on your feet! With Lord Soren's permission, I'll see you to a guest room." He glanced at the vampire, who nodded but made one correction.

"Yes, but show her to a suite close to mine. Harley is my newest Chosen, and I expect her to be treated with the proper respect." His direction brooked no argument.

"Yes, sir!" Jordan turned to Harley and scrunched his nose, making an adorable face. "Lucky girl. You're going to love it here. I'm a Chosen, too, serving Lord Aldric. He's an insatiable beast, but so are all three of them."

"Jordy." Soren's firm voice cut through the young man's chatter.

"Yes, sir?"

"I'm sure Harley is much too done in to listen to you rattle on all night."

"Oh! I'm sorry." He blushed becomingly. "Right this way."

Harley noted how Jordan glanced to her hand and the floor

near her feet. He must've noted that she had no possessions and, thankfully, didn't mention the lack. What little she owned had been left behind with her truck, which had no doubt been stolen and stripped for parts by now.

As Jordan led them up the stairs, she was aware of the vampire and Leila on their heels, and found herself grateful that they encountered no one else on the way to her new room. She'd had about all of the introductions and excitement she could take for one night. The bed was going to feel great.

At the second-floor landing, the young man showed her to the suite and opened the door, waiting for her to enter first. It was all she could do not to exclaim out loud at how freaking unreal her quarters were. Thick rugs accented polished hardwood floors, and a fireplace graced the wall opposite her king-sized bed. A sitting area with two stuffed chairs graced a spacious spot by the window, for reading or simply for gazing. Through a set of double doors was no doubt the bathroom, and if the space was anything like her bedroom, an army of vampires could probably bathe or shower in there.

Knowing what sort of resort this was, that was likely the point.

"I think you'll find everything you need here," Jordan declared, waving a hand. "But if you don't, give me a shout. I'm right down the hall, three doors on the right. Oh, and you'll find some big T-shirts and pajama bottoms in the dresser drawer, if you need something to sleep in. Tomorrow I'll make sure we get you some real clothes. In spite of what you might think, we don't go naked *all* the time around here."

"Jordy," Soren warned, exasperated.

She touched the younger man's arm. "Thank you, Jordan."

"Jordy, please. That's what all my friends call me."

She gave him a grin that didn't quite hide her exhaustion. She wondered how Soren's older brother kept this bundle of energy contained, and decided Aldric must be a strong man to keep up with him. "Jordy it is. Now, if you all don't mind, I'm going to shower and fall into bed."

"No problem. Good night, then!"

"Good night, Harley," Soren murmured.

Jordy bounced out, and Leila swept out after him, followed by Soren. Good riddance to the woman's departure. Soren could've stayed, though. But tomorrow was soon enough to get a good start on satisfying her curiosity with her new boss. Right now, she was going to fall over. Any second. Doing a face-plant on the bathroom tile wasn't the way to make a good impression.

Quickly, she ran the hot water, stepped in, and soaped her body. It felt heavenly and she groaned, rinsing away the night's activities, including the last traces of the aphrodisiac cream. Did Soren have any of that stuff on hand? She wasn't sure whether to hope so.

By the time she toweled off and slid between the crisp, clean sheets, she was more than ready to let go and drift pleasantly into dreamland. And she was almost there, too. . . .

When the unmistakable moans of carnal pleasure began to drift from the other side of the wall. With a sigh, she tried to settle in and get some sleep, but loneliness closed in.

Sounded like it was going to be a long fucking night. In more ways than one.

"I can scent your arousal, darling," Leila observed, smirking as they moved away from Harley's door. "Don't worry. I've got what you need."

"I seriously doubt that." Soren walked slightly ahead of the witch and made it to the door to his room in a few strides. Harley's suite was situated right next door to his, as he'd wanted. In hindsight, that could be more of a problem than he'd anticipated. But maybe not. His new Chosen definitely wasn't a prude, or taken aback by how he and his brothers lived.

But dammit, feeding from Harley had left him hard and aching. The witch wasn't about to let an opportunity pass.

Slender fingers wrapped around his arm. "It's not as though you have a choice, now, is it?" she pointed out with a sly chuckle. "You're sworn to see that my every desire is satisfied. Correct?"

At his door, he paused, gritting his teeth so hard his jaw hurt. He longed to shake off her touch, but didn't. She was right. He owed her for bringing Harley here, the woman whose scent and taste called to him like no other. He had to please Leila if he was to have any chance of getting to know Harley.

Opening the door, he stepped inside his suite without bothering to flip on a light. The moonlight streamed in through the bare windowpanes, plenty for a vampire to see. Walking over to the window, he stared through the glass into the night, understanding how a caged animal felt. This witch played a dangerous game, and he must play with even more skill in order to learn her secrets.

Probably at great cost to himself and his brothers. But he had no choice.

Leila's arms slid around him from behind and she pressed against his back, breasts brushing him through his shirt. Not nearly as full and luscious as Harley's, rather small, in fact, but his body began to warm. Insistent fingers found the button of his pants, then the zipper, making short work of both and parting the material. Pushing it down off his hips.

Harley. Her kiss had been potent, the sample of her blood such an insane rush of wicked joy. Nothing like Helena's nice, if muted, flavor, though a part of him had longed for them to taste the same. To take comfort in the familiar. But so far, Harley was more of a temptation than Helena had ever been, and it left him confused.

Leila lifted free his cock and balls, cradling the heavy weight of him in one hand, and it was easy to imagine Harley undressing him like this, touching his naked skin. Back at the club, he'd wanted that badly, had been primed and ready to sink his cock into her heat, but he'd restrained himself and instead concentrated on showing her how good it could be.

As Leila manipulated him, his cock lengthened. Hardened. She stroked him, and the dreaded darkness returned. Holding back his desires earlier worked against him now. The beast inside him stretched, awakened, and listened with a purr to her every word.

"Ooh, you want me. I have the proof right in my hand, throbbing with desire. Isn't that so?"

He wanted to deny the hated truth, but couldn't. The witch and this *thing* had him under their control, and he tried to fight. But he had no leverage, nothing whatsoever to hold on to. No foothold on his sanity when they teamed up against him. Against his will, the beast unfurled to merge with him again.

Yesss, the beast hissed. *Give yourself to her.*

He struggled to stay in control even as he kicked off his shoes, stepped out of the pants, and turned around to face her. She slowly unfastened the buttons on his shirt, then slid it off his shoulders. It joined the pants, and he was naked, jutting toward her, so ready he hurt.

"This is good," she crooned. "It's taking you less time than before to submit to our bond and embrace your power. Each time we're together, you'll come around more quickly, and afterward your beast will take longer and longer to subside, until your transformation is complete. We'll be unstoppable then, my love."

He arched into her touch, letting his eyes drift closed as she squeezed and stroked. "Unstoppable how? What will we do then?"

Have to find out. Tell Aldric and Luc.

No! You will do only as your mistress bids. There is nothing that matters but our desires, and we know what your kind longs for. What you need.

I don't know what you mean.

Oh, but he was very afraid he did.

"Come to bed, my love."

He went with her, allowed her to push him onto his back.

"Wait here and spread yourself for me. Just like that."

She left his side and returned in a few moments, carrying a couple of items. It took him a few seconds to realize they were cuffs attached to chains with locks. When she crawled to kneel on the bed by his head and took an arm, he didn't fight her. His arousal was too great, the slit on the head of his cock oozing with pre-cum.

That's right, vampire. You want this, don't you? We want this.

Leila cuffed one wrist, then wrapped the silver chain around the iron railing of the headboard several times before snapping the lock through the chain. *Silver!*

He was held fast, no hope of escaping until she let him go. He was totally at her mercy, and the knowledge only heightened the thrill.

"You look beautiful bound this way," she said, smoothing a hand over his chest. "Tell me what you want."

"Ride me," he said hoarsely.

"Perhaps. When you beg for it." With a predatory smile, she moved between his spread thighs and swallowed his cock. Or most of it.

He bucked, groaning at the glorious feeling of her tongue and throat massaging his rigid length. She was driving him crazy, bobbing down and up, getting him wet. Sucking him like he was her favorite dessert.

The torture lasted a couple of minutes before she raised her head. Her expression was hungry, and he needed to feed her. "Oh, gods, fuck me," he rasped. "I need it. Please."

Sitting up, she moved into place and straddled his hips, positioning the weeping mushroom head at her opening. Slowly, she slid down, impaling herself on him. Inch by lovely inch. Her pussy clasped him, hot and wet. Dripping for him.

"Shit, yes. Let me have that pretty cunt."

His dirty talk spurred her on, and she rode him faster. "You like me taking this big cock, don't you?"

"Yes. Take what you want."

"You'll give me anything," she commanded.

He gritted his teeth, trying to fight her hold over his mind. This was wrong. She was going to gain control of his mind and use him to further her agenda. Hurt others.

"No," he whispered. "Not anything."

"You will, because I can give you what you desire most." Her pussy continued to work him. She rode him, hands splayed on his chest, black hair falling around her. Such a slut, a bad girl. "Even now, I'm giving you the will to overcome your stupid morals and take it."

She knows. Your mate knows that your greatest hunger is to sink your teeth and cock into your prey and drink, fuck, and drink until the fragile human heart stills. This is the need that every vampire hides. Do not deny it!

"It's not true," he moaned. But it was. Cum boiled in his balls at the thought of the one indulgence a vampire must avoid at all costs.

"Being a predator is your nature. The lion doesn't apologize to the antelope because he must eat, and neither should you." It was like she could see inside him. She understood. "Imagine how it will be. Have a sip of my blood and embrace who you are."

"It's wrong to kill. I won't harm anyone." The darkness of her blood beckoned. He wanted it so much it hurt. But he managed to resist.

"No, it isn't." She fucked him, grinding, her pussy juices slathering his balls. *So good.*

"I would never hurt him. Never," he insisted. He wouldn't hurt an innocent young man like Jordy.

"You lie, my love. I'm going to prove it to you."

"How?" His breathing quickened, along with his groin. Any second, he was going to blow.

"I'll arrange for him to meet you soon. He lives to please, and so he'll never suspect. Such an innocent, trusting soul. And when you have him underneath you, helpless, you'll experience your true power and fill him with the gift of your cum as you drain him."

With a shout, Soren's orgasm exploded, filling Leila's clenching pussy. They rode out the shocks together until she slumped over his chest, spent.

True to her word, the beast didn't subside right away. Its claws were sinking deeper into him, their consciousness, their insatiable hunger, becoming one. How much longer did he have?

"Very good, my mate," she praised, kissing his cheek. "You're coming along so well. Very soon I'm going to show you the glories of taking what you want. And eventually, you'll give me one of the tools I require to achieve my goals."

"What's that?" The gleam in her dark eyes gave him a chill even before she answered.

"Your child."

6

*S*oren was losing his mind.

The beast had finally gone quiet—after Leila had spent half the night fucking them both into a coma. Sitting up, he rubbed his sore wrists. "What is she? Tell me, you bastard!"

For once, the gods-damned beast ignored him when Soren wanted to talk. "She's not human, is she?" he demanded. Still no answer. Sliding out of bed, he tossed the sheets and blankets aside. "Fine. I'm going to see Aldric, then. If he doesn't know what the hell this woman is, if she even *is* a woman, he won't rest until he helps me find out."

You cannot do that. Her destruction is your own.

His footsteps faltered halfway to the bathroom. "Stop speaking in riddles and explain for once," he muttered in frustration.

That was not a riddle, stupid vampire. What part of you can't destroy her without destroying yourself *isn't clear to you?*

His gut churned. "Destroy myself in the literal sense. As in dead."

Ah, you're catching on. The bond between you and Leila can be broken by killing her—if you could learn how it's done. To do that you'd have to discover her secret, and that I will not tell you. For severing the bond and ridding the world of her means you die, too. And if you die, so do I, something we cannot allow to happen. Do you want to die?

"Of course not," he snapped, shoving his fingers through his hair. "Who does?"

But he would do it, he realized. If he managed to retain one shred of his own mind, in the end he'd sacrifice himself to keep his loved ones safe. Carefully, he concentrated on forming a mental shield between the beast and his thoughts. One small piece of himself was all he needed to do what he must when the time came.

He tested the shield, prayed it held. Hoped that neither the beast nor the witch learned they weren't the only ones with secrets. Soren had a big one, too, and if she learned that her efforts to have him sire her child were totally in vain, she might turn her attentions to one of his brothers instead. She could not find out.

He had to play her game, and play it better.

Gripping the counter by the sink, he stared into his own eyes in the bathroom mirror and searched, despite the shield, for any hint of the hated voice in his head. Any sign of the beast that was slowly taking over his consciousness. If he'd been expecting something out of a horror movie, perhaps a hideous, demonic face masking his or a maniacal light in his eyes, he was relieved to find that wasn't the case. He just looked like Soren, if frazzled around the edges.

Suddenly, talking with Aldric right away wasn't quite as pressing as the need to see Harley. The lure of her was a physical pull, a draw he hadn't felt since he'd first laid eyes on Helena so long ago. As lonely as he'd been, as much as he'd hoped for a way to bring back his mate, he'd never really thought to experience that connection with another woman. Was it Harley's beauty that drew him in? Her taste that left him wanting more? Or her feistiness, so unlike demure Helena?

He didn't know. But he wasn't going to unlock the mystery of Harley by standing here ruminating when he should be taking action. Decision made, he turned from the counter and grabbed the silk robe hanging on the hook behind the bathroom door and walked out. In the hallway, he stood outside her door, knocked, and waited. Shuffling sounds came from the other side and then it opened a crack, revealing a sleepy Harley. She was naked, from what he could see of her arm and a tantalizing curve of hip and leg.

Her hair was mussed, shadows under her eyes as though she hadn't slept well. But she brightened on seeing him and gave him a smile. "Good morning."

"Good morning, Harley. How did you sleep?"

She shrugged. "Not too bad, I guess. You?"

The woman was lying, but he chose not to make an issue of it. "All right, when I finally managed to close my eyes." That was no lie—Leila had kept him awake into the wee hours. "There should be a robe in your closet. Why don't you put it on and join me for breakfast? Then I've got something in mind for us after."

"Is that an order?" The curve of her luscious mouth and twinkle in her eyes hinted that she wasn't opposed to the idea of being told what to do.

"Yes. Your first official one in your new home," he said, pleased. "Hurry. I don't have all day."

He did have plenty of time, actually. Thankfully, Leila had been gone when he woke up, and he found himself free to enjoy his day. But as he pushed the door open wider, it filled him with satisfaction to see Harley's firm, delectable rear as she hustled to do his bidding. He liked that she had fire yet seemed to need a dominant hand.

Digging in the closet, she found the green silk robe and pulled it on, wrapping it around her and tying it at her waist. He approved. It matched her eyes and hugged her figure nicely, and it showed off the taut tips of her clearly outlined nipples. Sometimes a bit of covering that hinted at the beauty beneath was just as sensual as wearing nothing at all.

When she headed toward the bathroom, he held up a hand. "Where are you going?"

She blinked at him. "Just to brush my hair. It's messy."

"Did I tell you to go brush your hair, or complain that it's disheveled?" he asked sharply. It wasn't a big deal—except he wanted to know how far her need for dominance really went.

Her pupils dilated, and the unmistakable scent of arousal reached his nose. "No, master, you didn't."

Master. There was that word he loved to hear from his Chosen. It made him hard as fucking nails every time. "Then get your pretty ass over here and let's go eat."

"Okay," she said in a husky voice.

She joined him, and, slipping an arm around her waist, he ushered them from the room. "I think I'll reward you for your swift compliance." He considered for a few moments as they descended the stairs. "I'm going to speak with Nikki, our cook's assistant. Wait here."

Striding to the kitchen, he found Nikki stirring a bowl of

eggs. The young man looked up and smiled hesitantly, no doubt still wary of him after the rendezvous with Leila. "Lord Soren. What can I get for you this morning? Want an omelet, or would you like to put in a special order?"

"Make that breakfast for two—omelets, some fruit and muffins, and juice. Instead of the dining room, however, I want the tray brought to the bathhouse," he directed. His stomach growled in appreciation, and he thanked the gods that vampires could eat what they wanted.

"Yes, sir," the boy answered brightly, setting down the bowl. He gave Soren a look of undisguised curiosity. "Is this for you and the new Chosen you brought home? The whole estate is buzzing about her."

"Yes, and you'd do well not to listen to gossip about Harley, much less spread it." His dangerous tone caused the younger man to pale.

"No, sir! I wouldn't," he stammered. "I was just wondering, that's all."

Giving the kid some slack, Soren clapped his shoulder. "Just a reminder. This female is special to me, and I won't have her harmed in any way."

"I understand, sir. I'll send that tray right over."

"Good boy."

Leaving Nikki to his work, Soren rejoined Harley, who was chatting with Jordy. On seeing Soren's approach, the boy bid her a quick good-bye and hurried back to whatever he was supposed to be doing.

"I think he's a little intimidated by you," she remarked as the Chosen vanished through a doorway at the end of the corridor.

"I don't know why. I've never done a thing to Jordy." He frowned.

Oh, but you want to, the beast rumbled. *And you will.*

Not now. With great effort, he squashed the intruder and offered Harley his arm. "Shall we?"

"I can't wait to see what you have in mind."

He led Harley toward the back of the house and turned down the hallway that skirted the gardens. The outside wall was glass from floor to ceiling, giving a great view of the lush, tropical flora and fauna that flourished in the Deep South. He watched her admire the scenery, taking pride in his home. It was as close to paradise as they could make it, and he loved sharing it with someone special.

At the end, he pushed through a set of doors, and beside him she stopped to stare. "Oh, wow. This is unbelievable."

"Isn't it?"

He took in the space as though viewing it through her eyes. The bathhouse was enclosed, the pool a large L surrounded by palatial columns, plants, and flowers. The vaulted ceiling soared overhead, making the room seem even bigger than it was. Fragrant steam rose from the surface of the pool, testifying to cozy heat for those who ventured in. At the moment, they had the place to themselves.

He waved a hand. "This is one of my favorite areas of our resort."

"I can see why! It's amazing. Are we getting in?"

He didn't miss the enthusiasm in her question, and grinned. "Of course. Ladies first."

Without hesitation, she shed the robe and waded in, the water lapping at her ankles and thighs as she carefully negotiated the steps. It wasn't too deep, barely more than waist high, and she walked out a ways, slapping her palms on the water's surface like a playful child.

Chuckling, he followed suit, leaving his robe in a heap next to hers and venturing out. The warm bath felt so good, soothing muscles that had gotten much exercise of late. Reaching the spot where she stood splashing, he grabbed her around the middle, pulled her back against his front, then bent to nibble her neck. She giggled.

His erection rested along the crease of her butt, eager to be buried in her snug channel, but he didn't want to rush this. He wanted to know this intriguing woman inside and out.

"The water smells so good," she commented, dipping a hand in and bringing a scoopful to her nose.

"Herbal bath salts. They're supposed to promote healing and relaxation."

"I don't think they work."

"How so?" He nuzzled her ear.

"You're not relaxed." To prove her point, she ground her bottom against his rod and tilted her head to the side, baring her neck in submission.

Laughing softly, he let his teeth graze over the delicate skin but didn't bite. The prize would be sweeter for the anticipation. "Not yet, beautiful. Let's eat our breakfast."

He gestured to a servant who'd arrived bearing the promised tray. The man placed it poolside and addressed Soren. "Will that be all, sir?"

"For now. Thank you."

The man nodded and left, and Soren took her hand, leading her to a built-in bench that was set just a foot or so below the water line. Taking a seat, he pulled Harley onto his lap and positioned her sideways, one arm holding her tight.

"If this isn't the height of decadence, I don't know what is." Smiling, she placed a palm on his chest. "I feel so spoiled."

"I believe you deserve to be pampered some after what you've been through." The idea of her being alone in the world, homeless, jobless, and struggling to survive, made his gut churn. Yet she'd survived, where Helena would not have.

Harley shook her head. "I don't know about that. I just did what I had to do and went with the hand I was dealt."

The truth of that hit him hard—Helena would have been eaten alive if left to survive on the streets. She would never have been as resourceful or bounced back as well as Harley, and she would've died before consorting with demons or allowing herself to be placed on the auction block. The shame would've killed her. Another resounding difference between the two.

"You're an amazing woman," he murmured.

Succumbing to temptation, he crushed his mouth to hers, tasting as his fingers skimmed down the slick swell of her breast to find a pert nipple, puckered and tight from being wet and then exposed to the air. He played with it as he swirled his tongue with hers, stroked, teased, and pinched until she arched against him, whimpering for more.

Pulling back, resisting the urge to impale her then and there, he caressed her cheek. "Food first, then play."

"Or food *while* we play," she suggested in a husky voice, wiggling on his lap.

"Perhaps. Now hold still." He tried to be stern, but managed only to sound as needy as his companion—a fact that didn't escape her, from the heated look she gave him.

Reaching out to the tray at the edge of the pool, he took his fork, cut off a bite of omelet, and speared it, bringing the savory morsel to her lips.

She frowned. "I'm not an infant. I can feed myself."

Her mutinous expression was cute, with her jaw set and green eyes glittering, but he forced himself not to smile. That would undermine his authority and ruin the lesson. Instead, he arched a brow and returned her glare with a stony look. "Are you defying me, Chosen?"

Startled, she blinked at him, annoyance vanishing. "No. I'm sorry, master."

Softening his tone, he relented some. "I know. The more you're with someone, the easier it is to get comfortable, forget who's in charge. I don't want you to walk on eggshells around me, but you must remember I'm in control. Always."

"I'll do my best, sir. Though I admit I'll probably forget again, because I've been on my own for so long," she said. She took the bite he offered and chewed, humming in pleasure. "That's fantastic."

"Our cook is the best." He fed her more, and decided that just observing her while she ate was an orgasmic experience. He liked the way her pink tongue flicked out to catch the bits, how she closed her eyes as she enjoyed the meal. He liked taking care of her needs.

All of them.

After he'd fed her the omelet and fruit until she protested that she was full, he questioned her between bites of his own meal. "Tell me how it happened that you ended up on your own."

"I already told you that my boyfriend got me fired and—"

"No, before that. Where is your family?"

She looked away, but not before he saw the flash of pain. "They're all dead. My parents and younger brother were killed in a car accident several years ago. They had a modest income and not many credits saved, so I used what I'd managed to save from my job at the newspaper, then sold the house to pay off the bills."

"What about aunts and uncles? Cousins?" He tried to sound casual, though he was dying to learn what had become of Helena's branch of the family after the Fontaines had lost touch with them, as well as *if* and how Harley was descended from her.

"I have a few cousins scattered around, but we were never close and I don't know how to contact them. As far as aunts and uncles, they're all gone, too."

Damn. No information there regarding his dead mate. He wasn't going to learn more unless he told her about Helena outright, and he wasn't ready to do that. Not yet. Setting down his fork, he turned all his attention to the woman in his arms.

"I'm sorry for what you've had to go through," he murmured, kissing her lips.

"It's been difficult. But I've come through it, thanks to Val . . . and you."

Harley was far from out of the woods where Soren was concerned, but he didn't have it in him to tell her that he might just be the greatest nightmare she'd ever faced. No, he was much too selfish to ruin this developing closeness. He wanted her, and it didn't matter at the moment who she was or where she'd come from.

She was simply his.

And it felt right.

Putting his back to the pool's edge, he turned her to face

him so she straddled his thighs. His cock was nestled against her curls, the swirl of the warm water adding a welcome caress. He ached so badly, but was more determined than ever not to rush this wonderful interlude. Cupping both breasts, he thumbed the stiff peaks of her nipples, loving her breathy gasp and how she pushed into his touch.

Continuing to pluck at one nipple, he slid a palm down her stomach, below the surface of the water, to grip his cock. He fisted it tightly, moaning as he pumped the shaft with agonizing slowness, letting his imagination run wild.

"Do you need some help with that?" Harley asked, lips turning up.

"I'd love some." He took one of her hands, but she pulled back.

"Not like that," she said with a mischievous grin. "I'm going to be a mermaid, seducing my sexy sea captain."

"Really? How?"

"Watch."

With that, she pushed off his lap and moved to stand in the deeper water a few feet beyond the bench. Taking a deep breath, she lowered herself until she was completely submerged. In fascination, he eyed her rippling form as she swam toward him, long auburn hair streaming behind her like a banner. When she reached him, she tugged on his calves, urging him, he thought, to scoot to the lip of the bench.

He did and was rewarded.

Slender fingers squeezed his balls and began to manipulate them, a damned good feeling in the medium of water. But when she took the head of his cock between her lips and began to suckle him . . .

He nearly came undone. If anything had ever felt as fucking terrific as being sucked underwater, he couldn't recall what it might have been. "Shit," he moaned, lifting his hips. If any sea captain had encountered a mermaid like this one, he hadn't stood a chance.

That hot, tight cavern enveloped his dick like a silken glove. She took him deep inside, down her throat, doing something mind-boggling with her tongue and the muscles of her throat to massage his length, driving him to the very precipice. Gripping her hair, he indulged in fucking her, using her as his naughty hole.

In and out, making her swallow all of him. To the root. His balls boiling.

But he didn't want to come yet, and he had to let her up for air. Worried that he'd let her go too long, he forced her head up, grabbed her, and hauled her back into his lap. She heaved a lungful of air, and he wiped her face and her soaking tresses clear of water.

"That was incredible," he praised. "Are you all right?"

"Better than." To prove it, she reached between them and grasped his throbbing shaft. "Is this for me?"

"It is, and I hope you're ready, because I can't wait another second."

His hands spanned her waist and he lifted her slightly, then took his cock and brought it to her pussy lips. She needed no further encouragement and sank onto him inch by inch, lashes fluttering closed.

"Oh, Soren. Master."

That damned word! It tossed him into the abyss every single time. Capturing her mouth with his, he began to fuck her with slow thrusts. There was nothing finer on earth than the joining of two bodies, lost to passion. The tips of her nipples lapped at the water and grazed his chest as they bounced together, her fingers digging into his shoulders.

It wasn't going to be long before he lost control, and he relished the moment as much as he dreaded it. He didn't want this moment to be over, but his body demanded completion. That he mark this female as his.

His to fuck. To drink. To do whatever he wanted with, because she'd given herself to him.

He increased the tempo until he was slamming into her, putting as much force into it as he could, given their position in the pool. When the tingling started in the base of his spine and he knew he couldn't hold off anymore, he pulled her head back, bared her throat, and struck.

Her scream of ecstasy, her pussy clenching around his cock, drove him over the edge. As her rich blood flowed over his tongue, his release erupted, shooting spurts of hot cum deep into her womb. He drank until they were both sated and then withdrew. She slumped against him and he just held her for a while, enjoying the intimacy of being buried in her after what they'd shared.

"You, sweetheart, are amazing."

She cuddled close, and he heard the smile in her sleepy voice. "No, that would be you."

He kissed the top of her head. "Why don't we bathe and get dried off? Then I need to make some rounds and check on the guests."

"Whatever you want, master."

A grin teased his lips. "I think you already know how that gets to me."

"Does it?" A finger trailed down his chest, her fingernail scratching lightly at his nipple.

He shivered and moved her off him with regret. "You know it does, naughty girl. Come on."

Grabbing some soap from a built-in ledge nearby, he scrubbed them both from head to foot. They had fun dunking each other while rinsing off; then he led her from the pool and fetched them two big fluffy towels from a rack.

Once they were both reasonably dry, he left the towels poolside for the staff to pick up and grabbed their robes. After helping Harley with hers, he shrugged his on and took her hand, leading her down the glass corridor once more. When they reached the staircase, he gestured toward it.

"Go and get dressed. I'll see you later," he promised.

"Aren't you coming up with me?"

"No."

"But you're still in your robe." Her brows furrowed.

"Exactly. Our guests frequently see me in less, darling. It's part of their entertainment," he said.

"Now I know what you meant by *make some rounds*," she muttered. She looked so miffed, he couldn't help but laugh.

"Yes, now you do. Go," he ordered, sobering. "Remember who's in charge."

"Yes, master."

She obeyed, but not before shooting him a rebellious look and marching up the stairs. Fire. He liked that. So unlike Helena, his Harley. In every way.

"A delicious piece of ass, is she?"

Soren turned, squelching a curse. He hadn't heard Leila sneak up on him from behind, and he hated that. He noted the skimpy shorts and top she wore, as well as the fact that she really did nothing for him. Without the black magic she wielded to use his mind and body, he'd never look at her twice.

"I'm not discussing her with you," he said evenly. "Especially our sex lives."

Closing the distance between them, she parted his robe and palmed his softened cock. "Really? What a shame. I suppose I'll have to content myself with other adventures regarding my mate— for the time being."

"Leila," he ground out, removing her hand. "I have guests to tend."

"Of course." Smirking, she raked him with her hungry gaze from head to toe. "You do that, and I'll see you later. Remember your task, though."

He worked not to show his exasperation. "What task is that?"

Leaning close, she whispered, "Take the one you've been waiting to taste. Bury yourself deep and drain him dry. You want it."

"No." His protest was spoiled by the quickening in his groin, in his blood.

"You do. I can see the truth. There's no point in resisting what you are and all you can be," she urged. "You'll do it. When you can't stand it another moment, you'll fuck him—"

"I can't."

"—and you'll kill him."

"I won't."

She spun and sauntered off, tossing him a knowing smile over one shoulder. Then she was gone.

He wanted to deny what she'd said. But the beast that had

been blessedly quiet during his time with Harley awoke with a vengeance. It stretched and growled in dark anticipation of doing exactly what the witch commanded.

Admit you want to fuck, to kill. To be what you were meant to be, and more.

"Yes," he whispered helplessly, the blackness descending.

He was left alone, his mind struggling against it, but his body aching for it—the taste of his prey's total surrender.

And the elixir of death.

7

$\mathcal{S}$oren toweled himself off, drying his hair as much as possible. He dressed in jeans and a mesh shirt that showed off his chest and abs, a teasing look the guests liked, and he didn't mind indulging them. After all, they were paying. Then he brushed out his long hair, leaving it to finish drying naturally, and went in search of his oldest brother. He'd been putting this off for a couple of days, ever since the interlude in the bathhouse with Harley, and that was too long.

He found Aldric at breakfast, chowing down on Nikki's blueberry muffins and sipping milk while reading the morning newspaper. So normal and good. For a moment he stopped in the doorway and watched, a lump growing in his throat. He'd risked his family for his own selfish quest. If only he had it to do over . . . Would he do anything differently?

The witch had led him to Harley, who might or might not be descended from Helena's family. The two females appeared as opposite as night and day, and he still wasn't sure whether to be disappointed. Honestly, he was a fool for thinking they might be one and the same, or that he'd be happy if they were. Wasn't it time to make new memories?

"Are you going to stand there all day or come sit down and eat?"

Soren blinked and pushed from the doorway, giving Aldric a wan smile. "Sorry. I'm not quite myself this morning." *Understatement of a thousand lifetimes.*

"What's wrong?" His brother's sharp gaze pierced his, studying him. No idiot, his sibling.

"Female trouble." He reached for a muffin.

"If you're out of tampons, I'm not going to the store."

"Fuck you," Soren muttered, taking a bite of the fluffy breakfast treat. "Mmm. Nikki's outdone himself."

"Yeah. I think Alasdair's going to give him more training as a pastry chef. Kid seems to have a knack for sweets."

"I'll say." He polished it off, licked his fingers, and reached for another.

"So, what gives?" Aldric glanced around, making certain no one else was within earshot. "Leila giving you problems?"

"Yeah, you could say that."

"How?"

Careful, vampire.

"Shut the fuck up!"

His brother blinked. "What?"

"No, no, not you." His appetite gone, he set the second muffin down and buried his face in his hands. "I wasn't talking to you."

"O-kaay," his brother drawled. "Then who were you talking to?"

"I don't know who or what he is," Soren whispered. "I just call him *the beast.*"

Aldric fell silent for a long moment. Lowering his hands, Soren raised his head to see his brother gazing at him with naked worry, all traces of teasing vanished. "Is this connected to the thing you said was growing inside you since you drank from the witch? The darkness?"

Do not, vampire.

"Yes. It's more accurate to say the beast *is* the darkness." He gave a bitter laugh. "It's meshing with me, taking over my mind. She and my beast want me to do horrible, evil things, and I *want* to do them. Long to do them so badly it hurts."

I warned you! Instantly, razor-sharp agony ripped through his head. With a cry, he slumped sideways, barely aware of falling from his chair to land in a heap on the floor.

"Oh, gods! Soren?"

Aldric was at his side in an instant, pulling Soren into his arms, cradling him. Shouting words Soren couldn't understand because his brain was being skewered and turned inside out. "Help me," he rasped. Or thought he did, but couldn't be sure.

Footsteps came running. More shouts. Someone yelled for a towel, but that didn't make sense. The pain was too much. His body shook, and vaguely he realized he was convulsing, the shudders racking him from head to toe. Strong arms held him close, kept him from moving too much, and the soft towel was pressed under his nose.

"Come on, bro. Come back to us." Luc's strained voice penetrated the thick fog of pain, and Soren looked up, trying to focus on his younger brother's face. Gradually, his blurred vision began to clear. Blue eyes and short, spiky blond hair came into view, and Soren realized Luc was the one holding the towel.

"Easy," Luc said softly. "You got a helluva nosebleed. What happened?"

His voice was a pathetic croak. "My head. Thought it was being torn apart."

"The beast?" Aldric guessed.

"Yeah. I pissed it off by running my mouth."

"Beast?" Luc frowned, glancing between them.

"I'll explain it to you later," Aldric said, shaking his head. He smoothed a strand of hair from Soren's face. "I promise we'll find a way to fix this. Can you sit up?"

"I think so."

He pushed upright with his brothers' help, but had to pause to wait out a wave of dizziness. When it passed, he nodded, and they pulled him to his feet. "Thanks. You guys, I don't deserve your—"

"Knock that shit off before you even start," Aldric growled. "We've always had each other's backs, and we're not going to let some two-bit whore bring us down. Speaking of her, where is the witch?"

"I don't know," Soren told him, taking the towel and wiping the last of the blood from under his nose. For now, the beast had subsided. "She's been disappearing for a couple of hours or more right before dawn every morning. I have no idea where she goes or what she does."

"Well, we'll find out and put a stop to whatever she's doing."

"She may succeed, thanks to me."

Aldric opened his mouth to answer, then stopped, noticing the small gathering of anxious Chosen and other house staff. "Let's finish this in my office."

He and Luc followed the vampire leader down the hall and into the office, where Luc closed the door behind them. None of them bothered to sit. This wouldn't take long.

Soren spoke quietly, hoping the presence inside him didn't rip into his brain again. "My beast is strong and becoming more difficult to suppress with each passing day. He has no empathy for others and is not reluctant to kill to further Leila's aims—whatever they are. In fact, I don't believe he really cares about her goal as much as he does killing for the erotic pleasure of the act itself."

"Blazing Hades." Luc's eyes were wide. "He's appealing to your predatory nature as a vampire, urging you to go feral."

"Yeah, that's a pretty accurate summary." He wanted to be sick as he made his final request. "I swear, I am trying to fight it, but if all else fails—"

"Don't even say it," Aldric hissed. "I'm not going to consider failure an option."

"You have to. Promise me that if this thing takes over before we can stop her and there's no hope of redemption for me . . ." He couldn't finish. But he didn't have to.

Aldric's face was pale, lines of stress bracketing his mouth as he nodded. "I promise. But I won't give up on you easily."

"Neither will I."

Gods, how he loved his brothers. "I know."

"Now get out of here, both of you! Can't you see how fucking busy I am?" He swept a hand toward the top of his desk . . . where there wasn't a single paper in sight.

Luc gave a terse nod, turned, and stalked out—but not before Soren had seen the suspicious moisture in his eyes. He followed, closing the door to the office, and stopped dead. His vampire hearing picked up a faint, telltale sniffle, the sound of his big, badass brother giving in to his emotions. Guilt hit Soren hard, threatened to cut him off at the knees.

Taking a deep breath, he turned the corner.

And ran smack into Jordy, who blinked big brown eyes at him, looking very much like a deer in the headlights of a speeding car. A tantalizing deer that awoke his slumbering predator.

"Lord Soren," Jordy greeted him cautiously, his usual bubbly self not in evidence. "I was just about to see if Lord Aldric needed anything from me this morning and—"

"I think my brother would prefer not to be disturbed," Soren said, his voice low. It wasn't really lying, was it? "He just ordered me and Luc out of his office."

"Oh." The boy looked away, obviously ill at ease.

"What is it?"

"Nothing."

He should send Jordy away now, before it was too late.

Instead, Soren took his arm, squeezing. "Don't lie to me," he warned. "I can smell it." Jordy gazed up at him in trepidation, and the beast reveled in his fear.

"Leila told me to meet you this morning but wouldn't say why," the young man blurted, his gaze darting around as though to make sure no one else listened. "She's weird and she scares me. So I wanted to talk to Aldric."

No, the beast said. *That won't do. Rein in the boy, and take what's yours.*

Soren hardly recognized the seductive purr as his own voice. "Now, why didn't you just ask me? I'm sorry she alarmed you, but there's no need to worry. I just haven't fed, is all, and Leila and I hoped you could take care of that for me."

Big doe eyes rounded. "But I serve Lord Aldric, and you know your brother is pretty possessive." Realizing his blunder, he stammered. "Not that I'm really anything special to him or that I'm refusing you! I'd never do that."

"Good. You know that as a Chosen, you're expected to serve any of us, however we require." Technically the truth, but he knew that Aldric had a big soft spot for Jordy. Taking him would enrage his brother—and please his inner predator. "Come with me."

Jordy was visibly startled by Soren's abrupt order, but could do nothing but obey as his master led him away. Soren caught his fearful look at Aldric's closed office door, and was gratified when the boy didn't call out.

He's ours. A juicy little morsel who'll scream for you.

How he longed for that. Jordy's lithe young body succumbing to him, a pleasure formerly denied anyone but his older brother. Well, that selfishness ended right now. If Aldric wanted the boy to himself, he should've claimed him off-limits long before today.

Excellent, vampire. No one has the right to keep this pleasure from you.

Picking up the pace, he dragged Jordy down the hall, away from the office and past a housekeeper, who gave them a sidelong look but wisely refrained from comment. Near the end of the corridor, he opened a door and shoved Jordy inside the room, which happened to be a conference room reserved for important meetings. No one would need it today. Except Soren.

Jordy stumbled, catching himself on the edge of the long table. Gripping it, he turned to face the vampire. "Lord Soren, I don't think—"

"We don't employ you to think," he said, advancing on the trembling young man. The unmistakable scent of fear and desire from his prey spurred him on. "So unless you're voicing your unbridled ecstasy, be silent."

"Y-yes, sir."

Grabbing Jordy's arm, he spun the boy around to face the table and pressed into his back. The slight form under him was warm and pulsing with the very life he wanted to devour. It was wrong to want to take that life, but the power of it held him in thrall. He could make it good for both of them. So good.

He nuzzled the soft skin of Jordy's neck, grazing it with the tip of one fang. The body under his shivered, driving him on. Reaching around, he slid his palm over the boy's hip to cup the telltale hardness at his crotch and chuckled darkly. His for the taking, this one. So vulnerable and fragile.

Working swiftly, Soren opened the young man's jeans. Freed him and stroked the silky cock, grinding his own erection into the pert, firm ass. He didn't need to fuck the boy to ensure that he remained under his thrall. But he would. Simply because it pleased him and his beast.

And it would drive oh-so-uptight Aldric mad with anger.

He pushed Jordy's jeans to his thighs, then kicked the boy's feet apart as far as the constriction of his pants would allow. Then he unzipped his own jeans and released his cock and rubbed it into the crack of that fantastic butt. His prey whimpered and backed into him, proof that he wanted this as much as his captor.

Holding Jordy close, he probed between the splendid cheeks and encountered the base of a butt plug. He'd been ready for Aldric's desires, had he? Well, too fucking bad for his older brother. He held the sweet thing now, and he wasn't letting go until he'd drained every drop of blood and cum from the Chosen.

Removing the plug, he tossed it aside and replaced it with his fingers. Worked them inside the hot channel to find it slick and ready. He sawed three fingers in and out just to drive the boy mindless. The slender body bowed backward, his tousled blond head on Soren's shoulder.

"Please, master," Jordy breathed.

"Yes? What do you want? Tell me."

"F-fuck me. Drink from me. Please."

"With pleasure."

That's all he needed. The boy had asked for this out loud. No one could fault him for what he did to the gorgeous Chosen. With a hiss, he pressed the head of his swollen, aching cock past the tight star, into the equally snug passage that gripped his cock with spine-tingling friction. He began to pump slowly, making sure to angle his thrusts to hit the boy's gland, drawing the sweet thing deeper under his spell.

"Ohh," Jordy moaned, melting in Soren's arms. "I always wondered what this would feel like, giving myself to you."

"Good?" Thrust.

"Yes, master! Oh, please . . ."

"Please what?" Glide, so slow. In to the balls.

"Bite me," he rasped. "Drink."

"How much?"

"As much as you want." Jordy's hand reached back, buried itself in Soren's hair, pulled his head down.

Taking his cue, Soren struck. Sank his fangs into the delicate throat and moaned as the rich blood gushed over his tongue. Jordy cried out, his cock jerking in his captor's hand, spilling his seed in a rush. He came again and again as Soren took his life's blood in great draws.

The boy weakens. He's yours! Finish him!

Yes. Soren's balls drew up and his release exploded, filling the boy's ass with his cum as he drank. The throb of his cock pulsed in time to the human heartbeat under his palm. Growing less and less strong. Fluttering, struggling to beat.

"Soren, the maid said you were—"

Jerking his fangs from Jordy's neck, he turned to snarl at the intruder. *Harley.*

"Oh, gods," she cried, sprinting forward. "What are you doing? Get off him!"

With more strength than Soren would've thought possible, Harley grabbed his shirt and yanked him backward. Then she stepped around him and shoved, disengaging him from his prey and sending him stumbling back several steps as Jordy slumped to the floor, unconscious.

"What the blazing hell are you doing?" she shouted, getting in his face. "Drinking that poor boy to death? What's wrong with you? This isn't the kind, caring vampire I thought I was getting to know!"

He stared at her, his brain a whirl of lust and confusion. "Harley. I was just . . . I don't know what came over me." His gaze went to the slight form crumpled on the floor. "Oh no."

"What the fuck is going on in here?" Aldric yelled, striding into the room. Spotting the Chosen, he rushed over to kneel at the young man's side. "Jordan? Fuck!"

"What have I done?" Soren whispered, pulling at his hair. "Will he be all right?"

Aldric didn't answer for several minutes as he slit his wrist and gave the young man a few drops of his blood. When at last Jordy stirred and opened his glazed eyes, Aldric turned his furious gaze to his younger brother. "He'll recover, no thanks to you. Touch him again, ever, and I'll rip your lungs out. Do I need to contain you?"

"No," he croaked. "It won't happen again."

Scooping a limp Jordy into his arms, Aldric stood, his expression forbidding. "Keep a tight rein on that thing inside you until we know what we're dealing with, or I won't have a choice."

"I understand." Soren hung his head in shame as Aldric strode from the room.

"What thing is he talking about?" Harley asked.

"Not now, okay? I need to think."

Gods, he'd nearly killed that sweet boy. And he'd loved the dark thrill. What the hell was he going to do?

"If that's what you want," she said quietly. "Just know I'm here for you."

"Thank you."

She nodded and walked out, leaving him alone and bereft in his own horrible company. If it hadn't been for Harley, he would've murdered an innocent. She'd been so brave, hadn't hesitated to jump him and shove his ass off Jordy. Then she'd gotten right in his face.

Something Helena *never* would have done.

They weren't the same. If he'd had any doubt, he didn't anymore. But where did that leave the two of them?

He laughed bitterly. It left Harley with the short end of the stick. He shouldn't have brought her home. It wasn't fair for her to have to face his madness, but he was too selfish a son of a bitch to send her away.

Whatever might come, Harley belonged to him.

And he had a sneaking feeling she was his in ways no piece of paper could name.

Harley stalked through the mansion, at loose ends. Everyone she'd met had been beyond nice, including the stern Aldric and sunny Luc, but Soren's vanishing act since the incident with the too-cute Jordy had her on edge. She wasn't sure why. Soren was responsible for her, but that wasn't the reason she was crawling in her own skin. Not totally.

He'd said she was his Chosen, but he hadn't come for her today. What if he did, and lost control as he had with Jordy? His brothers and the staff had been walking around with grim faces, but no one had said a word to Harley as to where her new master might be. She was worried, and prepared to get nasty if that's what it took to gain an answer as to his whereabouts.

Rounding a corner, she ran smack into a broad chest and looked up. *Well, speak of the devil.*

"Oh! I'm so sorry, Lord Soren," Harley said as he steadied her. "I was looking for you, but I didn't mean to run you over."

"It looks like I'll survive."

His smile made her weak in the knees, and she fumbled for a reply that would sound halfway intelligent. Saints, he was gorgeous. She'd always been a sucker for a man with long, silky hair, and she wondered what it would look and feel like draped over her body as he made love to her.

But hard on the heels of those thoughts, burned into her brain, was the image of his draining that helpless boy. The picture just didn't fit with the male she'd believed him to be.

Now she was just gawking stupidly. She hadn't had this much trouble talking to him before. Maybe she was just tired. Oh yeah—tired of the noises of scorching sex coming from his room at all hours.

"I'm surprised to see you up so early," she blurted.

"Why's that?"

Great. My big mouth. From his bemused expression, he was enjoying her discomfort a little too much, which irked her a lot. The acrobatics tended to keep her awake. Awake and jealous as hell. "Well, I'm assuming you don't have a cat in heat locked in your room every night. Wild guess."

He actually had the grace to appear embarrassed. "I apologize for the racket. I'm not used to having to keep quiet in my own home."

Now she felt sort of bad. "Don't apologize. It's no big deal."

"Truly, I can have you moved to a quieter wing if you'd like."

"No!" Her outburst startled her, and she cleared her throat. "That won't be necessary." The idea of being farther from him was painful, for some reason.

Blessedly, he changed the subject. "I have an idea. I've been keeping a low profile since the mistake with Jordy." He grimaced, as though the memory pained him, as well it should. "Would you like for me to give you the grand tour?" His engaging grin set her heart thumping. This wasn't the same vampire who'd turned and snarled at her, holding Jordy's limp body as though he were a jackal guarding a kill.

She gathered her courage. "That sounds fabulous. Where shall we start?"

"Hmm. I'd say the kitchen, but that's Alasdair's domain and he rules it with an iron fist. If you get hungry between meals or at night, send word to Nikki, the assistant. He's always happy to deliver food and drink whenever you'd like."

"Good to know. So, what about the cottages? I've been outside, but just right around the house, and I'd love to look around."

"You bet."

Soren held out his hand and she took it, loving how small hers felt in his much bigger one. What was it about holding hands with a man that made a woman warm and trembly inside?

The contact shivered through her nerve endings in a good way, made her feel special. Like he'd chosen her. And he had. He'd picked her to remain here and serve him. She couldn't wait to experience all he had to teach her.

Despite the voice in her head, urging her to be cautious.

The vampire led her down the hall and turned, then hurried through a sunroom where a few people were gathered at a mahogany dining table, munching on bagels and muffins and sipping juice, coffee, or milk. Most glanced up and called a cheerful greeting to Soren, and a couple asked to meet the newbie.

Soren simply smiled and promised, "Later!"

The vampire kept going through a glass patio door and out into the sunshine. She shot a sidelong look at him. "You won't burn in the sun?"

His lips turned up. "Haven't spent much time around vampires?"

"Not really, except for my time at the paper when I covered social events. Most of those were in the evening, and everyone is out at that time."

"Understandable. And it's not like we're out on the street corner, advertising what we are. Aldric refuses to play that up to bolster our business. He says the resort makes plenty of money, and I suppose he's right." He made a thoughtful sound in his chest. "Anyway, newly turned vampires should be careful in the sun."

"No vacation in the Bahamas?" she teased.

He laughed, squeezing her hand. "Exactly. Born vamps, however, don't need to be especially concerned. I'm not going to sunbathe, but I'm not worried about disappearing into a pile of charred ash. Makes for good movies, though." He winked.

"Wait. You were born a vampire, not made?"

"Yes, me and my brothers. The Fontaine family can be traced back thousands of years. Vampire children are rare, and the fact that there are three of us is almost unheard of. There aren't that many Fontaines left, though."

"Aren't you immortal?"

"Yes, but we can be killed. The sad fact is that death catches up to most of us sooner or later."

Too true. The sobering thought tried to put a damper on her morning, but she shoved it aside. They walked past the pool area, almost empty at the early hour, down a winding path bordered by beautiful flowers and trees. At the first break in the foliage on their right, the path split off to form a pebbled walkway to the first cottage. It was small but very pretty, a white oasis of tranquillity surrounded by more colorful flowers, trees, and shrubs. A covered porch was built across the front and sides.

"Oh, my," she breathed. "This is spectacular."

"Isn't it? We wanted to incorporate privacy and luxury with the fun to be had in other parts of the resort. So guests can play in public, semipublic, or private. Whatever's their preference. Come on."

They kept walking, and he pointed out more cottages here and there. Eventually the path widened into a clearing and they came to a pretty gazebo.

"This is a popular romantic spot," the vampire told her, pulling her up the steps.

"I can see why!" She turned to him, feeling playful. "Hey, are you hinting that you want to make out with me?"

"Make out?" He laughed. "What a human term. If you have to ask, I wasn't doing a very good job, was I?"

Pulling her against him, he captured her mouth and buried one hand in her hair. His tongue parted the seam of her lips, and she whimpered at the taste of him. So good and right. A spark ignited in her belly and quickly kindled to a flame that burned for him as it had for no one else. Not Val or Zen or anyone she'd been with. This sense of belonging was new and powerful, as wonderful as it was confusing.

She didn't know why she should feel this way so soon, but it was as if a missing piece of her soul had been found. From a kiss. How ridiculous and yet . . . real.

His fingers brushed down her cheek and dipped into the V of her borrowed blouse. "Bringing you here as my Chosen might be the best decision I've ever made," he murmured.

Her pulse sped up and arousal peaked her nipples. "That's all I've thought about since the night you brought me here," she admitted. "But what about Jordy?"

Regret etched his features. "You don't know how sorry I am that I lost control with him. That wasn't me at all."

"And your mate?" The last word was almost spat from her mouth like a nasty bug.

His golden eyes became hard as stones. "The priestess is *not* my mate, though she pretends we are for her own reasons."

"Priestess," she repeated. "As in voodoo witch?"

"Exactly."

"Witches are kind of weird, especially her kind, and that sure explains a lot of her creepiness." A chill slithered over her skin. "But not all of it."

Still holding Harley against his body, he stared intently into her face. "Something isn't right about her besides the obvious. Something is . . ."

"Off?" she suggested. "Like a piece of fabric that's been ripped in half and sewn back together crooked?"

"I couldn't have put it better. She has this effect on m—" His eyes closed and he swayed a little, clutching his head.

"Are you all right?"

After a moment, he opened them again. His pallor wasn't good. "Whenever I start to talk about Leila too much, my head hurts as though this thing inside me is stopping me."

"This is the same *thing* you referred to after you attacked Jordy?" She stared at him in dread.

"Yes, though the pain isn't as bad right now. Maybe that's because of you," he speculated aloud. "And I haven't had any blood since almost going too far with him, either. Guess I'm feeling too hungry."

"Poor thing," she sympathized, smoothing the hair from his eyes. "What do you need me to do?"

"Exactly what you're doing—just let me enjoy you."

"I can handle that." She hoped. As long as he didn't lose it again.

He took another kiss, and she palmed his cheek, exploring his jaw and brow. She liked the strength and character in his features. Her journey moved downward to his chest and she rubbed his mesh shirt, admiring how the fabric played peekaboo with his supple skin. Fun as that was, however, she wanted more.

Seeking the edge of his shirt, her hand crept underneath and slid up. His stomach was tight and flat and ridged with muscle, his chest smooth. The vamp arched into her touch like a feline being petted, and she smiled.

"Someone likes that."

"Want to feel how much?"

Taking her wrist, he guided her hand to the impressive bulge in his jeans. Apparently, his dizzy spell wasn't going to deter him from being a naughty vampire. Fine by her. She gave his crotch a squeeze, rubbing as he spread his legs wider. Encouraged by a rumbling growl of appreciation, she unfastened and unzipped him, and pushed the denim out of the way.

Next, she lifted his cock and balls free, salivating at the sight of him erect and ready for her attentions. Without hesitating, she hit her knees and tasted the weeping slit, then swirled her tongue around the head to catch all of the salty goodness.

"Gods, yes," he moaned. "Suck me. Take it all."

She gave it her best shot. Sucked him down, laving him like a yummy stick of candy, eager to get all of his essence. Slowly, she worked him in, sucking him deeper and harder until she took him to the base. Fondling his balls, she kept increasing the suction until he laughed hoarsely.

"Harley, sweetness, you're killing me here." Disengaging carefully, he helped her to her feet and kissed her again, hard. "I like the taste of me in your mouth. A lot."

"If you'd let me finish, there would be even more," she said, grinning.

"Maybe next time. At the moment, I want you over there, bent over with your legs spread."

He gestured at a bench and walked her over to it. Excitement rising, she unfastened her borrowed jeans and pushed them down, along with her underwear. Then she grasped the back of the bench, bending over slightly with her feet at shoulder width, and poked out her ass.

"Beautiful," he praised, moving in behind her.

His hands skimmed her ribs, causing her to shiver. Then

lower to her hips, and then on to worship the round curve of her butt. His palms played over her, fingers sliding into the crevice between her thighs, teasing her slit. The contact sent tremors of delight to every limb, curling her toes. Two fingers gently probed between her pussy lips. Slipped into her channel, getting the passage nice and slick.

She pushed back in silent invitation, hot for more. He set her body aflame without even trying, driving her to distraction. Suddenly, he took her arm, urged her to straighten, and spun her around.

"Hold on to me. Lock your legs around my waist."

She did, and he carried her a few feet to one of the gazebo's pillars. Placing her back against the support, he held her in one strong arm, brought the head of his cock to her opening, and pushed inside. She nearly lost her mind. Felt so good, Soren lunging deep. Filling her.

"Oh yes! Master . . ."

Holding her firmly, he began to glide in and out, fanning the flame into an inferno. Fucking her with even strokes, he pumped faster. Deeper. He owned her, and she loved submitting to him when she had a choice, not because she was required by some twisted slave system. She was glad he and his brothers believed in free will.

This was where she was supposed to be. Right here with him. She knew she'd do anything he wanted and gladly.

His strokes sped up, sending her need higher, driving her mad. The pinnacle loomed close, her womb quickening. The rush of electricity washed through her body and her release exploded. She cried out, pussy clenching around his cock, pushing him over the edge, as well.

"Fuck, yes!" he shouted, emptying his balls. Then he struck.

She'd almost forgotten Soren was a vampire. But when his fangs sank into the curve of her neck and shoulder, the bolt of pain took her breath—and was followed by an exquisite tidal wave of ecstasy. As intense as before, but with less pain each time, as he'd said. A second release turned her inside out and then left her a limp rag in his hands.

She knew how Jordy could've allowed him to take all he wanted.

On and on he drank in great pulls, bathing her with his cum. Cock jerking, he wrung every last drop from his orgasm and finally withdrew his fangs, licking the tiny wounds closed.

"Thank you, baby," he whispered reverently. "You give me such a gift."

"You're welcome." Her knees wobbled as he slipped free and set her on the floor again. "I can see why you like to take your Chosen here in the gazebo."

"This is the first time."

She laughed, but saw that he looked thoughtful and serious. "Is there a reason you haven't gotten down and dirty here until now?"

"Because until now, I never wanted to." He tilted his head, studying her. "My father built this structure with his bare hands and mated my mother here. This was the last place I saw them before they were killed, more than fifty years ago."

Her hand went to her throat. "Oh, I'm so sorry. How . . ."

"They traveled to visit friends and were trapped in a house fire." Looking away, his lips curved into a sad smile. "In the beginning, when my grief was raw, I used to wish one of them had survived so my brothers and I wouldn't be totally alone. But I knew from experience that I was being selfish. That neither of them would've wanted to live without the other. It's how I felt when my mate died. Thank the gods I had my brothers and parents to get me through her death."

He pulled up his jeans and she hurried to do the same, feeling too exposed in this new type of intimacy. For a few moments, he seemed lost in his own memories.

She didn't want him upset with her for prying, but she sensed he might be willing to talk about his mate. "Tell me about her."

That gained his attention, and to her relief, he smiled, the shadows gone. "Helena was a sheltered girl. Sweet and demure. Nothing at all like this place or the people in it, which is why my parents introduced us. And part of the reason I fell for her so hard, so fast."

"So she moved in here? What did she think of the resort and your . . . feedings? Was she a vampire?"

"You ask a lot of questions." An amused grin played on his sexy lips.

"I've heard that before," she said, thinking of Valafar. "I apologize."

"I'm just teasing. Yes, we lived here, and she was human. She wasn't ever really into the open, kinkier aspects of our nature, but she understood what we were. I couldn't have stopped feeding from the Chosen, but I would have refrained from sex with them or the guests if she'd ever asked it of me."

"She didn't mind? You must've felt very lucky."

"Of course I did. I mated a woman who knew the depraved predator I am and loved me anyway. And I loved her. When she died, I believed my life was over." He sighed. "She was attacked by demons while I was away. By the time my brothers found me and rushed me home, I was too late to save her."

"I'm so sorry. I know about loss, and it hurts like hell. Couldn't someone else have turned her?" she wondered aloud.

"Helena wouldn't let them. She wanted to speak with me first, and wouldn't listen to their pleadings. It took me a long time to forgive them for not forcing the issue."

"Or her for refusing?" she inquired softly.

"That, too," he admitted. "And ever since then, I've been searching for a way to bring her back to me. Decades of agony, as one witch after another failed to help me."

A sudden, brutal moment of clarity crystallized in her brain. Her eyes widened. "Your bargain with the priestess . . ."

"I was looking for a spell, a trade—anything to bring back Helena."

"Her last name. Tell me," she demanded. A memory of his face in the limo, pale with shock, came back to her.

"Vaughn."

Harley sucked in a sharp breath, pain lancing her chest, confusion clouding her thinking. "Helena Vaughn was my great-aunt," she said, numb.

"Gods." He ran a hand through his long hair. "I'd almost begun to hope there was no connection other than a coincidental last name."

"So *that's* why you were asking me so many questions about my family and my past when we were in the bathhouse! Are you saying you thought at first I was my aunt, brought back from the dead? Or that you wished I was? That's just sick."

"No! I didn't mean it like that! Well, maybe at first, but I saw almost right away that you're nothing like Helena, and I was glad," he said with vehemence. "I swear to you, I wouldn't have you any other way than just as you are. I know now that you and she are two different women, even if I didn't before."

She stared at him, letting the words soak in. Gradually, she saw the truth in his eyes and relented. "I'm glad you can tell that, because it's true. There's no one in here but me," she said, tapping over her heart.

He nodded. "I'm glad we have that put to rest. Now, what do you say we tour some of the places where I *have* gotten down and dirty, many times?"

Harley let him take her hand and pull her from their sanctuary, unable to help but smile at his enthusiasm.

8

Soren grinned at Harley as he began her tour. For the moment he could forget he was in heaven and hell, living two simultaneous lives that were tearing him apart. Housing two minds—his and the beast's—that were at war for dominance.

Harley's eyes gleamed like a delighted child's as he showed her the various adult-play facilities in the entertainment building; the main house was for family only, off-limits to resort guests except by special invitation. The particular room they were visiting happened to be empty at the moment, since it was favored more at night than during the day. At this hour, many people were out sunbathing naked by the pool.

"Oh, a media room!" She ran a hand over the large theater recliner outfitted with surround sound and drink holders and then gestured at the big screen taking up the length of the wall. "Guess everyone needs a break from the kinky stuff, huh? Nothing like movie night, complete with popcorn."

He snorted. "Baby, we show adult movies in here. Porn. See that bowl over there on the coffee table?"

She peered at the crystal bowl filled with colorfully wrapped discs on sticks. "Lollipops?"

"Look closer." His beast chuckled in derision while he did his best to ignore the damned thing.

Walking over, she picked up a stick with a round, flat red circle on the end . . . and started laughing. "Condoms. I should've known."

"For the humans." Soren grinned. "One of the perks of being a vampire is not needing them. Come on. I have something even more interesting to show you."

At the back of the media room was a door, and behind that a stairway descending to one of Soren's favorite areas. The passage was dimly lit by gas sconces, enough that they could see where they were going, yet still maintaining the proper ambience of stepping into a darker world. Of course, being a vampire with superior vision, Soren could've made his way in the pitch-black if need be, but humans could not.

At the bottom, the hallway continued straight ahead for a short distance and came to an end at a closed door that was facing them. To their right was another door, and he opened it, ushering her inside a long, rectangular room that was completely dark. A group of comfortable sofas and a couple of recliners faced a window that took up one wall, clearly set up to view the scene in the room beyond.

"That's a one-way mirror," Harley observed in a hushed voice. A man and woman cuddling in the corner paid her and Soren no mind. Their attention was riveted on the scene in the room beyond.

"Yes. This is our voyeur's salon. You can watch the goings-on or be watched, whatever is your desire."

Soren noted that like the couple in the corner, Harley was focused on the threesome beyond the window. Two males had a woman sandwiched between them; one fucked her mouth while the other reamed her from behind. The trio was clearly having a raunchy good time, their heated arousal searing the air, both from their activity and the novelty of having an audience.

"Would you like to do that?" he murmured into her ear. "Allow two males to take you, make you scream, knowing we have a salon full of aroused people glued to the scene? Perhaps wishing they could join in?"

She let out a deep breath. "I-I'd like that."

"Have you done threesomes before?"

"Well, with Valafar and Zenon . . ."

Her gaze found his, and from the heat in her eyes, he knew she had enjoyed it. A lot.

"Ah, we'll invite Valafar to join us, then. At the club he expressed enthusiasm for visiting the resort—and checking up on you." He took her hand and led her from the viewing salon and back up the stairs.

"Really? I thought he couldn't wait to get rid of me."

She still sounded a bit miffed about that, and he smiled. "I don't think it was his desire to make you feel cast aside. I believe he had your best interests at heart, strange as it is to think that a demon would care for anyone's well-being besides his own."

"His entire clan is the same way. Sort of . . . progressive. No less lusty, but definitely not brutal like other demons I've observed and read about."

"Yes, well, even the prince's clan can be violent if need be. If push comes to shove, they'll protect those they love same as anyone."

"The prince? What prince?" She frowned in confusion as they reached the media room once more.

He paused, hoping he hadn't betrayed a confidence. But Valafar hadn't said he must keep his status as royalty a secret, just that he kept a low profile these days. "Prince *Valafar*, leader of the entire Southern Coalition of demons, not that he cares for the title of late. In the demon world, he's Aldric's equal in rank."

"Holy shit," she breathed, wide-eyed. "I had no idea. He's dominant, but he doesn't act all pompous about his position, not like you'd think a prince would."

Soren shrugged. "Neither does my brother." Beside him, she fell quiet and he studied her. "What is it?"

She shrugged. "When I mentioned Val being dominant, it made me think."

"Of what?"

"How I loved it when he told me what to do," she confessed, reddening a little. But she didn't back down from the topic. "He exerted control over me but not in a hurtful way. It made me feel safe. And the same was true of the wolf shifter in St. Louis. How strange is that?"

"There's nothing strange about a submissive enjoying giving that control over to another," he said, his voice gone husky at the image she conjured. "Did you like what happened to you up on that stage in the club?"

"Yes," she whispered, then cleared her throat. "I was embarrassed at first. Then Kai rubbed that cream on me and it lowered my inhibitions. But that's not actually what sent me over the edge."

"You really loved being a slave, deep down." Saints, this woman was going to kill him. His groin got heavy and hot.

"I did. I liked not having a say, being displayed and used."
She shook her head. "How twisted is that?"

"It's not," he said, taking her hand. "Here with me, you can
have whatever your heart desires. Whatever makes you happy
sexually, I can make it a reality. All you have to do is tell me."

"What if I wanted that again?"

"Being bound and fucked?"

"Yes. I want to be your captive," she said, warming to the
idea. "And for others to watch."

"Give me a while and I can set it up—if you'll trust me." She
shouldn't, but he wanted to give her this. While he was still in
charge of himself and could be with her. Guide her.

"I do. Let's do it." Her eyes lit with excitement.

He was helpless to deny her. "All right. Meet me here in an
hour."

In just under an hour, he'd arranged for a tantalizing show
in the dining room with five participants, including himself and
Harley. Quite a few of the resort's guests were on their way to
attend as the audience, to observe the devouring of the evening
snack. He strode back to where Harley sat on a stuffed chair,
waiting. She looked up expectantly at his approach.

"Come with me," he ordered in a firm voice.

"What am I supposed to do?"

"Just do as you're told. We're going to the dining room,
where some guests are waiting. Don't disappoint me."

"Yes, sir."

He didn't miss the shiver, the gleam in her eyes as she said it.
His female wanted this, and he would deliver.

.   .   .

Harley could barely contain her excitement as Soren ushered her into the big dining room. She wasn't certain what he had in mind, and she eyed the crowd taking their seats around the long table. An assortment of fruits, dips, and cheeses graced the table, and some of the guests were availing themselves of the bounty. What sort of kink had he planned?

Then her gaze fell on the rack taking up quite a bit of space just beyond the head of the table. The rack was apparently the focal point of the room, and all chairs were turned so the guests could view the proceedings. A young, dark-haired man who worked in the kitchen and a woman she'd seen around and guessed to be a Chosen, plus another big male she'd never seen before, stood near the rack, awaiting Soren's instructions. The vampire joined them.

"Come here," Soren told her. She moved toward him and then stopped. "Undress."

She complied, hands trembling. She shook more with arousal than fear. The lust in Soren's eyes magnified her own, and she couldn't wait for what came next.

"To the rack," he said. "You're our afternoon snack—mine, Trisha's, and Nikki's—and one of our guests will participate while the rest watch."

"Your what?" She gaped at him.

"You heard me. Do as I said."

Quickly, she stripped, aware of the hungry attention focused on her. Legs weak, she backed up to the wooden contraption and raised her arms, spread her legs. Trisha and Nikki fastened her wrists, rendering her helpless and exposed. It felt so much more intimate than the club, which had been dimly lit, the faces in the crowd blurred. Not so here in this room, in close quarters. The shock of it was electric, and her nipples hardened to points.

"Good girl," Soren crooned, thumbing one pert peak. His hand skimmed down her belly to her clit, rubbed the nub in full view of everyone, making it wet. "Isn't she stunning? Look at her hot little cunt, ready to be sucked and fucked. She'll submit, because she belongs to me."

A couple of males at the table groaned, and hands began to touch partners, roaming.

His words were hypnotic, as was the sight of Trisha bringing forth a jar of familiar cream. *Oh, I am done for.* That wicked stuff would make her squirm, heighten her already simmering libido.

"Trisha, dearest, leave no area of our little slut unattended."

"Yes, master."

The Chosen began to spread the cream, and did her job well. She paid the most attention to Harley's breasts, kneading, plucking her tender nipples. It felt so good, Harley arched her back into the delicate touch, seeking more. Then the slim hands found her pussy, smeared it over her slit. Dipped into her channel, teasing. Then sought and found her back passage, preparing her there, just in case.

By the time Trisha was finished, Harley was about to cry in frustration. Soren liked this, and used it to his advantage.

"I believe she's ready," he told the audience. "Watch as Nikki and my loyal Chosen show my new female the ropes."

Trisha knelt in front, between her legs, as Nikki did the same behind her. Four soft hands skimmed the outsides of her thighs, a soothing motion. But nothing she'd ever experienced came close to being licked and sucked from both the front and back at the same time.

"Oh," she moaned, straining in her bonds. "Fuck!"

"That's what they're going to do, baby. Feast and fuck. Give yourself to them."

She had no other option. The knowledge of that was a powerful aphrodisiac, even more so than the honey-almond stuff on her skin. She was theirs to eat and fuck. Their treat.

And they did eat her, skillfully. Trisha's nubile little tongue laved her clit and folds, while Nikki's mouth suckled and licked her asshole. The dual sensations nearly sent her over the edge, but Soren wouldn't allow that. Not yet.

"Nikki, you may fuck her from behind. Trisha, dove, let our vampire friend take your place." He looked at Harley, eyes smoking with desire. "This is Roth, a friend of mine and a frequent guest. I trust him."

Just like that, Harley trusted Soren's judgment, even through the haze of lust. The handsome, dark-haired vampire wasted no time crouching at her feet and suckling her clit. The spirals of pleasure were becoming almost too much, and she didn't want to come. *Have to hold off a little longer.*

When Nikki pressed his cock between her folds and pushed his impressive length deep, she nearly lost the battle. The young man wasn't small everywhere, and was definitely no boy, despite the sweet, innocent face. He knew how to use his tool, and began plunging it mercilessly into her pussy until she began to whimper.

The skilled mouth eating her, the fucking! She couldn't take it.

"Soren, it's too much!"

"How do you address me?" He pressed close to her side, his lips by her ear.

"Master! Please, master, it's too much!"

"Do you need to come?"

"Yes! I'm begging you!"

"Then come," he purred. And sank his fangs into her neck.

She screamed her pleasure, coming all over Roth's face as he licked and nuzzled her mound. When he sank his fangs into the soft, vulnerable flesh of her inner thigh and began to drink, she yelled again, the orgasm jerking her like a puppet. Out of control. Nikki buried himself deep and emptied his cum into her pussy, hugging tightly to her back.

Several audience members joined in the shouts of ecstasy and others applauded wildly. But all she cared about was the triple stimulation that she wanted to go on forever.

But it had to end, and when the vampires released her, sealing her wounds, she sagged in the bonds. Nikki kissed her shoulder and withdrew, as well, carefully. Someone—she wasn't sure who—cleaned her with a warm cloth.

"You did wonderfully," Soren praised, speaking for her ears only. "I'm so proud of you, baby. You are mine."

"Yes," was all she could manage. That and a weak, satisfied smile in return.

Soren was hers. No matter what some witchy ghoul hoped or had bargained for. He called to her as no other male ever had.

He was *her* mate. She opened her mouth to tell him so, but decided against it for now. She didn't know how he'd react and didn't want anything to spoil this blissful moment.

"Ah, I found you," a voice called.

Soren inwardly cursed to see Leila enter the dining room and breeze toward them, derailing such a splendid moment. He turned and gestured for Trisha and Nikki to unbind Harley, and then quietly told her to get dressed.

"Thank you, old friend," Roth said, clapping him on the shoulder. "Your generosity astounds me, as always."

"Enjoy the rest of your stay. Perhaps we'll catch up later."

His friend left, and so did Nikki and the Chosen. They shot Leila a look of disgust behind her back before hurrying out. He couldn't blame them. Harley continued to dress.

The corner of his mind not controlled by his beast was really starting to hate the sound of Leila's voice, not to mention the sight of her. She wore a short black skirt and knee-high boots, and a sheer tank blouse that left little to the imagination.

Leila looked exactly like the witch he knew her to be.

At that uncharitable thought, he'd expected his unwanted alter ego to voice its displeasure with him, but it remained silent. In fact, most of the times he'd been with Harley, it had been subdued. Almost as if she eased its hold on him somehow.

Before he had time to consider that development, Leila took him by the arm. "If you're done fooling around, I need you to come with me."

Stepping away from her, he scowled and removed her hand. "I'm in the middle of something, as you can see," he said, annoyed.

Her eyes never left his as she ignored Harley. "Looks like you're done. Do I need to remind of your obligations to me?"

Bitch. "No," he said stiffly. He turned to Harley, letting his frustration show. "I'm sorry about the interruption. I'll see you later?"

"Sure." Her smile didn't quite reach her eyes, and when she glanced at the witch, the death glare she sent the other woman's way should've fried her on the spot.

He wished. "Have fun, then. And thank you for your gift," he said, referring to the scene.

"No, thank *you.*"

After giving Harley a kiss on the cheek, he spun and followed Leila, cursing silently every step of the way.

They wound through the house and he tensed as he realized she'd brought him to a little-used wing. And if their direction was any indication, he had a sinking feeling she'd discovered the one area he hadn't wanted her to find.

Sure enough, she led him into a private playroom used only by his brothers and close friends, and rarely at that. There wasn't a more secluded room on the resort, and his gut churned as she closed and locked the door . . . and he also realized they weren't alone. *Blazing Hades.*

Waiting for them was large male, ruggedly attractive, with long red hair. His scent hit Soren's nose and he tensed. *Wolf.* Any unarmed vampire would come out on the losing end of a battle with one of them. But the shifter simply stood there, expression unreadable, waiting for instructions.

"Arron, make my mate comfortable in the web," Leila instructed, waving a hand.

Soren blinked at the contraption taking up one side of the room and struggled to keep the dread from showing on his face. Someone had been busy. "I don't fucking think so," he said, his tone cool.

"Oh, but I do. You are entirely too resistant to the necessary change taking place within you. We're going to help you begin to accept your destiny." Sidling close, she touched his cheek. "Sleep."

"Wha—"

His brain whirled, and his legs buckled. Everything went black.

Conversation filtered through to him slowly. Not much of it made sense at first.

Are you certain he's the one? a curious male voice intoned.

Yes, Arron.

I'm not so sure, Leila. His will is strong.

Are you questioning me, you stupid wolf?

Never that, my queen. Merely . . . cautious.

Soren struggled to understand. Queen? What the fuck?

He's the last descendant of Azrael who possesses the strength necessary to survive the change. My last hope of overthrowing Aldric and Valafar.

Prince Valafar doesn't give a damn about politics anymore, and Aldric would've worked with you if only—

Shut up, she hissed. *I don't need your opinions. I want action, damn you!*

Fine, he soothed, though his tone was strained. On edge. *He is beautiful, even for a vampire, which I suspect is testament to his superior lineage. May I?*

With an effort, Soren opened his eyes.

Leila and the wolf were talking about him? Superior lineage? Descendant of *who?*

No, I want him awake during all phases of the transformation. It is the only way to ensure that the resistance within him is broken, vanquished, and the demon resurrected. You'll soon take your delights—never fear.

Their voices faded, and he suspected that he'd been left alone.

Delights? Blazing hell, he had to wake up. His mind was clearing rapidly, but his body was heavy, lethargic, as though he'd been drugged.

Forcing himself to remain calm, he took stock of his situation. The room was damned cold. Where the fuck were his brothers? But he recalled that hardly anyone ever visited this wing of the house. He was screwed.

He shivered, teeth chattering, realizing for the first time that he was naked. And immobile. He tried pulling his arms and legs into his body to conserve warmth, but couldn't move them. His wrists and ankles were bound—no, *stuck*—to something that was holding him suspended in an upright position. The web he'd seen before she rendered him unconscious. He was hanging spread-eagled, feet not quite touching the floor, each wrist and ankle bound with sticky threads.

He rested for a while, letting his strength return. When he finally managed to open his eyes and focus on his surroundings, he wished he hadn't.

The room, formerly used for lighter consensual play, had been turned into a torture chamber. There was no other possible description. The walls were affixed with chains and manacles designed for prisoners awaiting their gruesome end. The room itself bristled with every imaginable device capable of causing pain. A table in one corner had leather straps at each end, wound around hand cranks at the head and feet. Dark stains bathed the wood where a man would be placed, screaming as he was being pulled apart.

Where had the witch gotten these awful devices, much less smuggled then into the mansion undetected? By using her magic? If so, he'd terribly underestimated her.

Soren shivered harder, horror spreading with the icy cold through his limbs. Menacing whips, chains, and blades of every sort hung in neat rows on one wall. A metal vat large enough to hold a man rested over the remnants of a fire—not in use, thank God. What—or whom—might be boiled in the thing, he didn't want to guess. More grisly tools adorned the space at intervals.

A coffin filled with spikes pointing inward. Choke collars

attached to a pulley system. A large ax and chopping block. Many earthen jars containing God knows what. And resting on a table in front of him was an implement with a handle and several longish leather strips attached to the end. Instantly, he knew what it was and why it had been removed from the wall and placed where he could see it.

A cat-o'-nine-tails.

"Jesus," he whispered, eyes wide.

Surely they didn't intend to use any of this stuff on him. They were playing head games with him, trying to scare him. They'd succeeded.

Was this part of the *transformation* Leila had spoken of? The second part of her plan to break him? As though the beast he'd acquired wasn't bad enough.

"Son of a bitch."

Heart pounding, he swallowed the wild urge to call out, to give in to rising panic. No one would hear him, and no way in hell would he give her the satisfaction of seeing him lose it.

Keep your head, he told himself. There had to be a way out of this bargain he'd made with Leila. *Think!*

Soren closed his eyes, letting his mind drift back to his first encounter with her, in the modest shack in the swamp. Soren concentrated, digging into the fog, searching for an answer to his dilemma. Something evaded him, something important.

The deal was that she would give him back the love of his life, and in return he would give Leila anything she wished. Creature comforts she could easily obtain for herself using magic. No, that wasn't truly what she wanted.

The Council seat. Power. Those were her true aims, and she needed Soren to get them. Why?

His lineage. Descendant of Azrael. Surely not . . .

The archangel of Death?

Oh, gods, He didn't know how that could be true, but Aldric probably would—if Soren ever got the chance to ask him. And if it was true, and the witch—or whatever she was—succeeded in turning him into her monstrous creation, everyone he loved was doomed. Under the beast's and Leila's influence, he'd destroy them all. She would rule the Southern Coalition first, and then move on to taking the entire continent.

That was her ultimate goal: total power. And Soren was the instrument. If he was truly a descendant of Azrael, no wonder he'd become such a threat to everyone around him. Soren *was* death, and with the proper amount of influence, a tool of evil.

As their children would be. That explained why she wanted to conceive. To pass on their legacy of destruction.

Her destruction is your own.

That's what his beast had said. Anguish pierced his heart, drowning him in despair. His death was the only salvation for himself and his loved ones. Leila wasn't human at all, was much more than a priestess. Valafar had some answers, and Soren would get them. He had to discover how to kill her.

And then himself.

He hung his head, drifting until voices penetrated the gloom beyond the heavy door, moving closer. As he looked up, it swung inward. Leila entered in a swirl of black silk, but as before, it was the tall man trailing in her wake who commanded his attention.

The pair halted a couple of feet from him. Soren noticed how Arron remained a step or two behind her, his posture straight and proud, head up yet holding his silence. Clearly, he deferred to her only with great reluctance.

He was very tall, his bearing regal, and Soren could easily

imagine him as a leader of his kind. Auburn hair streaked with gold swept well past his broad shoulders. His brows arched over eyes of the clearest sea green, framed by long, dusky lashes. Faint lines bracketed his wide, chiseled mouth, indicating a man who'd once smiled a lot. *In the past*, Soren thought, because he couldn't imagine what anyone stuck with the bitch-demon would have to smile about.

"Would someone mind telling me what's going on?" Soren asked, striving to keep his tone neutral. "You won. I surrendered. So why the macabre little show?"

Her companion's expression betrayed nothing, but Leila smiled evilly as she spoke. "My pet, have I done anything for mere show thus far? Not to worry, we'll make a believer out of you yet." She turned to the man just behind her.

"I'm already a believer, so you can let me down before my brothers or one of the servants catch you both." It was an idle threat and she knew it.

She leveled him with a look of malice. "You are not truly mine yet, or you would've finished Jordan as you were told. As for your brothers, Aldric has been called away on Council business indefinitely, and Luc will be out of commission very soon."

Fear rode him hard, and he pulled futilely at his bonds. "What are you planning to do to Luc? Let me down from here, you bitch!"

"Now, that's not very nice," she said with a mock pout. "Arron, darling, you may proceed."

Soren fought the fear clogging his throat as Arron retrieved the cat-o'-nine-tails from the table. He'd made a horrible mistake in underestimating Leila once again.

"How many lashes, my queen?" the man inquired, voice devoid of emotion.

"Twenty."

Arron's lips thinned and a muscle in his jaw tightened. "As you desire."

Soren felt the blood drain from his face. *Twenty lashes from a whip with nine tails! Oh, gods . . .*

The man moved around behind Soren, and the vampire's mouth went dry. Numbing disbelief that this was happening to him suddenly transcended the fear. There wasn't anything he could do to stop it. Determined not to cry out, he tried to brace himself. Nothing could have prepared him for the eerie whistle of the tails flying through the air just before they struck.

White-hot, agonizing pain ripped through his back, stealing his breath. Tears sprung to his eyes, blinding him. The excruciating shock rocketed to every nerve ending. Before he could recover, another blow fell. And another.

The room began to slide away, a buzzing noise filling his head. He thought he heard a low, animal moan escape his own lips but wasn't sure. Warm wetness began to slip over his buttocks and down his legs. He was being torn apart, inches at a time.

See what you've brought down on us? the beast raged. *Now you'll learn.*

When the blows finally ceased, he hung limp, chin on his chest. His breathing came in harsh gasps and tears streamed down his cheeks. By God, he wouldn't beg. *I won't.*

"It is done," Arron said from behind him. A shuffling noise indicated that he was preparing to take his leave, but her voice halted him.

"It's done if he answers a simple question. Soren, where do you and your brothers keep the famed swords?"

The swords? Of course she wanted them in her possession; they could kill any creature in existence. "Fuck. You."

"No," she said coldly. "He isn't finished. Twenty more."

Soren jerked his head up, struggling to see through the hazy film clouding his vision. His pulse hammered wildly. Even a vampire might not survive another round if he lost too much blood.

For the first time, Soren heard a hint of tension—even animosity—in the other man's voice.

"Leila, I don't think—"

"It's not your place to do the thinking, damn you! Do it! And when you are finished, come to my room."

"Why are you doing this?" Soren rasped.

She looked at him, malice shining from every pore. "In order to fully appreciate the gift I'm bestowing, you must experience the depths of torment. By the time you've seen the error of your ways and given in, you'll be begging for the agony to end."

She whirled and stalked from the room, slamming the door in her wake. Arron came to stand in front of him, and Soren was surprised to see sympathy in the depths of his green eyes.

"I am very sorry," he said softly.

Hope flared. "You don't have to do this. You're not like her, Arron. I can sense it."

He hesitated before answering, anguish etching his handsome face. "You are correct. I am nothing like Leila. . . . I am much, much worse." With that, Arron moved back into position.

Panic returned, and he abandoned his vow not to beg. "Please, for the love of the gods, don't do this—"

The blow set his back afire and shattered his senses. The leather tore into his flesh again and again, until he could feel nothing except blood running down his legs, dripping off his feet. Until he could see nothing, and the beast roared at his surrender.

Until he understood, at last, that there was indeed such a thing as a fate worse than death.

Harley was sunning herself by the pool, chatting with a handsome faery, when she spotted a big male with a familiar black head of hair making his way to her side. Breaking off her end of the conversation, she smiled at Valafar and gave him a jaunty wave.

He returned it, but appeared far too serious as he approached and stopped at the foot of her lounger. "Hi, pretty," he greeted her. "I need to speak to you. Alone." He shot a pointed glare at the other male, who quickly left for greener, and friendlier, pastures.

"Now, you didn't have to scare off my new friend! What gives?" When he didn't respond to her teasing tone, she began to worry. Her smile wilted. "What's wrong?"

"Have you seen Soren?"

She curled her lip. "Not since the bitch-witch decided her play toy was spending way too much time with me and hustled him off someplace. Why?"

He paused. "How about Luc?"

"No, I haven't seen him today. Maybe Aldric is around?" she suggested.

"He's been called away on Council business," Val said grimly. "Council people are disappearing left and right, and no one seems to know where the blazing Hades they've gone!"

She frowned. "Soren said you didn't have much to do with the Council, *Prince Valafar*. So why do you care?"

He sighed. "So he told you about me? I *hate* the bullshit that goes on in the Council and I'm too old to stomach it anymore.

But when members of my clan start to vanish, and then I investigate to find out that high-ranking members of the city are going missing all over, I have no choice but to find out what the fuck is going on!"

"Maybe Leila ate them?" She was only half joking. "I hear she has quite the appetite."

"You're probably closer in that guess than you realize." He didn't crack a smile.

"What do you know about her?"

"Plenty, but I need to speak with Soren first. He has to know what he's dealing with before it's too late." Val's fists clenched at his sides.

That had her pushing from her lounger to poke him in the center of his broad chest. "If it's so dire, why haven't you told him already? He's made some sort of awful bargain with that sneaky woman, and I have a feeling it's one skewed in her favor."

"What do you know of this bargain?" he demanded, ignoring her question.

"She agreed to bring back his lost mate—*me*, they think—in exchange for his putting her up in style and pretending to be her mate. But I don't know what else he has to do or what she gets out of it."

Val's expression darkened. "No doubt the only thing she's ever really wanted: power. Very few know this, even the Fontaine brothers, but the Coalition tossed her out of the Council centuries ago for her nefarious practices. She changed her name and appearance decades ago, and has been trying to worm her way back in ever since."

Harley goggled at him. "Centuries? Changing her looks? How old is she and what the hell *is* she?"

"Ancient and lethal," he said cryptically. "Let's find that vampire of yours."

Why wouldn't Val say more about Leila, or whatever that thing was? A shiver of fear went down her spine as he took her hand and led her to search for the vampire who was starting to get under her skin.

9

*S*oren had never been brought low enough to pray for death, and he wouldn't start now. He wouldn't give that she-devil the satisfaction. He would take every abuse she meted out and more. If she wanted a monster, she'd get one. In spades.

He'd turn her own creation against her.

The beast seethed. *You can't do that.*

"Watch me."

Hang on; concentrate on that, he told himself. *Feel nothing.* Pain, grief, despair—gone. All of it. Nothing left except the hatred that fed the beast awakening within.

His companion shifted and rolled in his chest like a caged thing, uneasy. *Eager.* A chill whispered along his spine, but he tamped down the cloying fear that once unleashed, he wouldn't be able to control it. That it would consume him completely, his identity lost forever, even to himself.

The gamble wasn't a choice. If it got to the point he could no longer control the beast . . . somehow, he'd do what needed to be done.

Chin resting on his chest, he stared absently at the inky pool widening under his feet. What was Harley doing right now? Was she having sweet daydreams of their rendezvous in the gazebo, or was she enjoying the pleasures at the resort? Did she miss him, wonder why he wasn't back yet? Gods, he'd give anything to take her to his bed tonight and wake up tomorrow, all of this nothing but a nightmare. . . .

"You must learn to guard your thoughts, vampire."

He jerked his head up to find himself looking straight into Arron's knowing green eyes. "I've got a better idea. Stay the hell out of my head. How does a shifter do that, anyway?" He winced at the lack of force in his voice, betraying his weakened state.

Arron lifted a tawny brow. "Stay out? Impossible. Your musings couldn't resound more loudly if you stood at the very summit of the Temple of the Gods and bellowed them to the entire city. You have much to learn."

"And I suppose you're going to teach me?" he gritted. In spite of his resolve to block out the pain, it returned in sickening waves. Lack of sleep in the days since he'd brought Leila here, and now this torment, had left him faint with exhaustion.

Arron's full, sensuous lips turned up in a ghost of a smile. "I'm going to enjoy your lessons, and so will you."

"Yeah? Wake me up when the fun starts, 'cause I'm not real impressed so far."

The smile vanished. "Take care to curb your foolish sarcasm in Leila's presence. You will gain nothing, save prolonging the torture until she believes you've been beaten into submission— physically and emotionally."

Soren blinked, trying to hold the dizziness at bay. "What the hell does she want? Is death the fate Leila has planned for me?"

Arron looked away, his expression solemn. "Perhaps."

The wolf was lying. "I heard the two of you talking earlier," he whispered past the agony radiating throughout his body. "Why does she believe I'm a descendant of Azrael? How is she going to use me?"

"All will be made clear to you in time."

"You know," he hissed, "I'm getting damned tired of that answer. What's she going to do—turn me into some sort of demon from Hades? Is that what I somehow agreed to when we made our so-called bargain?" The man gazed at him with such sorrow, Soren's blood ran cold. "Sweet, merciful gods . . ."

"Never make a deal with the devil, vampire. The game favors the house, without exception." He paused. "One thing more— no matter what, do not let her get her hands on your family's swords. When your mind betrays you, remember that, if nothing else."

It was too much, and he couldn't think anymore. Couldn't reason out this madness and what he'd done to deserve it.

All he'd wanted was to have his mate and be happy.

"I've lost everything," he rasped. "My mate—"

"You have another, at least for now." Arron gave him a look filled with pity. "Your mate is the least of your concerns, unless she gets in Leila's way. As your brother has done."

Fear liquefied his guts as he remembered. "Luc. What has she done to him? Tell me!"

"Your younger brother is dead," he answered quietly. "I am sorry."

"You— You're lying."

"I'm not. I heard her order the attack myself. The assassin was a werewolf in half form. Luc never stood a chance."

The wolf spoke the truth; it was in his eyes, his voice. No one escaped a half-form wolf. The blood drained from Soren's face. Hanging his head, he fought the urge to howl. To go mad and tear apart everyone in sight.

Do it, the beast purred. *It will make us feel better.*

No. He would not give in to the sorrow and rage. That's what she wanted.

Soren strained against the bonds. "Where is my brother's body?"

"I—I don't know. Leila sent me to confirm the kill . . . but it wasn't there."

Hope rose, nearly clogging his throat. "Then how do you know he's dead?"

"From the amount of blood on the ground where he was attacked, I cannot see how anyone could've survived."

"Then he could be alive." He had to hold on to that slim hope.

"I do not think so. Nonetheless, it is curious. I cannot fathom why his body would've been taken or by whom."

"What did you tell Leila?"

"Nothing. For now."

This was all too much to take in. Yet he had a feeling he hadn't even scratched the surface of crazy. He hadn't stepped through the looking glass; he'd been slammed through the gods-damned thing, headfirst.

Luc. The fun-loving, adventurous brother, the bright star everyone wanted in their orbit. Dead. How could that be possible? *Please don't let it be true.*

He sagged against the bonds as exhaustion claimed him. Sometime later, he was vaguely aware of being freed from his prison, of Arron's strong arms catching, then lifting him.

162 † JO CARLISLE

Sharp voices, raised in argument.

By the saints, he's been pushed nearly past endurance! Surely you cannot mean to kill this man who is so valuable to your purpose?

I'll do whatever I damned well want, my impertinent wolf. Curb your tongue, unless you'd prefer my wrath fall upon the son you hold dear—

No! Please, I'll do as you say.

Crude laughter rang in his ears, and Soren could feel Arron's anguish as clearly as his own. The guy may have been black-mailed by the bitch queen to beat the hell out of him, play sub-servient to her every desire, but he hated every minute of it. Arron's loathing of her thickened the air between them, dark and palpable. That, at least, gave Soren some comfort.

Cool air rushed over his naked body as he was whisked away, floating. In moments he was lowered and rolled onto his stom-ach. His cheek rested against cool silk, and his battered body cried out in relief at the heavenly softness of the mattress. Even through his blurred vision, he could sense they were in Soren's quarters, and that gave him some relief.

Leila came to sit near his head, running her slender fingers through his hair. "There, my mate. All is as it should be, and you will soon take your rightful place beside me as ruler of the Southern Coalition. We will kill Aldric, place our own followers in the Council seats, and ascend the throne together, you and I."

What? He knew she lusted after power, but if she thought for one second he intended to help her murder his remaining brother, she was truly deranged.

She gave a low, throaty laugh of amusement as if he'd spoken aloud. "Darling, not to worry. By the time your transformation is complete, you'll possess the power and strength to bring Aldric to his knees."

"Impossible." he managed. "I cannot defeat my brother any more than you can." Had he offended her? He hoped so.

"You're wrong." Her voice tightened. "I don't know why your parents never told you. The blood of the ancients flows through your veins, like all males in the Fontaine family. The blood of your father, who was an incubus."

"A fallen angel?" He tried to rise on his elbows to stare at her, but she pushed him back down. "You're full of shit. My father was a vampire, like my mother!"

"Wrong. Your father is directly descended from Azrael, and an incubus like your late father lusts after many women. Why do you think he opened this resort? To feed his need—the need that all three of his sons inherited. Just like the great Merlin, a child is sometimes born of this unholy union, and that child is marked for greatness."

"Marked." His mind scrambled to follow where she was leading. No doubt he wasn't going to like it. "The crescent moon on Aldric's neck, and . . ."

"On your hip. Azrael's mark." She shrugged. "I would have preferred Aldric, as he's already on the Council and is a great leader. But the truth is, I failed to win him before, decades ago, when I possessed a different face and name. He's too strong-willed for me and Luc is too young, and so I watched you from afar for a long time. When you lost your true mate, I knew some-day when the timing was perfect, you would come to me. I fore-saw it, you see. And I knew I'd use your bargain against you. Soren, you can't fight me. Don't you understand?"

Gods help him, he was beginning to. "I sold my soul in exchange for my mate—"

"Needlessly," she revealed, toying with his hair. "Fate would've brought your Harley to you eventually, even if I hadn't taken you to Lash. I bided my time to bring you under control. And here you are."

A wave of helpless rage engulfed him. He'd bargained away his life *for nothing*. If it was the last thing he ever did, with his final breath, he'd make her pay for this.

"I failed to ensnare Aldric, but I won't fail with you. I will make that gift a reality for us both, starting now."

"If you can make me powerful enough to destroy Aldric, then why shouldn't I crush *you* instead?"

"Soren," Arron warned.

Leila leaned close to whisper in his ear, and her words froze his heart. "Sweet Luc is dead and Aldric will soon follow, but you have a very lovely lady whose sex still lingers on your skin. Perhaps I should invite her in here to play?"

"You bitch," he snarled. "If you go near her—"

"You'll do what?" she laughed. "Did you really believe I would create something I can't control? If you attempt to slip from my grasp, everyone you hold dear will be killed. *By your own hand.*"

No. "I will never hurt the people I love."

"Won't you? Think of what you nearly did to your brother and to Jordan. When every cell in your body is starved for blood and the beast has ripped the last shreds of humanity from your raging mind, who will stop you from satisfying your lust?"

"I will," he choked.

She smiled evilly, those black eyes boring into his. "No. You'll give yourself to the darkness and love every minute of it, starting now. If you don't, the consequences will be much worse."

His breathing hitched in panic. "Damn you, stay away from my family, from—" He didn't dare finish. *Oh, Harley.*

"Arron, let us begin." Her words punctuated the quiet like a death knell.

While she resumed stroking his hair, Arron spread his legs and moved between them. He gasped as the wolf's tongue began to lap at the backs of his thighs, his buttocks, his back, swirling lazy circles as he moved upward. Warmth spread through him, tingling, the fiery wounds on his backside knitting closed. A wolf, healing him? When finished, Arron rolled him onto his back. Soren tried to sit up and push away, but the warning look in his green gaze stopped him.

"Easy," Arron murmured gently, pushing him into the pillows.

The timbre of the shifter's seductive voice moved through his veins like several shots of whiskey.

"Please don't do this," Soren whispered.

Without a word, Arron took each of his wrists and spread and bound them. Turning his head, Soren saw they'd been secured to the heavy iron bedposts with thick silver chains. Before he could protest, his ankles were bound the same way.

Next to him, Leila untied the belt of her black silk robe, letting it fall away. Her small breasts bobbed close to Soren's face, a curious vial on a chain nestled between them. He swallowed hard.

"He's perfection, isn't he, Arron?"

Arron said nothing but stood and removed his own robe. Flinging his long auburn-gold hair over one shoulder, he seemed unconcerned with his nudity. Mouth dry, Soren watched as he retrieved a small clay jar from the bedside table and came back to tilt the object over him. The wolf poured a generous amount of thick, greenish oil onto his chest, stomach, and genitals. The stuff smelled heady and sweet, like spearmint, and oozed everywhere, luscious and soothing.

But he flinched as Arron's hands began to message the oil into his skin. Arousing him, stoking his desire. "No."

But his voice held little conviction and his protests turned to dust as the shifter took the head of Soren's cock in his mouth. Began to suckle him, deft tongue catching the drops leaking from the slit. Then taking him deeper, down that sleek throat. Sucking and massaging him with practiced ease, driving him insane.

Leila whispered in his ear as the wolf devoured him. "It's good, isn't it? You want more?"

"Yes." The admission escaped without his consent. He jacked his hips, eager.

"Our Arron is going to fuck you, my pet. Relax and let him have you. Free your mind and body to savor the wickedness."

He knew what she was doing—lowering his defenses through sex, and allowing the beast to reign. And he couldn't stop her. Didn't want to. Arron's big fingers breached his opening and began to slick his passage with the oil. He'd taken many males but had never been taken. It was strange and . . .

Incredible. The wolf's knuckle brushed the magic spot inside that drove his lovers wild, and now he knew why. "Oh, saints. Please!"

His cock jerked, hard and ready to explode. His balls were tight.

"What do you need?" Arron rumbled.

"Fuck me, hard and deep!"

Never before had those words passed his lips, and he couldn't wait. There was enough slack in the chains binding his ankles for the wolf to raise his ass and place the head of his cock at Soren's opening. He pushed, burrowing inside in a delicious burn that sent sparks shooting all through Soren's body.

The wolf began to pump, and Soren was lost. He exulted in the big rod plowing his ass and at being bound and at the male's mercy. He had no choice but to give himself and revel in being owned. Claimed.

Arron's strokes increased in tempo until he drove Soren into the mattress, his expert fucking spiraling the pleasure higher, faster. Finally he felt the tingling, the sparks sizzling out of control. A cry escaped him as his balls erupted and ropes of cum shot between their straining torsos, bathing them. Warmth filled his ass as Arron stilled, grinding into him.

So naughty, wicked. He wanted it again.

Arron withdrew, leaving him sated and sweating.

"See? You cannot fight your destiny," Leila crooned, reaching for the vial. She unscrewed the small lid and tipped the opening. A tiny drop of crimson liquid beaded on her finger, and she touched it to his lips. "Taste."

Just a harmless drop of blood, he told himself frantically. *Nothing more.*

His tongue flicked the moisture, a simple, involuntary reaction to having blood placed there. Just sustenance.

Nothing. And then . . .

His entire body shook. Slight tremors at first. Sweat formed on his forehead, trickled down his face. His breathing grew ragged, uneven, and his heart pounded in fright. Not just blood. Not even Leila's. Something ancient and terrible.

"What have you done to me?" he gasped.

If she answered, he couldn't hear over the roar of his own

blood rushing in his ears, increasing in tempo as the shaking worsened.

Poison?

No. Something worse, much worse.

That's sweet power, you mean sonofabitch!

"Who said that? Leila?"

Insane, raucous laughter. That of his beast. Of himself.

"You, my love." She smiled, her voice reverent. "I have waited for this day for so long. Have you any idea of the magnitude of the gift I'm bestowing upon you?"

"No. I don't want it." But the evil thing within him did.

"Taste, my love. The blood of Azrael, the archangel of Death. It took me centuries of searching to find and steal this vial, and now you, Soren, are about to become a hybrid of such greatness that only the gods themselves could vanquish you. Vampire, witch, demon, and archangel . . . not even the exalted Prince Valafar will be able to defeat you."

He turned his head away as far as the bonds would allow, but she succeeded in poking a finger between his lips.

The second drop detonated his body like a bomb. The blast ripped into his brain with nuclear force, seeking not just to destroy.

To annihilate.

His memories blew like shrapnel into the air. Harley. Aldric. Luc. His mother and father. Their beloved resort. The guests. Who would take care of them?

Screaming, he reached for everyone and everything he loved, but they whirled into space. A black vortex sucked them far away, out of reach.

Oh, gods, what was happening? *Help me!*

Like that fateful night decades ago when he'd lost Helena, he sent his cry for mercy to the gods. But no one answered, save the demon residing in his own soul.

"Nooooo." He strained against the bonds in helpless agony.

Yessss. The slumbering beast awakened, reveling in the torture, loving every moment of it. He looked up at Leila, saw the smirk of triumph on her face, knew that she called to the evil thing living inside him and that he'd lost.

Arron moved to sit near his shoulder, opposite Leila, his face grim.

"You belong to me. It is time to take your rightful place at my side," she said, pleased.

No, no! his mind screamed. But power, awesome and terrifying, surged through him in answer.

"I . . . I . . ."

Arron's lips brushed lightly against his. "All will be well. Do not fear."

He was wrong. Nothing would be all right again, ever. No stopping this now. It was over.

His soul wept, his heart shattered.

She straddled his hips and stretched atop him, breasts crushing into his chest. Grabbing a handful of his hair, she pulled his head back so hard that he thought his neck might snap, then sank her teeth deep into his throat.

Witch.

Demon.

Like one fateful night so long ago, when his horrified screams sought the gods, only the undead heard.

10

After searching everywhere for Soren to no avail, Harley and Valafar stopped short in the doorway to his suite.

Val frowned, scenting the air.

"What?" she whispered.

"I'm not sure. Something isn't right."

The prince moved into the room and walked over to Soren's bed. She followed, noting that the sheets were rumpled and stained. Soren lay on his stomach, naked, legs spread slightly and his arms above his head, hugging his pillow. Thin pink lines crisscrossed his back from shoulder to hip, as though—

"Your vampire has been whipped and then healed. I'm surprised he's into bondage or being marked—at least when he's on the receiving end."

"Yeah, me, too." Carefully, she sat on the bed next to Soren and laid a palm on his shoulder. His breathing was deep and even, but after a moment, he began to stir. Val stood beside the bed, arms crossed over his chest, watching in concern.

"Mmm."

"Soren? Hey, big vamp. I thought you were coming back. Are you all right?"

The vampire stretched and opened his eyes, blinking away the sleepiness.

"Your eyes," Harley gasped. "What's happened to them?"

The irises, normally a beautiful amber gold, were so dark that they were almost black. Worse, there was no recognition on his face as he rolled to his side and studied them both.

"My eyes?"

"They're usually golden," she said fearfully, glancing at Val.

"So?" The vampire sat up. "Who the fuck are you?"

"Shit," Val muttered.

Harley's mouth dropped open. *Soren doesn't remember us?* "What the hell has that bitch done to you?" she demanded.

"You mean my mate? I can't have anyone talking like that about her, even if it is true." His smile was predatory as he eyed them. "You two come to play?"

He was calling that vile witch his mate! She appealed to Val in a hoarse whisper. "What are we going to do? We have to help him!"

"Let me think." The demon paused. "My contacts haven't been able to locate Aldric, so it's possible that he's met with foul play or he's gotten wind of what's happening and is gathering forces. For now, it might be best if we humor your vampire until we have a solid plan. Perhaps involving him in some of his normal activities will help push the darkness to the back of his mind and allow his real self to get a hold again."

"You talking about me? What do you mean, my real self?"

"Soren—"

"Tread carefully," Val warned her. "His mind is fragile."

She nodded. "I'm Harley. You bought me at the slave auction and gave me a job as your Chosen. Remember?"

"I . . ." He faltered and stared hard at her, as though struggling to recall. Or perhaps he was fighting the thing inside him for dominance. "Vaguely, I think. Yes."

"You showed me around and promised me a scene with our friend Valafar, too." She indicated the demon, who stood by, trying to appear casual.

"I'm not sure." Soren shook his head. "But I'm not really feeling myself, so I probably forgot."

Boy, did you. And not in the way you think.

"No problem. If you're too tired, we can do it another time."

The vampire sat up and swung his legs over the side of the bed. "Of course not! I'm fine. Just let me shower and we'll . . . What sort of scene, exactly?"

"A private playroom," she said. Considering how unstable he was at the moment, she thought it best they steer clear of another public exhibition.

"Sounds perfect." His newly darkened eyes glittered like onyx, and she shivered. "How rough and raunchy do you want it?"

"I can take anything you dish out," she asserted bravely. Or stupidly, from Val's scowl. Ignoring her friend, she charged ahead. "I want to be mastered. Maybe even scared a little."

Soren tapped a finger on his lips thoughtfully. "I think some heavy bondage and a bit of S and M is in order for this one."

"Whatever you say, I'm game—as long as Val gets to participate."

"Absolutely. Wait right here, I'll be back."

He slid out of bed and walked unsteadily toward the shower.

Once he disappeared inside the bathroom, the demon voiced his concern.

"Do you really think it's wise to put yourself at risk in his hands with the kind of scene you've spurred him to enact?"

"Maybe not." She tucked a strand of hair behind her ear nervously. "But I do know that the real Soren recognizes *me* as his mate, not that witch. I'm betting on his soul knowing the truth, even though it's stained with Leila's lies and manipulations. Soren won't hurt me, and I'll get through to him."

"That's a huge chance you're taking."

"But I have to." She thought back to the incident with Jordy. "Soren lost control with one of the Chosen and came close to draining him. I was so damned scared, but I was able to get through to him. Maybe this darkness inside him was suppressed because of me, and if I can reach him, he can get control long enough to beat her."

"Do what you must, and I'll be there."

"Thanks."

When Soren finished showering, he dressed in jeans and a black T-shirt and called Val over. "Okay, this is going to be a big scene, and this is how I want to do it."

Keeping Harley out of the loop, the vampire spoke in hushed tones to the demon prince, who argued but eventually relented. The vampire left the room, and Harley waited to hear what to do next.

"All right, pretty. I hope you can handle what he's got planned." He chuckled. "I have to admit, my cock and balls are like stone just anticipating what we're going to do to you."

Her pulse sped up and her nipples tightened. "What will that be?"

"We're playing master and slave, and you don't have to guess which one you are."

"I'm surprised he'd pick that game, since he's so against the idea of slaves."

"But our Soren isn't in the driver's seat in his mind," he reminded her. "And besides, I think the plan excites you more than a little."

"You're right—it does. Now what?"

"We begin now. And remember, I'm playing a role, pretty," he said gently.

"Okay." She let out a deep breath.

"Take off all your clothes. Every stitch."

"But I've got to go outside to walk to the other building!"

"Do it, slave," he growled, snapping his wings open. The huge black feathers made him appear even more dangerous. "If you know what's good for you. And do not speak unless you're asked a direct question."

She undressed, hands shaking some as she kicked out of her shoes and pulled off her shirt and bra. Next went the jeans, and she stepped out of them, naked and feeling very vulnerable. Which she was. She just hoped Soren remembered he was acting.

Remember me, please. Don't let this thing win!

She followed Valafar on shaking legs down the stairs and out of the house. From the knowing smirks, the guests of the infamous sex resort were used to seeing someone being led stark-naked in broad daylight to a scene. It was a relief to gain the safety of the other building—but *safety* was a relative term. Her nerves were in full force as they descended the stairs.

Next Val led her down the hallway and straight into a play-room. She stood, checking the place out. Equipped with every imaginable device capable of eliciting erotic rapture, the room was a no-holds-barred sexual playground.

Gracing center stage, a massive four-poster bed loomed, almost identical to the one in Soren's bedroom—except this one had leather restraints, a collar, and chains. A sling attached to straps and pulleys was suspended from the ceiling off to one side of the room, and Harley couldn't fathom how the thing might be used. Wasn't sure she wanted to know, either.

Whips of assorted sizes hung from hooks on the black-painted walls. Dozens of candles had been lit, casting eerie, dancing shadows around the room. *Like a wicked cave,* she thought. A multicolored assortment of oils waited on the bedside table, fit for a yummy feast.

"Jesus Christ," she choked. "What am I doing?"

"Remember the rules, slave." Valafar flicked a hand. "Get on the bed. Question?"

Harley crawled into the middle of it, sitting on her knees, and gazed at Valafar, barely able to speak. "What do I do now?"

"Whatever your master desires," he murmured, his voice low and sensual. "Give him your wrists."

She offered them to Soren, who had returned. He reached to the headboard, took a pair of handcuffs secured to the bed by a length of chain, and snapped them in place. Next her lover brought forth a leather collar, also chained, and slipped it over her head.

"This is one of my favorites," Soren informed her, tightening the length to take out much of the slack. "I enjoy total control. The more you struggle, helpless to prevent me from doing anything I wish, the more aroused I become. There's something dangerous about the way I'll tighten it around your throat while

I fuck your ass. Something dark and decadent about knowing I could snap your neck if I please, even as we both come."

An electric thrill zinged down Harley's spine. A sense of unreality descended over her as Valafar picked up a strip of black silk, placed it between her teeth, and tied it behind her head. She'd stepped into a decadent dream, a willing offering awaiting the beast's appearance from the flickering shadows to devour her.

As long as that didn't happen literally, she was good.

Valafar bent to kiss her lightly on the cheek. "Don't be afraid, pretty. Just open your heart and mind to him. Accept him. You're his now."

He moved into the pool of darkness beyond the bed, watching as Soren walked into the dancing light, wearing only a loose silk robe of deep blue. The flames reflected the hue into eyes that glittered like black jewels from the planes of his angular face. Dark brown hair fell over the vampire's forehead into those arresting eyes, and brushed his neck.

With lean strides, he moved with the grace of a panther, letting the robe slip off his shoulders and to the floor. He stood by the side of the bed, his expression feral, like it hadn't been at the gazebo. He sported an enviable six-pack stomach and long, strong legs . . . and his enormous shaft stood out proudly at the ready.

She bowed her head and curled in on herself, instinctively trying to make herself smaller in the face of this wicked stranger. Unprepared, she started when Soren grabbed her chin and forced it up so that her eyes meet his gaze. His smoky voice held a thread of anger.

"Never do that again. Don't hide from me, ever. You're beautiful. And you're mine."

The vampire tunneled strong fingers though Harley's hair, then traveled downward to encircle the column of her throat. The wild throb of her pulse tripped in the delicate hollow like a jackhammer, betraying her trepidation, and this seemed to please Soren.

"Valafar is quite the lover, isn't he?"

A loaded question. Harley stared at him, transfixed, waiting for the cobra to strike. Soren gave a predatory smile.

"Cat got your tongue?" he teased, knowing damned well his captive couldn't answer. "We both know you couldn't resist having his cock inside you, any more than I could stop myself from fucking him if I had the chance."

A flicker of fear raced along her spine in response to Soren's words, and an involuntary whimper escaped. How much did he really remember? Soren knelt on the bed between Harley and the headboard, forcing her to move backward. The collar around her throat tightened a bit more, along with the pressure of Soren's strong fingers, reminding her that she was at this predator's mercy.

Helpless.

"Oh yeah. Val had you first, and for that I'm going to punish you. I'm your master and you belong to me," he said in a low voice. "I'm going to teach you all the meanings of *total submission* you never dreamed existed in your wildest fantasies. Or your darkest nightmares. You're my slave and will deny me nothing. *Nothing.* Do you understand?"

Harley swallowed hard, nodded. In spite of her fear, tingling warmth flooded her pussy and her arousal stirred. She was falling under this vampire's decadent spell. *Please let him remember.*

"Good, because I'll do to you whatever I desire, whenever I wish to do it. Starting now." Soren tested the chain secured to the cuffs on her wrists. Then he sat, reclining against the headboard with his legs out in front of him. "There. You have plenty of room to maneuver. Lie facedown across my lap and prepare to receive the first of your punishment."

God, is he actually going to—

"Yes, I'm going to spank that sweet ass," he smiled. "Get over here. *Now.*"

Harley shook as she moved to Soren's side and positioned her hips over his. A tiny shudder rippled through her when she spread herself on her belly, across Soren's lap, with her cuffed hands above her head and the vampire's heated cock nestled into her mound.

"Oh yes." One big hand pinned her in place while the other rubbed her exposed cheeks. "Let's see what you're made of, gorgeous."

Soren's open palm came down forcefully, and the shock of the blow took her breath away. She gasped but didn't have time to recover before there was another slap to her bottom. She cried out against the gag, but her captor chuckled.

"God, that's lovely. You should see how pretty and red your ass is. Feel how we rub against each other when I spank you?"

Another blow brought tears to her eyes, but her body was responding to the rough treatment—the scene she'd asked for. Every time Soren slapped her, his erection rubbed against her, each of them teasing the other. In a strange way, it made Harley feel connected to her tormentor.

"This is important, baby. Feel my power flowing through you," Soren purred as though reading her mind. "You must understand and accept your role and mine. You'll learn to bend to my will, eagerly. Before I allow you to leave this room, I'll have you in every way possible. I'm going to drown you in sensation, break you. And when you believe you can't take any more, Val and I will fuck you while you scream for mercy, drenched in our cum. Only then will you be broken to my satisfaction."

Harley whimpered. Master and slave. So wicked, the thrall of his mind control more addictive than cocaine. More and more blows on her ass. She moaned, tears seeping from the corners of her eyes.

Soren leaned toward the bedside table and picked up one of the bottles of oil. He spread Harley's butt and poured a generous amount on her hole. She flinched when the vampire inserted a finger and began to prepare her channel. After a few strokes, she was writhing in anticipation.

"You like that, baby? Let's see how you enjoy *this*."

Her master retrieved something else and parted her cheeks again. Something large, round, and slick probed her anus. Slowly, Soren began to work it in. The device was almost too large, and fiery pain mingled with intense pleasure as it stretched her to the limit. Filled her deeper, deeper.

Her ragged moan was muffled by the gag. "Ohhh."

A dildo, she realized. A really huge one. She was glad she hadn't been able to see it.

"That's it," Soren whispered, his voice thick with desire. "You're anticipating what I'll do to your body next, aren't you? Craving more punishment? There. The rubber cock is buried all the way inside your pretty ass. But you don't get relief yet. Not even close. It's going to stay inside you, torturing you. Roll onto your back."

Panting, Harley did as she was told. Soren moved off to the side and patted the pillows at the headboard.

"Here, lie down. I'm going to put a couple of pillows underneath your hips to lift you up. I want to see that dildo in your ass, knowing it's driving you insane with pleasure while I continue."

Harley scooted into position, not even daring to guess what he'd do now. Soren put the pillows underneath her, then tightened the chain on her collar to the limit. Next, he did the same with her cuffed wrists, pulling her arms over her head. Then Soren spread her legs wide, binding each ankle to a bedpost.

Harley blinked, panic warring with the liquid heat stealing through her. She was completely at the vampire's mercy now. No turning back. Soren's cock was hard, and he no doubt anticipated what he'd do to her soon.

"Fuck, yes. You're so beautiful, Harley." Soren moved off the bed and disappeared into the shadows for a few seconds. He returned, holding something long, slender, and black in one hand. He showed it to Harley, eyes glittering. "This is one of my favorites."

A riding quirt! Harley's heart pounded. She shook her head, nearly frantic, but not just with fear. Her pussy was wet, throbbing.

"I'm your master. With every blow, you will call me that in your mind. *Master.* You will engrave the word in your soul, and later, when I fuck you senseless, you will scream it as I fill your sweet hole with my cum."

Soren sat on his knees beside her. Harley strained against the bindings as the vampire ran the quirt between her legs, back and forth, letting her feel the length of it. Lightly, Soren—no, her master—began to flick the insides of her thighs with the very tip of the quirt. Then lightly against her little clit. Not hurting her, but reminding her that he could if he wanted.

Wonderful little electric sensations zinged through her cunt. She wiggled, groaning at the dual stimulation tormenting her ass and, oh, her pussy.

"Yes, give yourself over to your master. Totally," her lover hissed.

Master, her mind echoed.

The light flicks became more pronounced, took on a more stinging bite. Nipping at her slit.

Ohh yess. Master. Her entire body went molten. She arched her back, hips bucking, crying into the gag.

Master, please help me! Give me release!

Suddenly the flogging stopped. She wept in frustration as her master laid the quirt aside. Her lover moved in, bending his face close to her own, smoothing back her hair.

"Mmm, you're quite the little masochist, aren't you? Need to orgasm so badly you hurt, don't you? Not yet, beautiful. I want to savor you like this for a while. My slave spread before me, powerless against me, and begging for more pain, more pleasure. I own you now. Understand?"

Harley nodded, tears rolling into her hair.

"Excellent. Remember, do not come before I give you permission. I'll know if you do, because I'll scent your release, and the punishment will be severe."

Soren disappeared again. Harley's chest heaved as she fought back release. What was Soren doing? Her grinning master returned, holding two small silver clamps in his fingers. Opening the jaws of the tiny devices, he revealed serrated teeth that would inflict more pain. Harley's eyes rounded, and she struggled to no avail.

"Hold still while Val puts these on you." Rubbing the clamps over his slave's nipples, teasing them to hardened peaks, he smiled, then handed them to his friend.

Val held them up. "Such small, seemingly innocuous devices, aren't they? That's what makes them so perfect for reminding you how helpless you are to my wishes."

Guessing Val's intention wasn't difficult. Desperately, Harley shook her head, sweat beading on her forehead. The prince only laughed, and sprang the jaws of one clamp onto her left nipple. She cried out hoarsely, straining, as metal bit into tender flesh. The process was repeated on the other one, leaving her electrified with agony. Desire.

"Stop fighting," her master crooned. "Breathe deeply. Drink the pain. Allow it to become part of you."

She gulped deep breaths, her entire body quivering, hyper-aware of her vulnerability. The darkest corner of her soul begged her to submit to this devil. That newly awakened, perverse part of her opened like a flower in the rain. Daring her dangerous captors to do more, much more.

"Ooh, got some spunk left, huh?" Soren's eyes glittered in approval. "Good. I'd hate to break you too easily. I think we'll let you stew for a while. Miss us."

Harley blinked as Soren slid off the bed and grabbed his silk robe. *What?* Those sons of bitches planned to just leave her here, trussed like a game hen, every cell in her body aching for release?

Footsteps receded. A door closed in the inky blackness at the top of the stairwell.

Bastards! Closing her eyes, Harley groaned in misery.

And waited. It seemed an eternity before their footsteps returned.

"Did you miss us?" Soren smiled. Joining her, he cupped his captive's cheek.

Gods, yes!

Harley closed her eyes briefly, afraid of the ways her master would abuse her body. Even more frightened of her own awakening. But when she opened them again, her eyes conveyed the message *Fuck you! Make me bow to your will, damn you!*

Her master caught the challenge. And accepted.

Joining her, Val took one of the silver clamps between two fingers and slowly twisted the imprisoned nipple. Shock waves of pain shot to her brain, and Harley cried out, thrashing.

"Aahhhh!"

Smiling, the prince repeated the process on the other nipple. Then he bent and sucked each pouty nub, twirling the clamp with tongue and teeth, ignoring his captive's screams.

Val raised his head, and Harley knew only a moment of respite. Soren used the fingers of one hand to slide past her pussy lips and into her channel while the other grasped the end of the dildo. He began to work the toy, pulling it out slowly, pushing it in. Deep. In and out. Faster, harder, until it plunged ruthlessly into her hole, slamming her ass. Harley arched her back, moaning, reveling in the burn. The fingers fucking her pussy.

"Yeah, that's my girl. Take it all, but don't come."

Lost in hell, Harley strained to obey. She was hardly aware of the fake cock and ankle restraints being removed. Her legs were spread and Soren moved between them, hooking his strong arms under the backs of her knees. He lifted Harley's hips off the bed and draped her legs over his shoulders. The tip of Soren's huge cock probed her slick entrance, but he held back.

"Look at me," her master ordered, eyes smoldering. "I'm going to fuck my beautiful slave until you break. Until you sob, begging your master for release."

Harley stared as Soren reached out, tugged the gag from

between her teeth, and pulled it down to leave the material looped around her neck. She sucked in a sharp breath as her master pushed his cock inside, filling her completely. Their gazes met, held. Harley actually *felt* the mystical bond form between them, connecting their souls.

How, when the darkness held Soren just as captive as his restraints held Harley? Was their connection strong enough to vanquish the evil?

"Ohhh," she gasped, lifting her hips even more.

"That's right, baby. Open your body to your master. Beg me."

"Fuck me, please," she groaned.

Soren's eyes darkened as he began to pump. "Who's fucking you?"

"Master," she whispered helplessly. "Fuck me, master. Please."

"Good girl. Sweet . . . so sweet." His hips pumped harder, and he threw back his dark head. "Ah yesss."

Harley surrendered. Body and soul. She belonged to this man, would do anything he commanded. In a daze, she watched Soren fuck her, his tanned, muscular chest gleaming with sweat, strong arms supporting her thighs. Every stoke pushed her higher, driving her closer to the edge.

"Please let me come," Harley begged.

He grinned darkly. "No."

Harley groaned, helpless, her misery so great she almost missed the subtle flick of Soren's hand, signaling his friend into a different position.

Valafar spread his legs near her head, his movements lithe, graceful, his black wings tucked against his back. His eyes smoldered with lust, his long, thick cock iron hard.

Soren pulled out, and Harley whimpered at the loss, making

her master laugh. Soren loosened the chains attached to her collar and the handcuffs, just enough to give a bit of play.

"On your hands and knees facing Valafar, baby," her master ordered. "Spread your legs."

Harley quickly complied, and Soren positioned himself behind her. Her master parted her cheeks, slid his cock into Harley's ass until he was buried deeply once more. Curious as to what Valafar thought of her submission, she looked up at the demon, only to find affection shining on his face. Acceptance. Her own arousal throbbed anew, desperate for relief.

"Rub your face all over Val's cock and balls," her master whispered, voice hoarse with passion. "When the three of us are together, you will submit to him as my second. You will honor and serve him, same as you do for me."

Thrilled, she did as commanded, the action eliciting a moan from both of her lovers. Gods, she'd never dreamed of anything so wicked, so darkly beautiful, as being ravaged by two powerful males in quite this way. Burying her face in the demon's groin, she rubbed the delicate testicles, the smooth cock, against her lips, inhaling the musky scent of the male's arousal. She arched her back, spreading her knees farther, giving her master full access, showing her total submission. Soren gripped her hips and began to pump her ass slowly, torturing her past endurance.

"Lick Val's balls. Suck them."

Her eager tongue laved the taut sac, teased the twin orbs underneath the flesh. Then she took them in her mouth, sucking, loving Val's strangled groan.

"Now take his cock down your lovely throat."

Valafar tangled his strong fingers in Harley's hair, stabbing his cock into her mouth. Harley took all of him deep down her throat, until the demon's balls slapped her chin to the rhythm of Soren's thrusts.

Oh, gods! Both males filled her, fucking her hard and fast. Her arms trembled under the weight of their assault, her aching pussy scorching hot. Soren must've read her mind.

"You will not have release," he panted, pumping his hips. "We're going to drown you in cum, beautiful, so that you know who owns you."

Yes, yes. Harley's master slammed his cock into her ass while Val pounded his shaft down her throat. Harley took all the punishment they dished out, rejoiced in the pain, the ecstasy. But she hurt so gods-damned bad with the need to explode, she couldn't stand it. Tears welled in her eyes.

Her master shot off with a loud cry, sending his load deep into her ass. *Saints, yes, master,* her brain echoed, though she couldn't yell her joy. Valafar followed, spewing hot cum again and again, fingers wrapped in Harley's hair, grinding into her face. Harley swallowed every drop, licked him clean. When both of her lovers pulled away, the tears escaped to roll down her face.

"Please," she choked. "I need."

"I can see that." She heard the smile in Soren's voice. And something else: affection. It gave her hope. "A good slave bows to her master's every desire. You've done an excellent job. Come for me."

Harley came so violently, she felt as though the force would turn her inside out. She jerked hard, pulsing on and on. Spilling hot warmth until her body jerked in spasms of aftershock.

She closed her eyes, hardly aware of Soren pulling her from Valafar. Enfolding her in his strong arms, laying them both against the pillows, and cradling her against his chest. Harley burst into tears and cried hard, shaking, unable to explain why.

"Shh, it's okay, baby," Soren whispered, pressing tender kisses into his hair. "I'm here. I'll take care of you now, always."

"Me, too, as your friend," Valafar said. He scooted in close to Harley's other side, stroking her hair, kissing her cheek.

Harley cried until she was exhausted and the sobs tapered to hiccups. Both males continued to hold and comfort her, softly reassuring her of their love.

"Please remember me," she begged Soren, clinging to him. Sniffling. He'd called her baby, spoken to her with tenderness. He was coming back to her. He had to be.

"I do," he whispered. "After what you just gave to me, how could I not?"

"Thank the gods!"

Safe, warm, and happy for the moment, she drifted away to the deep, resonant tones of their voices.

And to the bittersweet knowledge that their happiness could be fleeting. Soon they would have to take action against Leila. But the witch was a powerful, formidable enemy. Soren couldn't hide indefinitely.

"I'll always remember you," Soren said. "Now sleep."

Wrung out, Harley succumbed to darkness, and knew nothing more.

11

$\mathcal{S}$oren's head pounded.

The effort of suppressing his dark half, of keeping it at bay, was taking a toll. Rubbing his temples, he sat up in bed and tried to make sense of the jumble of images assaulting him from the past twelve hours or so. Like puzzle pieces, he worked and reworked them until he had some that fit.

Leila and Arron. The torture. His eventual breaking at her hands.

And Harley. Beautiful Harley. *She*, not the pretender, was his mate. She'd submitted so wonderfully to him, her soul reaching out to his like a beacon of light. He couldn't help but respond. Latch on to that shining beam and gather it into himself, force the snarling beast into a corner.

On the other side of a sleeping Harley, Valafar stirred and opened his eyes. One of his black wings was stretched across her as though holding her, but he retracted it as he sat up. "It's morning already? Ugh." He wiped at his eyes.

"Don't do sunrise?"

"I don't do daylight, period," the demon grumbled. "Being nocturnal suits me just fine."

"Well, we have to get up if you're going to help me out of the mess I've gotten myself into."

"True." The prince slid naked out of bed and stretched his arms and wings, which brushed the ceiling. "I can tell being your friend is going to cause me no end of trouble."

"You're probably right. Hope you can handle it."

"I've dealt with bigger problems than you and lived to tell. I'll manage."

Soren thought for a moment, his heart clenching. "Gods, my brothers. We need to find out what's happened to Luc. The wolf, Arron, said he didn't find a body. And Aldric! Where could he be?"

"I've still got a few trusted members of my clan working on it. There are far too many disappearances for my liking, and I'd bet my wings that your demoness has her hand in all of it."

"A female demon? Is that what the witch truly is?"

"She a half-breed, actually. She's used her demon magic for decades to masquerade as a garden-variety voodoo witch. Her other half is something out of your worst nightmares."

"As if the first half wasn't mean enough? What the hell is the other?"

"I'd like to know that, too," Harley murmured sleepily, rolling onto her back to smile briefly at Soren. He returned it and reached for her hand.

"Gorgon."

Soren's brows furrowed. "Isn't that a creature from mythology?"

"An intelligent creature. They're rare, but they do exist. Like most citizens, you've never met one until now because they keep to themselves and mask their appearance. In true form, they've a face only a mother could love, as the saying goes."

Soren began to feel ill. "So she doesn't really look like a human? What's her true form, then?"

"Being half-demon, I'd suspect she'd have something of our features. An angular face, perhaps a pair of wings. But if she were only a demon, she'd still be attractive even when she wasn't masking her looks. For example, when I unleash the full power of my demon, my features become sharp and my skin bluish, but I still basically look like me."

"Makes sense."

The demon continued. "I've never seen Leila in true form, but I'd venture a guess that her demon's features would be combined with those of her serpent."

"Her *what?*" he croaked.

"Um, snake. You know that's what a Gorgon *is*, right? A snake woman."

He stared at Val in horror. "Like Medusa? With a head full of writhing snakes and a gaze that turns a person to stone?"

"Yeah."

"Oh, shit. I think I'm going to be sick." He'd fucked a snake woman. Had given her control over his body and mind.

"No time for that. You've got a much bigger issue at hand, and that's how to kill the bitch."

"I don't suppose you've got any ideas in that department?"

"You have a sword that will slay any creature," Val said. "I know you have been forbidden to use it, but surely in this case the Council wouldn't punish you—"

"It won't matter whether they do or not, my friend. We both know why."

Harley's attention bounced between them with growing alarm. "Why not? Won't you get in trouble for using the sword if you're not supposed to?"

Clearing his throat, he took both of her hands in his. Telling her this was so hard when they'd just found each other. "Baby, they won't really have to discipline me because of my bond with Leila. When she's killed, I'll either die with her or my beast will take over completely and I'll have to be terminated."

"No," she whispered, tears welling in her pretty green eyes. "I won't accept that."

"You have to, love." He leaned over, kissed her lips gently. "Even now the damned thing rages inside me. It's such an effort to hold him back, and the only reason I'm able is because of you."

"Then maybe our bond will be enough to break hers!" she cried, tears spilling over. "You don't know for sure."

Heart wrenching, he wiped them with his thumb, but they kept falling. "Maybe you're right. We'll have to hope it's true." Then there would still be the issue of breaking the law, and he'd wind up being executed, anyway, for taking justice into his own hands for a second time. But Harley didn't need to be reminded.

"I'm not going to ask where you keep your sword," Val said, interrupting. "But I'd suggest you get it and keep it close at hand. I'm going back to my clan to round up a few good demons. While I'm there I'll dispatch a few more to search for Luc and Aldric, and then we'll return to guard the resort."

"I should send the guests home, too, though I hate to do that. I'll give them a free pass to come back whenever they like."

"Do that," Val said, nodding. "Their safety must come first.

By the time the Gorgon returns, the grounds will be clear of innocent bystanders and we'll bar her from entry."

A thought hit him. "That's another thing—where is she returning *from*? She has a tendency to disappear for hours. My brothers were going to check into where she goes, but never got the chance."

"My guess? She needs to spend time in freshwater to keep her skin from drying out, so I think it's likely that she's found a pond to visit."

"Okay, so what next?" Harley asked. "Is there a way to just subdue her and turn her over to the Council, let them deal with her punishment?"

"We can try," Val said, his tone cautious. "But that might be much more difficult than killing her, because you'd have to cover her eyes first and bind her, and that means being in reach of the venomous serpents on her head."

"Scratch that idea," Harley muttered.

Val agreed. "Easier to get in a lethal strike and be done with it." Waving a hand, he clothed himself in jeans. "I'm off. You two get the guests out of here and then stay out of sight, if you can, until I return with reinforcements."

"Will do." Soren shook the big demon's hand, feeling a particular sense of dread when the prince vanished. He hated to be negative, but he couldn't see how this was going to end well, short of a miracle.

Harley touched his arm. "Why don't we have a shower and then tend to the guests?"

Most folks were nice about the disruption. Once everyone was gone, he and Harley went into the house. Soren led her to Aldric's office, where he swore her to secrecy about the location of the swords.

"I want you to know where they are in case you have no other option but to use one. But you can't tell a soul where I'm taking you," he said quietly. "Our lives could depend on it."

"I won't, I swear."

He pressed a panel next to a wall of books, and the bookcase slid open to reveal a room that was deep but not too wide. The inside of the panel, walls, floor, and ceiling were thick and lined entirely with titanium, forming a box that could withstand nearly any onslaught. At the end of the rectangle, straight ahead, was a long table. On the table were three aged leather cases awaiting the masters who had been forced to lock them away so many years ago.

Soren walked to his case, ran a palm lovingly over the leather with his initials hand tooled on the top. "I haven't opened this since the day the Council threatened to execute me if I so much as held it again."

"That's harsh."

"Is it? I killed the demons who murdered Helena, without sanction. Afterward, I was so mad with grief, my brothers had to chain me. It was months before I learned of my punishment."

"You needed to avenge your beloved mate."

"Yes. And I'd behead the demons again, if I could."

No sense putting this off. Flipping the latches, he opened the lid. Harley's reverent breath echoed his own.

"Soren, it's beautiful."

"As much as any instrument of death can be," he said with a humorless laugh.

"Why is that, I wonder? Swords are so romantic, and yet their purpose is brutal."

"It brings to mind an image that the wielder of the weapon is fighting for a just cause, even if that isn't always so."

He gazed at the workmanship, seeing it through her eyes, as

though for the first time, and agreed that it was indeed a work of art. The curved hilt was made of gold, with jewels encrusted in the center just above the grip. The broad silver blade was sharp as a razor on both sides—and blessed by a druid priest many centuries ago to always deal death upon any evil.

It would serve him well in his final stand.

A sudden sense of urgency stiffened his spine, like the hair rising on the back of the neck when one is being watched. "She's coming. Let's close up and get out of here."

Hurriedly, he shut the case and ushered her out, sword in hand. Out in the office, he sealed the room, relieved to have it hidden once more but still anxious to get out of this area of the house. If the Gorgon caught them here, she'd search until she found the hiding place.

They made it all the way to the foyer before the front door crashed open and at least a dozen demons rushed inside. Two ugly brutes grabbed Harley, who screeched and tried to yank away, to no avail. They were much stronger than a human female.

"Stay back!" Soren hefted the sword and the demons froze, eyes widening as they realized what he held. "Let her go before I cut you all down!"

"They answer to me, vampire."

The demons parted and Soren's gaze took in the awful sight before them. "Harley, don't look into her eyes."

"I won't!"

He gaped in disbelief. Where her feet should have been were snakes. They crawled along, acting as her "legs" to move her forward. Her torso was slim but entirely covered in blue scales, as were her bare breasts and arms. Her face was angular and blue snakes writhed on her head.

He'd fucked this wretched thing. And enjoyed it.

"Love the real me, mate?" She chuckled at her own humor.

"I'm not your mate."

"My blood calls to you." She sounded so confident.

And it was true. Regardless of her appearance, the beast inside him did crave another taste of the wicked rush of her blood and the dark place it took him. He battled that lust, using the disgust he felt to assist him. "No. You've nothing I want."

"Tsk, not true. I have your Harley," she said in amusement, pointing to the demons holding her prisoner. "I'll make your choice simple. Drop the sword and kneel before me, or watch as I have them tear her fragile human body limb from limb."

"Don't listen to her," his mate hissed urgently. "She'll just double-cross—"

One of the demons jerked her arm hard, making her cry out in pain, and that's all it took to unleash his beast. *Kill the fucker.* With a roar, he lunged forward and cleaved the offender's head from his shoulders. The bastard was dead before the rest of his body hit the marble tile.

He swung at the second, who'd let her go and backpedaled, but not fast enough. Soren plunged the blade through his black heart and yanked it free to face the rest. But there were too many enemies, even for a former Warrior of Exodus with a magical sword.

The demons dog-piled him, and he lost Harley in the melee. She cried out again and he tried to reach her, only to have the breath pummeled out of him. The desperate situation and the demons' violence called to the beast that was always lurking, waiting to answer. For once he let it come, allowed the power to surge through him and explode. Snarling in rage, he shook a few of them off, but not all. Though he went crazy, fought like a mad animal, they managed to pin him again. He'd slaughter them all, if only he could get free.

Scrabbling for purchase, they clawed him, one getting a fist-ful of his hair and yanking back his head. The Gorgon yelled for the demon to stop, but its bloodlust was stronger. He raked his claws across Soren's throat just as a jarring blow snapped his head sideways . . . and he knew nothing more.

He could smell her blood.

Hunger. Lust.

Those twin devils rode him hard. He could sense her sad-ness, her anguish. They called to him, but not as much as the pull of her blood. The musky dampness of her sex.

He knew her. How?

The image rose. Moving between her thighs. She'd cried out his name. And what *was* his name?

I'll come back to you. . . .

His promise. Loss and grief flooded him because he knew he'd broken his word.

"Soren? Honey, please wake up."

Was *he* Soren? The musical sound of her beautiful voice beckoned him. To hear it again, he'd be whomever she wanted. With effort, he tried to obey, but his eyelids seemed frozen.

"Honey, it's Harley."

The name and her sweet voice teased the edges of a forgotten time. A lost world.

He opened his eyes and found himself staring into a lovely face. She was looking down at him anxiously, auburn hair falling around her shoulders. His gaze traveled to the wild pulse at her throat, and the scent of blood aroused him.

Hunger clawed at his guts, shredding them, blinding him to

everything else except making it stop. Snarling, he lunged, but was held fast by the bindings at his wrists and ankles. The woman scrambled backward, staring at him, her green eyes huge. Fighting the bonds, he roared in fury, the need tearing him apart. He had to have blood.

"Soren, stop! You're hurting yourself!" She clamped a small hand over her mouth, and tears streamed down her cheeks.

Her torment stilled him. He lay back, panting, the terrible pain twisting in his stomach.

She took a step closer, hope blooming on her face. "Baby, it's me. We—I'm your mate. Do you remember? Please. You beat this before and you can do it again!" This brought a fresh barrage of silent tears, and he understood that it hurt her to have to remind him of their . . . love? His mate? Her tremulous voice held the ring of truth.

He shook his head. "I don't know anything except I'm hungry," he rasped. "It burns. Help me."

"I know and I'm sorry, but you have to listen to me. Leila's going to change you into a demon, try to make you like her. She'll tell you that you're her mate, try to make you murder Prince Valafar and me, maybe others, too. She's a liar, Soren. No matter what happens, don't believe anything she says or does. *Promise me.*"

Confusion overwhelmed him. "None of this makes sense."

"It will. Just keep remembering what I told you."

A large figure materialized behind Harley. "I might be able to help."

Harley whirled to find a tall, sexy man standing there. A man who looked like he belonged onstage at Lash, with a cascade of long, gorgeous auburn hair, green eyes, and a full, sensuous mouth. His white shirt stretched across his broad chest, and black breeches hugged impossibly long legs, all the way to his black boots. Nervous, she took a step back, and her legs bumped against the side of the bed.

"Who are you?"

"I'm Arron, Leila's *servant*, for lack of a better word."

"Then I don't want your help," she snapped. "I don't trust you."

"You probably shouldn't, pretty little dove. But do you see anyone else offering to assist you?"

Damn. "Well, no."

"Then step aside and let me do what I must while there's still time."

Harley obeyed him, concern for Soren overriding her annoyance at Arron's overbearing attitude. She couldn't imagine this man as anyone's servant. Whatever Leila had over him, it must be huge. Which meant that he probably hated the Gorgon, as well. The idea renewed her spirits.

Soren eyed him, tensing as he approached. Arron placed a hand on his forehead and murmured something Harley couldn't understand. Instantly, Soren relaxed, the tension leaving his face.

"What are you doing to him?"

"Hush, little one. I will not harm your lover."

"Untie him. I can't stand seeing him like this."

"That would be foolish and dangerous. He must remain bound until he gains control again. Otherwise, he might harm us both."

"But Soren would never hurt me!" she gasped.

"The beast within him will rage to do things he doesn't

wish, things he will not be able to control. That is how I may be able to help. My blood is ancient and of great nobility. It will heal the wounds on his throat and might temper the cruelty Leila will inflict on his mind."

"Don't talk around me like I'm not here," Soren protested hoarsely. "I *don't* want to hurt anyone. I'm just so damned hungry. I need . . ." He trailed off, misery darkening his eyes.

"The bloodlust is at war with your soul. What you want doesn't matter one shit compared to what *is*."

Arron's words filled Harley with renewed dread. "She's really going to try to change him into some sort of monster."

"Yes. But let's try this, and it might help put on the brakes." Quickly, Arron sliced a wound across his wrist with a fingernail and held it to Soren's lips.

Soren lunged, latching onto the offering. Harley stumbled backward a couple of steps, a hand splayed over her galloping heart. Her mate swallowed eagerly, making low sounds of satisfaction deep in his throat, and Arron closed his eyes with a sigh, his own pleasure apparent. Soren wrenched away, his voice stark, blood dripping from his lips. "Now I know what drug addicts are really up against. What's in your blood, wolf? You're not just a shifter."

"You'll find out if it becomes necessary," Arron replied gravely. "These walls have ears."

Soren nodded. "I understand. Now what?"

"We win. The only other option ends with your death, and perhaps ours, too," he said, indicating himself and Harley.

A jet of fear shot through Harley, and she stifled a cry. "He's my mate and I love him. If he dies, so do I." If everything went wrong and Soren was lost forever, they'd have to kill the man who'd become her world in such a short time. One she was just getting to know. Tears welled in her eyes. If that happened, she'd gladly die, too.

Seeing her distress, Arron went on quickly and addressed Soren. "We're going to do everything in our power to ensure that doesn't happen. You *must* cling to what little identity you still possess while making Leila believe that she's succeeded in stripping it. You must fool her into thinking you have lost control, yet keep the beast reined in."

"Sure." Soren laughed, the sound brittle. "No problem."

Arron touched the other man's hair lightly. "Enough. Sleep now."

At his command, Soren's eyes drifted closed and his breathing eased into a slow rhythm. Harley watched him for a time, simply loving him. Knowing she'd never be able to live without him.

If Soren had to face death, he wouldn't do it alone.

Her decision made, she turned to Arron. "What are you? Please tell me, while there's no one around to overhear."

He turned to her, considering his answer. "I'm a wolf shifter. I have certain magical abilities. And I am half brother to Valafar, unbeknownst to many, for very good reasons." Hopelessness darkened his lovely green eyes. "I'm also a coward."

"No, Arron. A coward wouldn't risk plotting against Leila."

"If I'd taken the necessary risks ages ago, the entire Coalition might be safe now. Not only am I a coward, but I've placed my own selfish goals above the greater good for far too long. I can only hope it isn't too late to rectify my mistake."

Harley laid a hand on the sleeve of his shirt. Awesome power flowed from him like an electrical current, tingling her fingertips through the material. He looked down at her, and the sadness in his gaze touched her.

"What does she have on you, Arron?"

"My heart. My *son*."

They hadn't been prepared to be betrayed or outnumbered. They'd won, but the cost had been high. His clan's traitors had already taken the resort, with Leila in charge. Val had a new plan in place.

Several miles from the clan's compound, which lay smoldering in ruin, Val's great strength finally abandoned him. He sank to his knees, pitched forward, and lay prone. Paralyzing cold enveloped him, reminding him that while he might be damned near impossible to kill, he was as susceptible to pain as any being.

An eternity passed before heavy footsteps approached. Large hands grasped and rolled him over. Zenon loomed above him, expression clouded with worry, blond hair tangled around his handsome, angelic face.

"Come on, my friend. Don't do this. By the gods, flash-fry the evil bitch and be done with it! Every creature in the Coalition and beyond loathes her, and we all know that you would be within your right to do it."

Val shook his head. No one, not even Zen, knew that his reason for not destroying Leila—yet—went far beyond his sense of justice. No one had thought to question *how* Val knew so much about the Gorgon. Or suspected it was a bond of blood that held him back. *Arron.*

With Leila's death, the location of Arron's grown son would be lost forever. Arron, once a great leader of his wolves, had fallen to her blackmail centuries ago when she'd kidnapped and imprisoned his son. She'd lusted after Arron, but he'd spurned her, earning her wrath. Grief and determination to learn where she'd hidden the young man had been his downfall.

The proud wolf had traded his soul in exchange for Leila's promise to keep his beloved son safe. To this day, Arron had learned nothing of his whereabouts, and she continued to refuse him proof that the young man lived.

Thank the gods Leila hadn't managed to discover his and Arron's secret. One that would prove to be their salvation—or hasten their destruction.

That Arron was his half brother and nearly as powerful as Valafar himself.

"Well, if you insist on besting Leila fair and square, there must be a way to ensnare the she-devil without endangering yourself."

Val made several attempts to speak through frozen lips. "No time. You brought the chains?"

Zenon's jaw clenched. "Yes."

"Good. First, you'll find two small vials in my coat pocket. Take them and fill them with your blood."

"Great gods, what are you up to?" Zen grumbled. Not really expecting an answer, he performed the task with the aid of his dagger, then sealed the containers. "What now?"

"We make Leila think you're one of the clan who's betrayed me and joined her ranks. Take one to the Gorgon and tell her you caught me trying to hide it when you came upon me, and that I tried to bribe you to get my blood to her captive, Soren. Slip the other to Arron and let him know the truth. If everything goes wrong, if there's no hope, your blood is the silver bullet that will destroy them."

"I see," Zenon said quietly. The poison from the bite of a

pure-blooded demon like Zenon would induce slow, excruciating death.

Leila wouldn't stand a chance.

Neither would Soren.

"Take the chains and bind me."

Zen looked at him, alarmed. "But my prince—"

"Do it."

Not bothering to conceal his distress, Zenon did as he was ordered. It took all of Val's willpower not to cry out as the golden bonds began to sear his flesh like acid, even through his clothing. Raw agony, like nothing he'd experienced in centuries, tore at him.

Vaguely, he was aware of Zenon lifting him into his arms, before the blackness closed over his head.

Soren awoke suddenly, again shaking with the force of terrible hunger. Need scraped at his raw insides like broken glass. Arron's blood had quieted the beast's fury a little, slowing his slide into total insanity. A lion tethered by a piece of yarn.

Something soft and warm pressed against him. A whiff of French vanilla teased his senses, calling to the man inside the monster. His shaft rose, along with the gnawing in his gut, and he shifted—

To find himself unbound.

He'd been freed!

The warm presence wiggled to curl into his back, snuggling in like a contented kitten. *Harley.* Her name whispered through his brain like a breeze through gauzy netting, concealing memories that fluttered just beyond them. Dammit, why couldn't he *remember?*

She stirred again, pushing her breasts against his back,

sending a bolt of heat straight to his groin. The monstrous thing inside him came awake with a vengeance. Crazed with lust.

Take her. She's yours.

He was appalled at the direction of his thoughts. *No,* he corrected himself. *The beast's thoughts.* Gods, he didn't want to . . . didn't want—

Yes, you do. Use her love for you. Bend her to your will. Destroy her!

"No," he groaned. His cock hardened.

Oh yeah.

"Soren?" she murmured, her voice sleepy.

He turned over to face her, shaking her shoulder. "Dammit, why did you untie me?" Her eyes widened. She reached out to touch his cheek.

"I couldn't stand seeing you tied like an animal."

"How can you say that?"

"Because if you could honestly hurt me, then I've lost you. You're my mate, and if I've lost you, nothing matters. I love you, Soren," she whispered.

"Yes, you are. I love you, too." With all his heart.

"You remember us!"

"Yeah. That much, at least. The details come and go, but it's all going to return, sweetheart. Don't worry."

He leaned into her, kissed the tip of her nose. Need roared through his veins once more, swamping his senses. Cupping her face, he brought his lips to hers and drank her sweet taste. Saints, he wanted to taste so much more.

Pushing Harley onto her back, he rolled with her, his body atop hers. Her arms encircled his neck, drawing him in. He kissed her hard, his tongue sweeping into her mouth, licking until he pulled back, breathless.

"I need you."

Her lips curved. "Then have me."

As simple—and dangerous—as that. The beast reared its head, unable to refuse the invitation.

With a growl, he grabbed the soft fabric of her T-shirt with both hands and ripped the material. The swell of her breasts heaved as she looked up at him with complete love and trust. And desire.

With the flick of a wrist, he made short work of her lacy bra, and she spilled free. He had her pinned, at his mercy, and the demon inside him laughed at her naiveté.

"Lift your hips." He unzipped her shorts and slid them off, then removed her panties. "Now spread your legs for me."

She lay totally exposed before him. His to do with whatever he wished. His penis throbbed in anticipation, the rabid hunger to be joined with her, gorging on her life's blood, nearly blinding him.

"You won't let anything happen to me," she vowed, her belief absolute. "I love you, Soren. My mate, my love."

Soren fought the blackness washing through his soul as the beast claimed him again. Her words were lost in a swirl of chaotic sensation. His need.

"I see we've come at just the right moment. Arron, I told you to keep them separated, did I not?" she asked in a tone that promised retribution. "I'll deal with you later."

Leila strolled into the room, smiling cruelly, Arron beside her. She was in human form again, Soren noted. Her black silk robe hung open, leaving nothing to the imagination, the curious vial dangling on the strap between her breasts. Arron wore his white robe in the same fashion, his expression carefully blank.

"You! What do you want from me?"

The she-demon laughed, her pointed little incisors flashing. "It's time for the moment we've all been waiting for. Arron, take him. I'll see to our sweet little darling. Shall we?"

The beast within him stretched its claws like a cat in anticipation. Ready to assuage this tearing agony in his gut, the fire between his legs.

Soren slid naked from the bed, jerking as Arron gripped his arm. He glanced at Harley, taking in her state of undress, her vulnerability. Her green eyes wide with fear. Whatever was about to happen, the last shred of humanness in his soul wished she didn't have to suffer for it.

He let himself be led from the room on trembling legs. The chamber door shut behind them with a heavy, ominous thud as they moved down the darkened corridor.

The final battle was about to begin.

12

*H*arley made a concentrated effort to keep her chin up and appear defiant as Leila led them through a maze of corridors. Soren walked beside Arron, his face devoid of emotion, but she could feel the turmoil radiating from him like heat. His clenched jaw, the tense set of his shoulders betrayed him.

Their trek ended in one of the mansion's large rooms, as richly appointed as the bedroom she and Soren had been confined in. A dozen or more candles provided the only light that cut through the shadows. Instead of a bed, a pile of fat throw pillows sat on the rug, surrounded by four ornate sofas arranged in a rectangle, as if for an audience.

A golden bar hung suspended horizontally, with a length of chain at each end attached to the rafters. It had been lowered to just a few feet above the pillows. An earthen jar sat on the rug nearby. An image of what this room's purpose might be started to emerge, and Harley didn't like the picture one bit.

Arron guided Soren to the center of the pillows, next to the

gold bar. "Kneel," he instructed, his voice giving away neither pleasure nor sympathy. Glaring at him, Soren did as he was told. "Now
raise your arms."

He did, and Arron bound his wrists to the bar overhead
with gold chains. The position rendered Soren completely vulnerable to Leila's wishes. The rage in his dark eyes made Harley
retreat a couple of steps. Leila was merely amused.

"I see you haven't lost your fight. Believe me, darling, it will
do you no good. Arron, let us begin my mate's anointing."

"Fuck you," Soren hissed. "I'm not your mate, for the last
damned time!"

Leila shrugged. "In your old life, that was true. But you don't
have that option anymore. You're about to become something
much more powerful than you've ever imagined. You'll embrace
it, and we'll rule the Coalition together." She turned to Harley.
"Lie back and enjoy the show, princess. Don't even think of trying to escape. If you do, your former lover receives the punishment for your actions."

"Damn you to Hades," Harley spat.

"Such a disappointing threat. Next time, try an original one
that actually means something to me."

Fuming, near tears of frustration, Harley sat down. The
pair moved to Soren, and he lifted his head in proud insolence
as Arron retrieved the jar and tilted it over his chest. Rivulets of oil
streamed down his skin, the taut plane of his flat stomach, and
lower. Their hands began to smooth it all over his body, slicking
every contour and crevice until the ripples of his muscles shone.

Soren stared straight ahead, quivering as their caresses
strayed between his legs, stroking his shaft. He swallowed hard,
shaking his head in denial as he swelled and filled, his cock
standing as erect as an exclamation point.

"No," he groaned.

Harley's heart ached to see him being used this way, forced into an encounter he wouldn't have chosen for himself. The Fontaine men oozed sexuality, and Soren was no exception. He could no more stop his reaction than he could stop breathing. When Leila threw a smug smile over her shoulder, Harley longed to rip her fucking head from her neck.

Their robes slid away and they sandwiched him, Leila's breasts grazing his chest as she twined a hand into his thick hair and kissed him, the other hand stroking his cock. He couldn't pull away with Arron at his back, caressing his shoulder and neck. "No . . . don't." Closing his eyes, he moaned, helpless against the relentless assault.

They pleasured him, lowering his defenses to move in for the final kill. Stroking and licking every inch of him until his eyes glazed over with lust he couldn't deny any longer. His arms shook in his bonds and his breathing came fast and shallow. Harley's throat burned with tears.

His voice, husky with desire, cut her to the bone. "Ohhh . . . oh, gods, yes . . ."

Lips turned up in a malicious smile, Leila removed her necklace and uncapped the vial. "Drink, Soren. Embrace your destiny."

"N-no. I can't."

"You must. Give yourself to the darkness, my love. It is time."

Arron moved behind Soren, pulling him against his chest and laying Soren's head back to rest on his shoulder.

Harley's heart knocked against her ribs as Leila brought the vial to Soren's lips and tilted it. With a groan, Soren drank all the blood inside, and for several seconds, nothing happened. He panted, leaning against Arron's chest, and seemed about to speak when his entire body seized as though zapped with a million volts of electricity. He bucked wildly in his restraints, head thrown back. Agonized screams tore from his throat again and again.

Tears streaming down her face. Hands clasped over her ears, Harley watched in horror. It was taking all of Arron's strength to prevent Soren from hurting himself. Both men's muscles bunched from the strain.

Blue lightning shot from Soren's fingertips, crackled through the air above their heads. The walls shook with the thunderous force of his pain and rage. Harley sobbed, positive that he would simply vaporize from the immense pressure.

Soren's body remained rigid until his screams subsided into hoarse moans. The eerie lightning receded, and Harley fought down a bubble of hysteria. His head fell forward, chin resting on his chest, and he sagged in the bonds.

"Please," he rasped.

Leila moved to him again, smoothing a graceful hand over his chest. "What, darling?"

Slowly, he shook his head from side to side, as though trying to focus his thoughts. "I need you. The hunger. It's killing me . . . hurts so bad . . ."

"Tell your queen what you desire." Her fingers kneaded his balls, eliciting a helpless groan.

"I have to drink. I'm so thirsty!"

"Beg."

"Please, I'm begging you!"

Leila smiled, her black eyes gleaming. "You admit that you belong to me? You surrender your body and soul to my will?"

His breath caught. "Yes."

Longing to cut out her black heart for touching Soren,

Harley opened her mouth to protest. Arron shot her a warning glance, and she snapped it shut.

"Say it, Soren!"

Soren raised his head, and Harley stifled a cry. His eyes no longer held even the faintest hint of amber. The light of his soul had faded completely. Those black eyes glittered with malice. Evil.

"My body and soul are yours, Leila. Take them both and we'll rule the Coalition together."

She rubbed her breasts against him. "Very good, my mate. But Prince Valafar is immortal. How will you destroy him?"

"I don't know, but there's a way to find out."

"Which is?" she demanded.

"If I drink his blood, all of his knowledge will be mine, including how he can be destroyed. But he has to be seriously weakened for anyone to get that close to him." He hesitated. "Please, I need—"

Leila's face darkened in fury at yet another obstacle in her quest. "We'll just have to bide our time until we find a way to bring him under control. Arron, release our fledgling prince."

Arron freed him and he fell to his back, breathing hard. Leila lay down beside him, then slowly stretched herself across his chest, looking down at him with naked desire before lowering her lips to his. This time, his mouth began to move with hers.

In that instant, Harley wanted to die. Nothing—not even the most hideous physical death—could've been as cruel as watching the man she loved lying naked with Leila. Willing. She didn't notice that Arron had come to sit beside her. He took her hand and gave it an almost imperceptible squeeze.

"She owns his soul, but not his heart, little dove," he whispered in her ear. "He resists her still."

"Not all of him is getting the message," she sniffed, wiping at the tears that wouldn't cease.

"Do not worry. Your lover will take nothing more from her than blood to survive. Because his senses are overwhelmed, he would react physically to anyone right now, even a troll. He can't resist our touch. He's locked in battle with the evil that has taken him."

Coldness enveloped her, and she searched Arron's lovely green eyes. "What if *she* realizes it?"

He glanced at Leila, who was kissing Soren as though trying to suck the air from his lungs. Careful to keep his voice low, he leaned closer. "She is blind to all except her obsession to destroy Valafar. That's why she doesn't hear us speaking to each other."

The awful pain in Harley's chest eased a bit. "Let's hope it stays that way."

Soren rolled, pinning Leila underneath him, his swollen cock pressed against the whiteness of her flat belly. Burying his fingers in her black hair, he tilted her head back and grazed her neck with his sharp eyeteeth. Then he sank his fangs deep into her throat. She screamed her pleasure, arching against him. He rode the pleasure, taking, taking.

To Harley, the act seemed as intimate as making love. *He's mine. I should be the one easing his pain, not his murderer!* Watching them cleaved her in two. Blindly, she turned and buried her face in Arron's shoulder. His arms went around her and he gathered her close.

"Shh, I know. Remember, the act means nothing but survival to him. There is no true passion between them. With you, it would be different. In your heart, you know this."

She supposed so, but she let Arron continue to hold her until

Soren rolled away from Leila and lay on his back. Harley peeked over Arron's shoulder. His eyes were closed. The lines of agony around his mouth had softened, but his arousal had not. Harley felt a hot little spurt of satisfaction that the bitch hadn't managed to coax his seed from him.

Leila stood and moved away from Soren, belting her robe just as a sharp rap on the heavy chamber door shattered the quiet. Leila stalked to the door, throwing it wide. "Trisha? What in great, blazing Hades do you want?" she yelled in the Chosen's face.

"I—There's a big m-man in the foyer. One of your new demons—"

Leila grabbed the girl's arms, enraged. "And you interrupted to tell me this, you little idiot? You knew I didn't want to be disturbed, damn you! What does he want?"

The young woman raised her elfin face to look directly at Leila. "He b-brought with him another demon, b-bound in chains of gold."

"The devil you say," Leila whispered. "Who the hell is it?"

"The demon is called Zenon . . . and he says the bound one is Prince Valafar."

Soren sat up on his elbows, watching with interest as Leila all but ran from the chamber, Arron on her heels. The door slammed and locked in Arron's wake, and Soren nearly smiled. Puny stone and wood couldn't hold him now. New, malevolent strength surged through his veins, and he longed to test it.

But first . . .

Harley glanced at him, green eyes wide and shiny with tears

from all she had seen. Her wounds ran deep, and the vampire he couldn't remember wanted to comfort her, love her. His beast only wanted her underneath him. *Mine.*

"Come here."

"Go beat yourself off, you jerk." She spoiled the barb by reaching to wipe a tear that had escaped from the corner of her eye.

His lips turned up. This must be why in his old life he'd loved this woman. "Well, now. That wasn't very friendly. Looks like I'll have to give that smart little mouth something satisfying to do."

He moved to sit on his knees, close to her back, and rested his hands on her slender shoulders.

"Get away from me," she snapped.

"Is that really what you want?" He kissed her neck, smiling when she shivered.

"Yes."

"Beautiful liar. Tell me to stop."

"Stop."

"Once more, with *feeling.*" His teeth grazed the delicate flesh at her nape, then traveled upward to the soft shell of her ear. She started to move away, but he held fast.

"Soren, we need to go see about Valafar. He's in trouble."

"Mmm." He nibbled a path from her earlobe to her neck, his hands sliding under her arms to cup her breasts.

"Leila has destroyed your whole life! How can you think about helping her kill Valafar? You have to fight what's happening! She's taken over your soul and killed your brother Luc."

Luc. The name delivered a crushing blow to his chest. Sadness rolled through him, drowning him in a giant wave. Blurred images sped past. Two tall, handsome men. A mansion. Horses. Sex, blood, and lots of it. Anytime he wanted.

This woman, spread in lovely submission between him and a black-haired demon.

He couldn't hang on to their meaning.

"I'm *trying* to fight!" He jerked her around to face him, rage joining with the darkness spreading across his soul like an inky stain. "You don't have any idea what hell is! It's *inside* me. I want to do terrible, depraved things."

Harley stared at him, paling. "What kinds of terrible things? Like you did to Jordy?"

"Yes!" *Jordy.* Yes. How could he have forgotten? He bent over her and tipped up her chin with a finger, forcing her to look up at him. "I want blood. More and more blood. I'll never be able to get enough. I need it filling my mouth, my cock. I-I don't want to kill for it, but I will—the hunger is so bad I can't stand it anymore."

After a moment, she flattened both palms on his heaving chest. "Better *me* than *her.*"

His balls tightened in anticipation. "But what if I can't stop?"

"I trust you."

He didn't need further encouragement. Slender, creamy thighs beckoned him to delve inside. To taste her pink, delicate sweetness. Auburn tresses fell in a curtain around her slim shoulders. Her stormy jade gaze revealed fear—and incredible arousal.

Soren knelt between her splayed legs, gripping her thighs and kissing his way along the inside, toward her center. Finding the tender nub, he flicked it with his tongue. Leisurely at first, then faster, darting into the soft folds to lap every drop of her honey.

"Ohh, Soren! Yes, yes."

She began to relax, closing her eyes, arching her back to thrust her breasts forward. Offering herself to him. The pressure in his balls, the fire licking his shaft, drove him to near madness. He wanted to crawl inside her, consume her. He barely heard his own command above the blood roaring in his ears.

"Lie down, hands above your head."

She complied, raising her arms and crossing her wrists. Soren maneuvered over her, pinning her wrists with one hand, her submissive position short-circuiting his brain with animal lust. If a more sexual invitation existed for one person to do whatever they wished to another, he didn't know what it could be.

With one finger of his free hand, he stroked her clit, gleaming and flushed from his attention. Liquid gold rushed over his hand, and she whimpered.

"Please!"

"Please, *what?*" he demanded.

She bucked against him. "I need—I want—"

He reveled in her soft moan as he guided the tip of his head to her entrance. "You want this?"

"Yes!"

Fingers digging into her flesh, he impaled her. Buried to the hilt, he rocked, hips thrusting. Grinding into her as fully as possible. Her muscles clenched, sheathing him, her little clit rubbing his slick cock.

"Harder!" she cried.

He slammed into her again and again, the pulse of her life force calling to him. His fangs lengthened. He'd take all of her. Letting go of her wrists, he wrapped her hair in his fist and pulled her head back as he fucked her. Exposing her neck and the sweet blood flowing there. She'd surrendered, ready for him. He smelled the musky perfume of her excitement.

He brushed his lips against her neck once, then sank his

teeth deep. She screamed, bucking wildly beneath him. Her rich blood welled on his tongue and he drew hard, pulling the nectar down his throat in greedy swallows. It filled him, engorged him, and the beast rose in triumph.

"Soren! Please . . ."

She was helpless beneath him, at his mercy. His willing captive.

You can't deny what you are. Ravage her!

He drank, riding her, and when she began to spasm around him, holding back wasn't an option. They exploded together, her heat flooding him as he shot his release deep inside her.

Do it! There will be many more to satisfy our hunger!

"Shit." Soren withdrew and rolled to lie on his back, gasping. Fighting the strong urge to pounce on her and finish it. Drain every delicious drop from her body. The beast craved the kill. The ecstasy of taking his pleasure as life faded away.

Soren closed his eyes in despair.

The constant assault on his senses, the lure of evil, was becoming impossible to resist. The beast was merging with his mind, methodically overtaking his soul. Sometimes, like this moment, he could discern between the two of them. Soon he would no longer be able.

Harley squirmed beside him, and he opened his eyes to see her lying on her back, gazing at him, dark auburn hair tangled around her face, a small smile teasing her lips.

Look at her. She'd willingly die for you. Drain her!

Yes, he longed to do it, imagined riding her again, ripping open her throat. Tearing the meat to get all of the—

"No!" He bolted to his feet, panic thundering in his chest. He was becoming Leila's creation. A murdering brute.

Her smile vanished and she sat up. "What's wrong?"

Shaking, confused, he clasped his hands over his ears. His voice cracked. "Who am I? Help me, Harley."

She hurried to him, took his face in her hands. Her beautiful eyes bored into his. Calm and reassuring. "You're Soren Fontaine, the man I love. *No matter what.*"

"I don't know who that is anymore." He swallowed hard.

She pressed against him, kissed away his tears. "Oh, honey, you will. Believe it. Please don't cry."

"I'm so fucking scared." Wrapping his arms around her, he crushed her to him, willing her strength into him.

"Me, too. But we're going to get through this together, if you'll just stay with me."

You've already lost, bastard.

He hugged her tighter. "Harley, if everything goes wrong, if there's no hope for me—" He broke off, choking on the words.

She pulled away, touched his hair, his face. "Then I promise I'll do whatever it takes to set you free."

He gave her a gentle kiss, lingering for a moment, letting her love wash over him, quieting his raging, black heart.

And understood that he was saying good-bye.

13

*S*oren pulled away from her, casting about the room, searching for something they could wear. "We have to get the hell out of here."

"Don't bother. We're locked inside, anyway."

"Not for long." He held up a pair of robes that had fallen behind one of the sofas and tossed one to her. "Put this on."

She slid her arms into it, securing the belt around her waist while he did the same. "Now what? Are we just going to walk through a solid wooden door?"

"Even better."

Bracing his feet apart, Soren held one arm in front of him at chest level, palm down. Harley was about to make a skeptical comment when the door began to shake on its hinges, as though a fierce hurricane screamed beyond the planks.

She gasped as the door bowed outward like a balloon, stretching, straining. The wood shattered with a deafening *boom*, like a cannon shot. Dust and splinters blew outward, into the corridor beyond. *Crap! The Gorgon's entire army must've heard!*

Soren held up his hand, flexing his fingers. He looked at her and grinned. "Pretty cool, huh?"

That was her Soren. Impish, like a mischievous boy with a new toy. Tears sprang to her eyes and she blinked them away furiously. This wasn't the time to think about that beautiful light giving in to the darkness. About the horrible promise she'd made to him if the beast won.

"Come on." Taking her hand, Soren led her into the dim corridor and paused. "Left or right?"

"Take your pick. I'm completely turned around."

"There's got to be a way out."

He turned to the right, moving stealthily, pulling her along in his wake. When Harley realized what he'd said, she drew up short, yanking on his hand.

"Wait! We can't leave Valafar behind to face her alone!"

Soren spun around. "We have to. If I stay, Leila will force me to extract the secret of how he can be killed."

Every instinct shouted to run, to get Soren as far away from this hellhole as possible. But the solution wasn't that easy.

"If you go, she could torture him forever, literally. Could you really condemn another to suffer the same fate you made me promise to help you avoid?" she said softly. "And this is a guy who's trying to save your hide."

He raked a hand though his hair and dropped his gaze to the floor. "Damn."

"She won't quit, honey. If you get away, she'll enjoy having the prince at her mercy. She'll amuse herself for a while by making him suffer, but the novelty will wear thin. A power-hungry bitch like her will want him dead eventually. And when she tires of playing with him, she'll hunt you down again."

"Because I carry the mark of Azrael. We'll be right back where we started," he finished, miserable.

"Yes." She touched his arm. "This has to end. Maybe you can find a way to help Valafar without her catching on, and then *he* can help *us*. It might be the only solution."

He looked away, fists clenched. "It's a long shot at best."

"We don't have anything else."

"I know, I just . . . I want to run. Pretend none of this is happening. When I'm alone with you, I can keep the beast under control. I want our life to begin," he whispered.

Our life. Not his. Deep down, he still carried her in his heart. "Can you use some of that magic of yours to pinpoint where they've taken Valafar?"

He closed his eyes and breathed deeply, scenting the air. After a few seconds, he opened them again and nodded, his black gaze troubled. "I think so. But, Harley, from this point on, don't believe *anything* you see or hear. I can't hold out much longer. Don't trust anyone, especially me."

Fear zinged through her. "Then who'll help me?"

He brushed a strand of hair from her cheek and looked deeply into her eyes, as though memorizing her face. "You."

"Against a bunch of crazy vampires and demons?"

"You don't have a choice." Soren grasped her hand and turned with a heavy sigh, leading the search for the doomed prince.

Aldric became aware of a hand on his shoulder. Shaking him hard. He moaned and opened his eyes to see a large demon hovering over him, and automatically reached for a sword he hadn't carried in ages.

"Easy, Lord Aldric," the demon said, eyeing his condition. He checked the bandages on Aldric's leg as he spoke. "Do you know where you are?"

"No." He thought. "I was on my way to quell an uprising between two packs of shifters when I was ambushed by a few of your kind."

"Rogues," the demon spat. "Traitors. Valafar will have their heads—if he can be rescued, along with your brother Soren and his mate."

Fear made Aldric lightheaded. "Tell me what's happened. All of it."

When the demon had finished speaking, he was numb with rage. Grief. "Luc has not been found?"

"I'm afraid not."

"Then he lives. I won't believe otherwise."

The demon nodded. "Still, something has to be done about Leila first. The traitors must die."

"They will, believe me," he replied coldly. "I'll need to sneak onto the estate and retrieve our swords."

"Leila has Soren's, but I know of a couple of double agents who can get the others."

"I'll need the other two swords, and someone I can trust to carry Luc's." His throat damned near closed at the thought of Luc being gone. Maybe forever.

"You'll look no further than Zenon, then. He's the best, aside from the prince himself."

"Find him and bring him here. We have a battle to win."

"Consider it done."

. . .

Soren led them through a dark wing of the mansion. Torches had been lit at intervals along the gray walls and cast a ghostly dance of light and shadow across the vast space. He paused before a door, placing one hand on it as though testing it for something, then opened it. The gloomy depths bristled with torture devices straight out of a ghoulish horror flick. The difference was that these were real, capable of killing someone slowly and inflicting great pain while doing it.

She couldn't help but notice Soren flinch and avert his eyes from a spiderweb contraption in the middle of the room. On the floor underneath it, a black pool of something resembling blood marked where a man might've been suspended and tortured. *Oh, gods.*

She touched his arm. "What did she do to you?"

He shook his head. "It's in the past."

Staring at the stain, Harley decided he was right. Neither of them could change what he'd already suffered. She could only pray for a swift end to the nightmare.

They heard a low moan from a far corner of the chamber, followed by raised voices. Soren snatched her wrist and bent to hiss in her ear.

"Remember what I told you. I'm not the same vampire you loved anymore. Your only priority is to get yourself out alive, whatever you have to do."

"And you, too."

Sorrow and regret flickered in his eyes before he hardened his gaze. He tightened his grip and led her deeper into the chamber, looking for the source of the noise. His search ended at the door to another room, this one slightly ajar. Inside, they could see Leila and Arron standing over Zenon.

The triumphant sneer on Leila's face marred it with ugliness. "Get up, you worthless dog, and tell me the truth! You expect me to believe that you found Prince Valafar—the most powerful demon on earth—lying on the ground, helpless as a swaddling babe? Do you think me a complete idiot?"

"Yes! I mean, no! I—"

"Arron, he needs more persuasion."

With a flick of his wrist, Arron sent a blue bolt into the man's prone body. Harley watched in horror as her friend screamed, twisting, damp blond hair tangling around his face. When his pain subsided, he lay panting on his side. He saw Harley and shook his head almost imperceptibly, as though trying to convey a silent message.

"I'm telling the truth," he wheezed. "The prince was drained when I found him, but I think I know why."

"Talk fast, Zenon of the demons, or I'll have Arron separate your head from your shoulders."

"Valafar was on his way to our clan to gather reinforcements to defeat you when the traitors ambushed him and he was badly injured. He was in no shape to fight me when I bound him and brought him here."

"I think Zenon speaks the truth," Arron said.

"But it doesn't explain why he would bring his leader to us, trussed like a game hen. I don't know you, so why would you seek an alliance with me against your prince?"

Zenon pushed up to a sitting position, gritting his teeth as he winced in pain. "I don't seek an alliance. But I am no friend of Valafar. He meddles in my private affairs instead of ruling the Southern Coalition as he should, leaving us to fight for our survival. Ensnaring us in this mess with you, which is none of our concern, was the last straw. I want him neutralized, and I don't care how you do it."

Zen was lying, Harley knew. He and Val were the closest of friends. What were they up to?

"And you seek no payment?" Leila asked, eyes narrowed in suspicion.

"What would I accept from you?" Zenon said coldly. "Coin is of no value to me, and my clan would starve before accepting food from a Gorgon. No, I simply wish to leave Valafar as your captive, and the only recompense will be the satisfaction I feel when he suffers."

Harley studied Leila, wondering how she would react to Zenon's bold slur. He'd practically said she would poison his entire family given the chance. Harley didn't doubt the accusation for a second.

Leila paced, robes swirling in her wake, and considered Zenon's words. Suddenly she turned, her smile malicious. "Demon, if that is the only payment you desire, then I shall do my best to reward you. Go now and relish the moment Prince Valafar's screams of torment reach the Coalition. Arron, show our guest out."

Arron helped Zenon to his feet, then took his arm and steered him toward the door as Harley and Soren stepped back. After casting a furtive glance at Leila, Zenon reached into his pants pocket and pulled something out, hidden in his big hand. Without breaking stride, he handed it to Arron, who palmed the object and slipped it into his own pocket.

The men brushed past them and left without acknowledging their presence. Soren dragged Harley into the room, making the Gorgon aware of their arrival. He strode to the black-haired demon and she spun, brows arched in wary surprise. *Leila, wary?*

"Soren, my love. I don't suppose I need to ask how you managed to free yourself from the chamber."

He let go of Harley and stepped so close to Leila that she was forced to look up at him. His lips turned up in a sexy smile. "Darling, you made me, so you have to know it will take more than stone walls to hold me. Shame on you, leaving me *hungry*."

Harley rubbed her wrist and backed away. He'd dismissed her, just like that, as though she'd been nothing more than a plaything to keep him satisfied in Leila's absence. She was losing him to the darkness again. Or was he pretending? She couldn't tell.

He seized Leila, pulling her hard against him, crushing his mouth down on hers. She twined her arms around his neck and returned the kiss hungrily, as if to devour him whole. Harley could only stare, helpless. Whether it was an act on Soren's part or the real thing didn't make it hurt less.

Leila jerked back, her face angry. "You've been with *her*. I can smell her on you. It's time for her to die."

"Yes, I fucked her while I drank," he murmured into her mouth, nipping at her lip. "But we won't kill her yet. She amuses me. Admit it—you can't wait to see our little human slave squirming between me and Arron. Maybe even joining in the fun."

Harley went numb. In front of that bitch? He couldn't be serious.

"Mmm," she groaned, arching against him. Her hand found the bulge tenting his robe and rubbed. "You are a wicked one, my love. All right. We'll keep her alive for our pleasure, until we tire of her."

"I thought you might see things my way." He brushed his fingers across a taut nipple poking eagerly against silk. "Now, darling, I believe we have a date with a prince."

Leila grinned. "This way."

The witch took his arm and he went with her. Glancing at Harley, he nodded for her to follow. He avoided her silent question, his eyes darting quickly away to stare straight ahead. But not before she caught the profound sadness in their black depths.

And she knew.

Soren had just charmed Leila to the roots of her witchy black hair. He'd used her own weapon of sex against her. *And saved my life.* How far would Soren have to take this depraved game in order to defeat Leila?

Harley trailed in their wake as they passed into yet another room. She couldn't imagine how she'd ever find her way out if forced to run.

Her thoughts scattered at the sight of a tall male lying on a marble altar, bound in chains of gold, battered black wings hanging off on either side of him. *Valafar!* The chains had burned right through his clothing to the skin. His black pants were soaked with blood. Sooty lashes rested against pale, hollowed cheeks, and ebony hair fanned around his shoulders. Except for Soren, he was the most breathtakingly beautiful man she'd ever seen.

"Soren," Leila purred, "meet Prince Valafar, whose impotent rule has just come to a tragic end."

Harley tried to melt as far into the shadows as possible while Soren strode to the altar. No one seemed to be paying attention to her at the moment, and she preferred to keep it that way.

Soren stood looking down on the prince's still form with a slight frown, pretending never to have met him. Or perhaps he really didn't recall. "This is our kick-ass, bleeding-heart demon? How pathetic."

"Valafar is more than eleven thousand years old—so ancient no one even knows his continent of origin. Don't make the mistake of underestimating him," Arron put in from the doorway, his expression placid.

"Spare me," she snarled. "Come, my mate. I've waited centuries to learn the secret of how to destroy Valafar, and I'll wait no longer. Find out how to destroy the bastard and do it now!"

Soren's fists clenched, and a muscle jumped in his jaw. "I told you—I'll need his blood to read his secrets."

"Yes, yes, of course," Leila huffed, impatient. "Will this be enough?" From the folds of her robe, she brought forth a small vial similar to the one she used to wear around her neck. "Zenon said that our exalted guest attempted to bribe him to bring this to you, a vial of Valafar's blood. It was supposed to strengthen you against me."

"Hmph. Such a small amount might've helped *Soren* . . . but its only effect on me would be equal to a shot of good whiskey. Save it for a midnight snack." He grinned. "I need to consume a massive portion to strip his secrets from his brain, and that means taking it directly."

"Well, what in the hell are you waiting for?"

Soren knelt by Valafar's side, and Harley's heart pounded. He *wouldn't* betray the prince and condemn the entire Coalition to suffer the death and destruction of Leila's rule. He couldn't.

But the beast would.

He smoothed back the prince's hair, tilted his head back to expose his neck. He hesitated only a second, then sank his fangs deep into Valafar's throat. The prince's eyes opened on a strangled gasp and he moaned, arching into his captor.

Soren raised his head, chuckling knowingly. "That feels

good, doesn't it? Give yourself to the rush, to me. Give up your secret."

"No," Valafar whispered. "Don't—"

He bent again and drank, the seductive dance heating the place between Harley's legs even as it horrified her. The prince could do nothing to shield the onslaught on his mind and body. He groaned his passion, heedless of the chains burning his flesh. Soren held tight, sealing them together, swallowing his life's blood. Stealing the secret.

At last, Valafar went limp. Soren withdrew his fangs and placed a very gentle kiss on the prince's forehead. "Belladonna," he said.

Something flickered in the prince's eyes so fast, Harley thought she might have imagined it.

"By the gods, don't do this." Lines of anguish had deepened grooves around Valafar's mouth. "Soren would never have betrayed me." He closed his eyes and fell silent again.

"Belladonna?" Leila interrupted. "A flower? What the devil are you talking about?"

Soren rose and turned to face the group. "It's a plant that's deadly to humans and other creatures such as werewolves, but harmless to immortals. In most cases."

Leila's face lit with excitement. "And the prince is different *how*?"

"None but the gods of Olympus are allowed to enjoy the purplish-black fruit of the plant. Even though this demon was granted immortality at the Temple of the Gods, as the son of an incubus and a mere human woman, he's strictly forbidden to partake of belladonna."

A slow, evil smile curved her lips. "You mean, Prince Valafar can be poisoned? Simple as that?"

"Yes. What's more, should he willingly ingest the fruit at the temple itself, the gods will take personal offense. His death will be excruciating, darling."

"Eat the poison willingly?" She frowned. "Even if we take him there, why would he do that?"

Soren tipped her face up to his with one finger. "Think, love. Who means more to Valafar than anyone ever has?"

"Zenon? But the demon betrayed him."

"Even so, Valafar is loyal. He won't allow any harm to come to him—or to this human woman, Harley. He has a strange fondness for her."

"You're right. Arron! Take several of my guards to fetch Zenon. Tell him that if he holds out hope for any of their lives, he'll come without a fight." Arron nodded and left. She parted Soren's robe, ran her palms down his chest and stomach. He growled as she cupped his balls, stroking. His cock hardened in her capable hand. "You'll prove yourself to me tonight, won't you, my pet?"

"Yes, anything. Tell me."

"After Arron takes Zenon to the temple, we'll join them with the fallen prince and our little human slave. And we'll savor each of them . . . before you kill them all. A feast fit for a king, don't you think?"

Harley fought to breathe as his hands slid to Leila's breasts. He moaned as her nemesis stroked him, then looked boldly at Harley and smiled. Pumped on sex and evil.

It was over. He'd turned and sold out the prince. Sold out their love. Harley heard his voice from somewhere in the distance as he pressed his throbbing shaft against *her*. The bitch.

They sank to their knees together, shedding their robes,

naked in each other's arms. The tips of her nipples grazing his chest, her fingers buried in his beautiful sable hair. Hands grappling, mouths devouring.

Spots peppered Harley's vision, and she gladly let the blackness take away the pain.

Soren watched Arron leave; then his gaze went to Harley lying nearby. His tormented mind was reeling from the mix of emotions swirling through him. The lust, and the certainty that this was wrong. Trying to fight it, to remember his true name. The shock and horror on Harley's face made the vampire locked inside him cry out in agony.

No! Oh, God, who am I?

The demon in his black soul squelched the cry as Leila pointed to the pillows. "Lie down and ready yourself. You are my toy now, to use as I desire."

Shaking, Soren did as he was ordered. He lay before her, arms over his head, legs spread. Heat rushed to his cock and it hardened painfully.

"That's it, my love. Give yourself to the darkness." She knelt between his thighs and bent low. Her black hair fanned across his lap, her breath warming his groin.

"Leila." He made a helpless sound in his throat. *Fight this.* But he couldn't.

She smiled. "My darling, no one understands our kind. The need, the desire we share. Embrace the craving, and know that part of you exists only to quench it. Forever. Let's see how you taste."

Her little tongue licked his balls, teasing. He groaned,

spreading his legs wider. She took them in her mouth, sucking the sensitive flesh. Her teeth grazed them and a slight pain followed, quickly doused by a tidal wave of erotic pleasure.

"Like me tasting your blood there, do you?" she laughed huskily. "Tell me whom you belong to."

"You, my queen." *No!*

"What do you wish for me to do to you?"

Something broke inside him, and he knew his last hope for redemption was being ripped away. The man inside him was being silenced forever. But he had no choice.

"Whatever you want. Take me; drink from me."

She nipped his balls, suckling, driving him mad. Her tongue lapped the length of his shaft until he could stand no more.

"Please, please . . ."

Her mouth sheathed him to the very base. A wet, hot cavern sliding up and down. Black velvet between his legs, enslaving him.

"Ah yesss." He pumped his hips, filling her, climbing higher until—

She sank her demon's fangs into him, and lightning rocketed to every cell. He bucked, shouting in ecstasy, welcoming the wickedness rolling through his body. She took him deep, all of him. Sucking, drinking. There was nothing, nothing but his cock on fire. The ecstasy building to a wild crescendo, tormenting him.

His cock exploded and his body shuddered as he sent his release into her. She drank the very essence of him until the spasms ended. Then she licked him clean and raised her gaze to his, smirking in victory.

What have I done?

Shame engulfed him and sickness gripped his stomach. At the same time, his beast was roaring for blood.

How long he lay there, steeped in misery, suffering from this new, hellish desire, he didn't know. He was only vaguely aware of Arron's return, of Leila speaking with him.

"Is it done?"

"Yes. Zenon awaits us at the temple outside the city. He's under guard."

"Let him wait a while longer. I have need of you."

Soren could hear the satisfaction in her voice. *What is she up to now?*

"How may I serve you, my queen?"

"Before we leave, we must make certain that Soren is properly prepared. I've already begun, but his reserves are quite remarkable. It's your turn."

Soren rolled to his back, heart thrumming. Arron threw him a heated look, flinging a long lock of hair over his shoulder. "You wish for me to arouse his lust?"

"Yes, but do not allow him to drink from you. By the time we're finished, our new prince will be so crazed for blood, he'll slaughter them all."

Arron nodded his assent, moved to him. Sympathy sparked in his green eyes as he laid his beautiful body over Soren's, legs entwined. He bent his handsome face close, muscular arms on either side of his captive's head.

Soren shook his head, even as desire pooled between his legs once more. "No."

"Yes," Arron breathed into his mouth. Then claimed it.

The kiss electrified his nerve endings, then deepened, the wolf's expert tongue sweeping inside to devour him. His cry of denial was lost as the beast inside him embraced the passion, the erotic things Arron did to his body. All of the things Leila had done and more—much more. Again and again.

Until he was starving and out of his mind with the need for blood.

Leila had conquered him. Except . . .

A glimmer of hope shone beyond the despair.

Soren could still distinguish himself from the beast, just barely. Whatever it took, he'd destroy himself before he'd harm Harley or the others.

And when the time came, he no longer had any doubt that he would deserve his end.

"Wake up, pretty dove."

Harley fought to burrow back into her dreams. It couldn't be time to get ready for work. Just five more minutes.

"Harley, wake up."

Her eyes popped open. She wasn't back in St. Louis, in bed. And that wasn't Soren's voice. She sat up to find herself looking at Arron's anxious face. While she'd been out, she'd been returned to the same chamber as before. Except for Arron, she was alone. Alarm seized her.

"What's happening? Where's Soren?"

"He's getting ready to go to the temple. We haven't much time."

"For what?"

"To get you far away from here, if you wish. Leila would likely never bother with you again. She will have much more pressing interests after tonight's outcome."

"But what about Soren?" she asked quietly.

Arron shook his head sadly. "He must stay, at least for now. Unleashing him on the world in his state would be a disaster, and the future of the Coalition is resting on his shoulders. To be honest, things are looking dismal."

She crossed her arms and rubbed at the sudden goose bumps. "Thanks, but no thanks. I'm not leaving without him."

"The risk is tremendous. He is the beast now. How can I make you understand? The bright flame inside him that was goodness has been reduced to nothing more than a tiny pinprick of light. Even if he *wants* to fight against evil in the coming battle, he may be unable to do so. Leila has ordered him to kill you, dove."

"I still don't believe he'd ever hurt me or anyone else!"

"Yesterday that was true. But now . . . I'm sorry."

Her lip trembled and tears blurred her vision. She had to ask, but, God, she didn't want the answer. "Has he b-been with h-her tonight?"

Arron combed his fingers through her hair, brushing the strands out of her face. "Ah, love. He is her creation now, and has given his body to her, yes."

"Nooo." The sob was torn from her throat.

"Understand, his mind is no longer his own. He cannot control his sexual response, whether it's to Leila or me."

Startled, she gasped and raised her eyes to his. *"You?"*

"Yes, I've taken him, as well. I imagine this does not ease the pain in your heart much, but his actions are not the betrayal you think. You have a human's emotions and mores."

This was too strange. Her head was beginning to pound. "I don't understand."

"How can I explain? I don't generally prefer men. But most immortals, especially vampires, are sexual creatures by nature. Our responsiveness is far beyond what a human can experience or perhaps grasp. But beyond that, he has been in Leila's thrall ever since he took her blood."

"Sounds like an excuse to me." She sniffed.

"You must see what Soren is going through, what he's up against. I could enthrall you, too, dove, and you wouldn't be able to resist me even if you wanted to. I'm an immortal. I could place you completely under my spell and we'd have sex, and if we did, there could be no shame on your part because I'd given you no real choice."

Harley was beginning to understand what he was telling her. She nodded. "Okay. I think I get it."

"Good. Then we must go the temple—and pray we survive the battle."

"What about your son? If Leila is destroyed, you may never learn where he is." The dejection on his face saddened her.

"I have to face the fact that she'll never tell me. I'm breaking free of her. Tonight. I'll have to find my son on my own."

Harley cupped his face. "We'll help you. I'm with you all the way, and so is Soren. The man I love is inside Soren somewhere, and we're going to win. All of us." He looked away, his lovely eyes troubled. "What is it?"

"Zenon passed something to me in secret—a vial of his blood. I gave it to Soren earlier, when Leila left the room. If all goes wrong tonight, if he can no longer fight the evil, he can choose to consume the poison."

Her hand went to her mouth. "Does it work fast?"

"No, dove. A vampire can't suffer a more hideous death, even by fire, than from drinking the blood of a pure demon."

"My God." She thought back to earlier. "But wait. He drank from Valafar."

"His blood isn't pure. Zenon's *is*. Let us hope it doesn't come to this. Are you ready to go?"

"No, but I don't suppose we have a choice."

"You have one."

"No, I don't," she said firmly.

"There's the spirit. Wherever his soul is, Soren Fontaine is a lucky bastard."

And where is your soul, my love? She thought in anguish. *Where are you, Soren?*

Gathering her robe and the last shreds of her courage, Harley trailed Arron from the chamber.

14

*L*eila used her power to translocate the group to the temple, which was situated on a point next to the bay outside the city. As they materialized, he could feel Harley's gaze on his back, sharp as a laser beam. Soren couldn't look at her. He was the lowest of scum, not even fit to stand in her presence. Her misery tore into him, but he didn't dare react. The minuscule part of him that remained good and whole, he'd locked into a small box and hidden away deep inside.

For the moment.

Leila was keeping a close watch on him. Measuring the depth of her new prince's corruption, savoring her hold on him. And, oh, what a primitive, luscious initiation it had been. Soren shook from craving more, while knowing in his heart that more would never be enough. It sickened and shamed him yet made his blood quicken in anticipation.

Hang on, he coached himself. *Just a little longer and the suffering will end.*

If he could only get one of the swords, he would fall upon it when this was done.

Soren took in their surroundings, aware of Leila, Arron, and Harley standing behind him. They were at the bottom of a steep incline of steps leading up to the temple. He started up, and the others followed.

At the top, he found the temple to be a huge marble slab about fifty yards square. The roof was supported by ornate white Grecian columns, but three sides were open to the elements. Staring, he found it difficult to imagine that the gods of Olympus would condone an act of evil being performed in such a beautiful place. Then again, the stories went that many of them were selfish and mean.

"Grand ceremonies are held here, honors bestowed on those most deserving," Arron said, as if reading his thoughts. "Judgments are passed, as well, against those who violate the law of the Coalition. Executions are carried out. The gods typically do not intervene, leaving that duty to the prince."

"I see." He nodded.

The fourth side of the temple served as the front and hosted the altar. Clad only in black breeches and boots, Prince Valafar lay bound to the slab, awaiting his fate. Several male guards—Leila's demon slaves—stood sentry on each end of the altar. On the other side of Valafar, two males had also been stripped to the waist and were chained to the slick marble wall by their wrists, arms over their heads. The one with shaggy, dark blond hair must be Zen, but the other?

He crossed the vast space with quick strides, and his heart skipped a beat as he drew closer. The man's angular face was a younger version of his own, and wide blue eyes regarded him with a mix of joy and trepidation.

"Soren!" he called. "Boy, am I glad to see you! Are you all right? I got attacked by a werewolf and then rescued by some Valkyrie, and I'm not really sure how I got here. Hey, get us down—"

"Luc, he doesn't know you," Zen said gently.

Luc flinched. "He has to recognize his own brother! Tell them, Soren."

Soren skirted the altar and stepped close to Luc. "I have no brother."

He steeled himself against the shock, and pain etched on the younger vampire's face. Time was running out, and he didn't have a moment to spare for sympathy. Opening himself to the beast, he allowed the lust to flow. The stark hunger.

But he turned from Luc. Even as a beast, he would not slake his thirst on his own flesh and blood. Instead, he moved to the altar and addressed Leila over Valafar's unconscious form.

"You have the belladonna?"

"Eager, aren't you, my new prince?" She handed him a blue velvet pouch closed at the top by a drawstring.

"Why wait?" He smiled, hoping she couldn't see through the ruse. Praying she wouldn't smell his desperation. "Once he's dead, we'll move into his home. I was thinking we'd bring one or two of our slaves here each week and sacrifice them as a reminder to the Coalition of our new rule, our power."

"Hmm. His home is smaller than your estate. We'll remain there."

"Whatever you want, love."

He was going a bit over the top, but it was easy to see how much the prospect delighted her. In truth, the conjured scenario did something erotic to his groin, and the beast responded. He was playing with fire.

"A wonderful idea, my pet," she enthused. "You'll have the right to the first ceremony, beginning with our three captives."

Harley shrank back against Arron. Luc stared at him in horror, and Zen glared, his face murderous.

"I can hardly wait," Soren heard himself agree. "Arron, your blade, please." Arron hesitated, glancing at Leila.

"Go on. Let's see what Soren has in store for our poor Valafar."

Arron snatched the blade from his belt and handed the object to him, golden handle first. Soren palmed it, testing the weight. The wolf and his allies had come through. Little did the Gorgon know it wasn't Arron's blade at all.

But he had to carry on the ruse just a bit longer.

With lightning speed, Soren grasped the hilt and punched the tip of his very own sword into Valafar's bare shoulder. The prince came awake, his bellow of rage echoing through the temple. Several of the traitorous guards paled, as much as demons can, and stepped back.

Soren sneered, twisting the blade. Blood welled and flowed from the prince's wound and the sweet scent of it called to him. No, the darkness couldn't take him. Not yet.

"I have a snack for you, Valafar," he taunted, dangling the pouch in his free hand.

"Yeah? Wouldn't you know, I'm not hungry," the prince said between pants.

"Too bad. You're going to eat these berries anyway. Care to guess why?"

"Haven't a clue, but I'm sure you'll enlighten me."

"Because if you don't, the pain you're feeling will be nothing compared to what Zen will get next."

Soren gestured to the demon in chains. Turning his head slightly, Valafar saw his friend, and the fight seemed to leave him.

"If I surrender willingly, Zen lives."

"Agreed. He lives—as my slave."

"No! I meant—"

"Too late." Soren jerked the blade from Val's shoulder, averting his eyes from the tantalizing blood. Working open the pouch, he extracted several purple berries. "Enjoy them. And while you do, think about me carving your heart from your chest and devouring it for my evening meal."

He slipped the fruit into Valafar's mouth. Almost as soon as the prince began to chew, he choked, gasping for breath. Convulsions racked his body and his chest heaved. His struggles slowed until he lay still, eyes staring. Sightless. The whole thing had taken only seconds.

"You bastard!" Zen screamed, thrashing in his chains. *"Valafar! No, no!"*

"I knew the demon cared for his prince," Leila scoffed. "Liar."

Soren tossed the pouch back to Arron, but nonchalantly tucked the sword into his belt. He said a quick, silent plea to whatever god might be listening to have mercy, to please let his plan work fast. If it didn't, they were all fucked.

Zenon continued to rage, and tears were streaming down Luc's cheeks. "Oh, gods," his brother kept saying over and over. "Oh, dear gods."

Innocent Luc, he thought. The beast grinned and stretched, ready for the showdown.

"Valafar is really dead," Leila breathed. "I don't believe it."

"Arron, secure our little human whore beside these two," Soren ordered.

"Soren, don't do this!" Harley begged. She fought the wolf as he chained her, to no avail. "This isn't you, and you know it! *Soren!*"

He approached her slowly, like a cat stalking a mouse, a smile curving his lips. The pulse pounded in her neck as his hands skimmed her shoulders, parted her robe. Auburn hair framed her small face and enormous green eyes. Taut, rosy little nipples puckered. Strained, like his cock.

He lowered his head, flicked one peak with his tongue and swirled the rounded tip. She sucked in a ragged breath, trying to block his assault on her senses, and failed. His fingers slid down her flat belly to the thatch between her thighs and probed her clit. Succumbing to his seduction and heedless of their audience, she spread her legs.

"Come taste the slut," he said over his shoulder.

Leila joined them, her tongue attending the other nipple with expertise. "Ah, my prince, she's delicious," the demon bitch murmured.

"Ohh," Harley moaned. She was no match for the two of them.

The sudden urged to sink his fangs into Harley and drain her while she was bound and helpless seized him. He fought it down, but the beast was becoming nearly impossible to subdue.

Almost out of time.

"Yes, she's sweet. Enjoy her while I see to our handsome demon."

With Leila absorbed in her seduction of Harley, he moved to Zen, who was practically rabid with the desire to kill him.

"Let me down from here and I'll carve out your fucking heart," Zen hissed.

Soren looked deep into his eyes, willing him to get his message. "I hope you do. Now pretend I'm biting you." He pressed his body into the demon, palms skimming his sides. When his teeth grazed Zen's neck, the demon shivered and tried to pull away. Giving the beast some rein, he sank his fangs into Zen's neck, but only enough to make it look like he was drinking. He wasn't ready to die yet.

The demon was a good actor and gave a hoarse cry. Soren ground his hips, sealing them together. He walked the razor's edge between the pretense of evil and reality. The beast was rapidly taking over every corner of his soul.

Hoping no one could see, he reached between them and slipped the sword from his belt. Zen sensed what he was doing but not why, and began to struggle. Soren withdrew his fangs to whisper in his ear. "Easy. I'm not going to hurt you. Help me. This has to look real."

Soren put his arms around Zen, as if holding him in a lover's embrace. Though the demon wasn't aroused, he put on a good show. He moaned as Soren's mouth claimed his, their tongues dancing, exploring. Zen was so good at it, his actions were driving the beast inside Soren nearly out of control.

Quickly, Soren tucked the hilt of the blade into Zen's waistband at the small of his back, the sword's blade running behind one leg, hidden from view. He broke the kiss and gave the demon a sad smile, and kept his voice low. "When the moment comes, use it well."

Zen inclined his head to indicate his understanding, and Soren walked back to Leila and Harley. He spared a furtive glance at Val's body.

Dead. He'd been wrong, and he'd failed.

His fragile hold on his mind began to crack, like thin ice across a pond. Leila had Harley enthralled, fingers deftly stroking between her legs, teasing her clit. The demoness laved one nipple, then the other, nipping at her breasts. Drawing a bit of blood, licking it away. Harley moaned, helpless.

Looking up, Leila smiled at him. "She is ready. Kill her."

He closed the remaining distance and Leila moved aside. Burying one hand in Harley's hair, he pulled her head back. Her lovely eyes were glazed with passion, ready to submit to his will. To give him her life's blood. And he wanted it flowing into his mouth, his cells. All of it.

Soren sank his fangs deep into her throat. She bucked, crying out, but her words were drowned in blood. Streaming into his mouth, filling his hard cock. Throbbing.

"Yes, that's it," Leila breathed into his ear. Her hand cupped his crotch, stroking his erection through his pants. "Take it all. Drain her. Feel her heart slowing. This power, this ecstasy is all yours now, my love."

Yes! The beast exulted. *Kill her!*

The wickedness bled to every part of him like an ink stain. He could feel her heartbeat weakening as he drank. She was saying something again and again, the words finally penetrating the fog.

"I love you, Soren," Harley whispered. "I always will."

Soren. His name.

I love you.

He drew back as she slumped in the chains, eyes closed. His gaze fell to the tiny holes in her neck.

I love you, Soren.

He staggered back as if from a physical blow. "Harley?" He shook her shoulder gently and her head wobbled, hair obscuring her face. "What have I done?"

Leila sidled up to him, laid a possessive hand on his chest. "Don't worry, darling. The beast's first kill is always a bit shocking. It gets easier with each one. Kill the other two; then we'll feast on their hearts."

Feast. On their hearts.

On his mate's heart.

Cold rage suffused him and the beast demanded blood. But when it flowed again, it would belong to Leila and her cohorts.

Howling with grief, he shoved Leila away and whirled. He flung out an arm and hurled a blue bolt at the chains holding Harley's body. They snapped as the blast hit the wall, and she collapsed to the floor in a heap. Leila leaped at him, but Soren sidestepped her, freeing Zen and Luc in an explosion of flying rock and chain links.

The pair dropped to their feet, Zen whisking the sword from his back.

"What are you doing?" Leila screamed. "Arron, guards, stop them!"

The bitch is going to fucking die.

Turning, he shot another bolt at Leila. Missed. Instead, it slammed into a column next to her, taking out a large chunk of marble. The impact knocked her off balance and she staggered backward.

Shit! In frustration, he cast about for a weapon, wishing he hadn't given his to Zen. Power flowed through his veins like an electric current, but what damned good did it do if he didn't know how to control it?

Arron, who had been tensed and waiting, promptly relieved a surprised guard of his sword and lopped off his head with it. "Soren, catch!"

Soren caught the weapon and faced the advancing guards. It wasn't his own sword, but it would do. They split off, a group of them going for Zen and Luc, and the others standing against him and Arron. It seemed like daunting odds.

And then a familiar dark-headed vampire charged into the temple, leading reinforcements. *Aldric! Thank the gods.* The newcomers joined the fight as Aldric tossed Luc's magic sword to their youngest brother.

One big brute squared off with Soren, feet planted, sword at the ready. The confident grin on his broad face revealed just how short he believed the fight would be.

With one swift stroke, his opponent raised the blade and brought it down at an angle. Soren barely parried the blow in time to keep his head on his shoulders. He blocked several more, but the weapon felt awkward in his hand. He wasn't going to win a contest of swordsmanship, so he'd change the rules.

Tossing the weapon aside, Soren charged the giant before he could swing again. The vampire's eyes widened a fraction, and he wrapped his arms around the brute's waist in a flying tackle.

Caught off guard, his adversary toppled and they crashed to the floor. The vampire's sword skittered out of reach as they rolled, grappling. Soren landed several good punches before a flash of metal caught his eye. Pain lanced low in his abdomen. Straddling the demon's waist, he looked down at himself to see the handle of a dagger protruding from his own belly.

"Not so tough, are you?" the lug sneered.

Jerking the knife from his belly, Soren plunged the blade into his foe's heart. The demon's scream ended on a gurgle, then a final rasp as his eyes went blank. Soren moved off him, springing to his feet.

Blood everywhere. Flowing like a crimson river. It puddled underneath his boots, the stench of it driving him mad. Both beautiful and awful. He couldn't let the insanity claim him forever. Gods, if he could only hold out a little longer, he could finish this. The prickling sensation in his stomach told him that his flesh was already knitting closed.

Holding his head in his hands, he blinked furiously to clear the red film, the frenzy to feed that had descended over him once more. The scene before him was unfolding like a surreal, grisly nightmare.

Zen and Luc were fighting back-to-back, cutting a swath through the enemy, the Fontaine swords glowing with beautiful, sinister light. Zen had taken out one of Leila's goons and was wrestling with another, teeth clenched in grim determination, muscles bunching. Gaining the upper hand, he hooked an ankle behind the demon's leg and tripped him. They fell together, and Zen finished him with one efficient stroke to the heart. The demon's flesh sizzled and popped as the magical blade slid home, ending him.

What Luc lacked in practice with his sword, he made up for in sheer strength and resolve. Blades clashed, Luc's sword sending out showers of eerie sparks with each hit, and he drove the attacker back, unbalancing him. The kid was good, and Soren felt a surge of pride. The falter in his opponent's step provided the opening his brother needed. Grasping the heavy weapon with both hands, he swung, cleaving the demon's head from his shoulders. The severed neck blackened and burned.

Arron had just dispatched the last of them. He braced a booted foot on the shoulder of the deceased, yanking the blade from his chest.

In the middle of the carnage, Leila stood laughing like a loon, her high-pitched cackle raising the hair on the back of Soren's neck.

"Bravo, darlings! I knew those dimwits would be no match for such brave warriors." Dropping her voice low, she looked straight through Soren with a knowing smile. "My, look at all the blood you've lost from that nasty wound. You must be starving, my love. Why don't you begin with Zenon?"

"Shut up." Clenching his fists, he glared at her, hatred for his tormentor—and himself—bringing a hot rush of bile to his mouth. *Don't think of the hunger!*

"Death surrounds you. Can't you smell the sweetness? Can't you taste—"

"Shut the fuck up!"

Soren started for her, ready to rip out her throat, to end her miserable existence, when a movement along the wall snagged his attention. *Harley!* She was moaning, holding a hand to her temple, trying to sit up. Joy bloomed, but his happiness was short-lived.

Leila spun with a curse, outraged to see that her rival wasn't dead after all. She intended to do something about it, but Soren grabbed her arm, jerking her around. Wild power surged through him, and he flung her to the tile with enough force to crack the surface where she landed. She stared up at him, eyes wide with surprise as he fell on top of her with a snarl, grabbing for her throat.

His fingers wrapped around her neck like a vise. He probably couldn't kill her by strangling her—if he were still a normal vampire. But now? Fierce, dark satisfaction swelled inside him at the sight of the way her eyes bugged as he turned his black magic on her. Used the power against her that she'd worked so hard to force on him.

It flowed from him like a river of blood, burning the demoness like acid. Her flesh began to sizzle under his hands, and he laughed. "Die, bitch."

He was unprepared for the blow that sent him flying through the air. His flight ended abruptly as he crashed into one of the support columns, his head smacking against the stone. He slid to the floor, dazed, fighting to stay conscious. He'd used too much of his unpredictable new power and didn't know how to get it back.

The images before him split double, bouncing. But he could make out Luc, running to place himself between the demoness and Harley. The maniacal wrath on her features twisted them into ugliness. Zen raced after him.

"Get out of my way, before I send you to Hades!" Leila shrieked.

"You first, bitch," Luc growled. Feet spread, he held the sword in front of him like a born warrior. Behind him, Harley's green eyes were huge in her small face, taking in the unfolding horror.

Soren blinked, tried to push up, and fell again. With a flick of her wrist, Leila hurled a bolt into Luc that staggered him, in spite of his attempt to deflect it. Stunned, the sword slipped from his nerveless fingers to the floor with a clatter. Lips curled into a sneer, she reached into her cloak.

"I don't think so. Die, young vampire."

What happened next seemed like a series a slow-motion clips as Soren pushed to his feet.

Leila's hand slipped from the folds of her cloak and drew back a bloodstained dagger.

Arron and Zen leaped forward, shouting. Arron was closer, and stepped in front of Luc.

Held out his palm as if to reason with a child.

"Leila, sto—"

Arron's words broke off on a strangled gasp. He gazed down at himself, dumbfounded. The blade was buried deep in his chest. He took a halting step, then slowly sank to his knees. "Poison," he whispered. "The blade is poisoned."

Luc knelt beside him, catching him as he collapsed, cradling him gently. "Easy, dude. You're going to be okay."

Arron gritted his teeth hard and began to shake as Luc held him against his chest. A muffled sob from Harley urged Soren forward, step by painful step, until he stood between Leila and those she would have him destroy. Her face was drawn into a cold mask as she raved.

"See what your little whore and your sniveling brother have caused? They've made me kill my only friend!"

"Friend? You treated him like your possession," Soren said. "You've used his son against him like a weapon for hundreds of years, and now he's dying by *your hand*. You're a vicious whore, and if he doesn't walk away from here, neither will you."

Leila glared at him. "A very moving speech, not that it matters. After I kill them all, I will make you my slave. I will rule the Coalition alone as queen."

"No, you fucking won't."

The deep voice that came from behind Leila was filled with deadly promise, like the roll of distant thunder. A chill blew past Soren, as if someone had trailed icy fingers down his cheek.

Leila spun, her face blanching in shock. "No, this can't be," she whispered.

Soren looked past her to the altar, and what he saw made his knees go weak with relief. Valafar sucked in a giant breath and strained against the chains binding him. One by one, they snapped in rapid succession, reverberating throughout the temple like gunshots.

With great dignity, he rose. Steady on his feet, he straightened to his full height, stretched his fully healed black wings to their massive span, and approached the small group. The tread of his boots made a slow, ominous click across the marble. He raised his dark head, eyes smoldering. The new, moon-shaped scar on his cheek—exactly like the one on Soren's hip—added to the effect. He moved like a cat, exuding power, grace, and utter control. The demon prince held no weapon, but Soren knew he wouldn't need one.

Valafar's lips turned up, and he spoke to Soren first. "Sorry I'm late. The belladonna took a little longer to work than I expected."

"I'm just glad you made it," he admitted. "I could use some gods-damned help."

"What the devil is going on? How is this possible?" Leila gaped at the prince. "Soren took your blood, read your secrets. He said only the gods are allowed to partake of belladonna!"

Valafar stepped so close to her, she had to tilt her head up to look at him. Very, very softly, he enunciated each word so that there could be no mistaking his meaning.

"Yes, that's exactly what he said."

Leila froze, lips parted, terror leaching her color to gray. "But . . . but you were sired by an incubus and a human woman. How do you have the mark of Azrael?"

"Ah, you do not know my true history, thanks to Soren." He

smiled. It wasn't a nice smile. "I am indeed the son of an incubus who was a descendant of Azrael. The archangel's mark shows only when I allow it, such as now. But I wasn't birthed by the human woman you speak of. Soren lied to you about that, just as I trusted him to do."

Soren didn't envy Leila's position. Valafar was toying with her now, a cat with a mouse.

"Y-your mother . . ." she stammered, unable to finish.

"Is Hestia, goddess of Olympus."

A collective gasp sounded from the small group. Even Arron's eyes widened in surprise, and he and Valafar exchanged a glance that Soren couldn't decipher. Leila began to back away, shaking.

"F-former goddess!" She was desperate, grasping at straws. "Hestia resigned her throne on Olympus eons ago! That makes you nothing but the bastard son of a common affair."

"No, my conniving traitor. It makes me the beloved son of my parents—and a demigod. It makes me your prince, keeper of peace and justice in the Southern Coalition. I was charged thus by the gods of Olympus when they granted me immortality in this very temple, and it's past time I take my duties seriously. I'll do it gladly to prevent more parasites like you from squirming into my realm."

Valafar caressed her check with his palm. Transfixed, gazing into his stony face, she sank to her knees.

"My prince, have mercy," she begged.

"Your request comes centuries too late, demoness." Retrieving Soren's bloodied sword from near his feet, the prince lowered it, resting the tip at the V of her neck and shoulder. "Leila Maria Doucet, for your crimes—including the murders of countless innocents, the attempted murder of my beloved brother, Arron, and for treason against my throne—I hereby sentence you to death."

"Valafar, please! I'll do anything—"

"Soren Fontaine, for the wrongs you and your beloved have suffered at her hands, you have earned the right to choose the method of execution—and the right to carry it out."

Soren was struck temporarily speechless. He didn't deserve such an honor. He could no longer recall the vampire he'd been.

"No!" she screeched. "He betrayed you! He tried to kill you with the belladonna."

"Belladonna is a healing agent to a demigod. Soren saw my secrets, but he chose to reveal the one that would strengthen and free me, not destroy me. In spite of your pitiful attempts to crush the remaining good in him, you failed. I owe him a great debt. Sentence her, Soren. That's an order."

He studied Leila. Next to Valafar's awesome presence, she appeared beaten, small. How could he have allowed her to control the beast inside him? Was he so weak?

Considering her fate, he took no satisfaction in it. He believed only that the punishment should fit the crime. Death by beheading was too swift. This required something more in keeping with her hideous acts.

"Take the vial hidden in your robe, the one you took from Zenon."

She did, holding it aloft with a puzzled frown. "Valafar's blood? I don't see—"

"Drink it."

The prince nodded his approval of the sentence. "The judgment is fitting. So that there can be no question of subterfuge, the blood in the vial is Zenon's, not mine. You wanted my blood to strengthen you. As Zen is a pure demon, his blood will kill you. Do as Soren says."

"You tricked me!" Her fingers tightened around the vessel.

"You believed what you wished out of greed for my power, evil one. Proceed with the sentence," the prince ordered.

Her eyes cast about the area, frantic for an out. Soren tensed, and Valafar shifted on his feet. Whatever she had in mind, it didn't include going quietly into eternity.

Suddenly, she threw the vial to the floor. It shattered, the poisonous demon's blood spilling harmlessly. With lightning speed, she sprinted the short distance to Luc's discarded sword and snatched it up.

"Halt!" Valafar bellowed.

Instead, she spun toward Harley with a snarl, shedding her human form to appear as the hideous monster she truly was.

Soren's heart leaped to his throat as she went after Harley. He ran faster than he ever had, caught her by the head of writhing snakes streaming behind her, and wrapped his fist in the squirming bodies. Jerking hard, he yanked her off her feet and threw her to the ground.

"Soren, look out!" Harley cried.

Leila brought the blade upward, intending to shove it under his breastbone. He captured her wrist and they rolled, each fighting for control. Fighting to the death.

He rolled atop her, straining with all his strength. The tide began to turn in his favor, her grip weakening. Gradually, he twisted the knife into the soft flesh of her abdomen. And as their eyes met, hers widened. Before she could turn him to stone, he plunged the weapon forward, the blade parting her snake's skin like a knife filleting a fish. Sickened, he pushed off her and knelt, hands gripping his thighs. Her muscles contracted and she screamed. A slow, agonizing death for an evil being felled by the enchanted sword.

But she wasn't finished. Turning her head to look at him, she gave him a malicious smile, blood bubbling to her lips.

"My demise changes nothing. The beast will move within you always. Growing, filling you until you no longer care who you once were. I should know." She coughed, shuddered, and went on. "A part of me now lives in your soul. You are trapped, a slave to the evil inside you. Go forth in my stead, for that is your burden to bear . . . forever."

15

*S*oren pushed to his feet, lurching away from the damning truth. From all of them. "Oh, gods."

A slender hand touched his back, and the sweet scent of his mate teased his nose.

"Get away from me, Harley. I'm dangerous."

"I don't believe that. You have good left in you. Even Valafar said—"

He whirled, grabbing her by her arms, shaking her. He had to make her understand. "I nearly killed you! Any second I could lose control again to this—this *thing* inside me. There's only one way out for me. Don't you see?"

The stricken look in her green eyes almost felled him. "It's not hopeless. Valafar is a god. He can help. Can't you?" she said, turning to the prince.

Soren hung his head in shame. He'd given his body and soul to darkness and broken her heart, and would do so again. Still, she pleaded for his life.

Everyone waited. Seconds passed. Val shook his head. "I'm so sorry."

"There has to be something you can do!" Harley cried.

"Can't you just try?" Luc implored, his voice breaking. Against him, Arron's eyes were closed, his face pale, as he clung to life. "Please. You can't lose your brother, and I can't lose mine."

"Healing Soren is different, young one," Valafar said kindly. "I will easily mend Arron because his soul isn't bound to the depravity that consumed Leila. I am, however, forbidden to do the same for your brother for that very reason. Leila was correct about what will happen to him, and that leaves two options. Soren can choose to free his soul from their bargain by death, or fight the beast and possibly lose. If he chooses the latter and the beast wins, I will be forced to destroy him."

Soren hadn't expected anything else. In a strange way, hearing Valafar speak it aloud was an immense relief. Even if he could've been spared, he and Harley had no chance together. He'd never be able to live with his betrayal of her.

Harley walked into his arms and he held her tight, tucking her head under his chin. Wishing he could make love to her one last time and leave her with memories of tenderness, not of the savage he had become. He inhaled her essence, felt her heart beating much too fast against his chest.

Pulsing, the sweet nectar rushed like a river under her skin. Waiting to be tasted. His starving body reacted with violence, fangs lengthening, his cock growing hard. He lowered his lips to her neck and froze.

The ravenous beast demanded more than sustenance, much more. It craved the tearing of meat in his teeth and rich juices running down his throat.

Spread her legs and fuck her! Drain her. Take it all.

Horrified, he pushed her away.

"Valafar, get her out of here," he groaned.

"I'm not leaving you, Soren Fontaine, so forget it!"

The sword? No. It was an honorable death he didn't deserve, any more than Leila had. He stumbled away from her, past them all, to the altar. Fell to his knees before it, fumbling in his shirt for the vial Arron had given him. Not a minute to waste.

"Soren? What are you doing?" she called. He could hear her alarm, her footsteps moving up behind him. Could smell her blood.

"Harley, stay back!" Valafar commanded.

She wouldn't, he knew. With a twist, he removed the cap. Lifted the bottle to his lips . . . and downed the contents. Her forlorn scream echoed his own.

"Nooo!"

Fire seized his entire body. The inferno of Hades. It raced to every limb, burning. Eating him from the inside out. How long would it take? Convulsing in agony, he rested his elbows on the altar and clasped his hands, casting his eyes to the gods.

"Please forgive me. Take care of Harley—"

A horrendous spasm of pain slammed him again, and he fell in slow motion. Fell forever.

Harley rushed to Soren's side and knelt. Tremors shook his body, and his fingers clawed at the floor. Arching in spasms, he threw his head back and screamed, nearly stopping her heart. Sweat mixed with blood began to seep from his pores. When he relaxed again, she clasped one of his hands in hers.

She was barely aware of Valafar leaving them in order to attend to Arron. Of Zen producing a long coat and placing it around her shoulders, then retreating to hover nearby.

"Soren, honey, you're going to be all right. Just tell me what to do." She wouldn't believe he was dying. That she was about to lose the male she loved. The nightmare wasn't supposed to end this way.

As he gazed up at her, his eyes began to change. The black faded, swirled. He closed them for a moment, and when he opened them again, she found herself looking into *Soren's* eyes. A beautiful amber gold.

"Harley?"

"Soren," she choked. "Is it really *you?*"

"Yeah. Tell me that one day . . . you might be able to forgive me for what I put you through. For giving myself to that . . . that whore." He broke off, his face lined with torment.

Tears clogged her throat. "I never blamed you. Don't you see? I love you more than my own life, so there's nothing to forgive. Fight for us, Soren."

Another tremor coiled his body. He coughed, strangling on his own blood. Harley gathered him into her arms and held him through the torment, whispering her love again and again.

Luc and Aldric crouched beside her. Luc touched his brother's hair, and Soren smiled. "Hey, bro. Is Arron okay?"

Luc swallowed hard. "Yeah, he's going to be fine. So are you."

Soren didn't answer that. Instead, he pinned Luc with a questioning stare. "You'll take care of Harley and Aldric?"

"I don't need a keeper," Aldric said, but the statement was filled with sorrow.

"You know it. Hey, didn't really get a chance to tell you—I

met a woman. A Valkyrie, the one who saved my ass from the werewolf. I think she's my mate—no shitting. Can we even *have* a Valkyrie in the family?"

Soren barked a short laugh, but the effort cost him. His body shook with pain as Harley continued to hold him, stroking his hair, his face. Several moments passed before he spoke again.

"Take that happiness and run with it, Luc. It's too rare to give up. I love you."

"Gods, Soren." His brother hung his head and started to cry.

Aldric was more stoic, but the agony on his face spoke volumes.

"I can help you," Harley said softly. For him, she could do this. "I can take your sword and—"

"No! I don't deserve any mercy, and I won't let you carry that burden for the rest of your life. Just hold me, baby."

"If that's what you want. Anything at all," she sobbed.

Harley could feel him slipping away. Sand through her fingers, and she couldn't stop the inevitable. After a time, he no longer struggled. She didn't need anyone to tell her that the poison had almost finished its deadly work. His voice broke through her sorrow, barely audible.

"Harley?"

She gazed into his face, memorizing every feature. The way his sable hair fell in disarray over his face. His high cheekbones, his nose, the full, sensuous lips.

"Yes, darling?"

Fingering a lock of her hair, he spoke so quietly, she had to strain to hear. "I loved you from the first moment I saw you. For yourself, not because I thought you were Helena. Did I ever tell you?"

"No." The word came out on a sob. She wouldn't cry, but it hurt so damned much. "But I knew."

He gave her a weak smile. "Figured you did," he teased in a breathy rasp. "You're a smart babe, after all."

His body went limp in her arms, and his hand fell to the floor. He gazed past her in wonder, as if he saw something magnificent that no one else could.

"I love you, too, Soren!" Her shoulders began to shake.

Harley knew the exact moment he left her. The spark in his golden eyes flickered, faded . . . until they were empty as glass.

"Soren?" She shook him once. Again. "Soren? Oh, honey, no. Nooo!"

She held him close to her breast, because she could do nothing more for him ever again. The racking sobs overtook her, and she gave in to the grief. His loss flayed her, a thousand lashes of a whip, tearing her apart.

"Why?" she wept. "Why?"

Her heart shattered, blew into a million pieces, leaving her hollow. She wanted to die with him. How long she rocked him, she didn't know. After a while, a warm hand came to rest on her shoulder.

"Harley, you must let him go," Valafar murmured.

"I know." However, several more minutes passed before she'd calmed enough to do it. Loosening her grip, she eased his head into her lap. Very gently, she placed a hand over his face, closing his eyes forever. "Good-bye, darling. I'll love you always."

She couldn't stop touching his cheek, attempting to comfort him, even though he no longer needed it. If not for the rivulets of blood coating him, the result of the poison that had caused his insides to hemorrhage, he might've been sleeping.

Sitting against the altar, Aldric held a weeping Luc in his arms. At least the brothers would be okay, and they had each other. With the passage of time and a lot of love, their grief would ease.

For Harley's part, she'd never love another. In fact, she didn't intend to stay on this earth without him. "Can you change this?" she asked Valafar without preamble. "Can I take Soren's place?"

"I'm afraid not. It doesn't work that way. Besides, would you condemn him to a lifetime of the grief you're feeling now? The loss of not one mate, but two in his existence?"

"Of course not," she whispered, feeling guilty for even considering it.

"But there is something I might be able to do."

She stared at him, not daring to hope. "What?"

He took a deep breath, as if considering the wisdom of what he had to say. "Soren's eyes. They changed to gold just before his death."

"Yes, they did." She stared at him. "His sacrifice was complete, and the darkness was gone!"

"Exactly. I said I couldn't intervene to save him because the beast ruled him, but he rid himself of it. Given his bravery and selflessness, I'm willing to try to bring him back."

Hope flared. "Anything. Please!"

Arron, who'd held his peace until then, walked over, running a hand through his long, fiery locks with a worried frown. "Valafar, my brother, you can't seriously think of breaking the law."

The prince clenched his jaw, glaring at Arron. "In the Coalition, I *am* the law, and I have the power to do this."

"At great cost to yourself," Arron argued. "Even if the gods choose not to execute you for it, you might never recover! Your enemies would converge on you like rabid dogs!"

Fledgling hope shriveled in her breast. She could have Soren back, but at the possible cost of the prince's life. Misery swamped her anew. "I can't ask that of you."

"Ah, sweet Harley," he murmured, a bit somber. "You don't have to ask. What's eternity without love, anyway?"

Cocking her head, she wondered what a sexy, ancient demi-god could possibly have to be sad about. As soon as the thought occurred, she felt stupid. The prince clearly didn't need to bring more trouble to his door by helping them, but his honor would let him do no less. An eternity of taking on the world must be draining, no matter how powerful the man.

"Valafar—"

"Cease hounding me, little brother," he snapped. "I've been out of swaddling clothes for nearly eleven thousand years. If I need coddling, I'll go to Mother." He looked at Harley. "Hold Soren tight. He'll need to sense your presence and be assured of your devotion if this is to work."

Under any other circumstances, Harley would've been amused by their squabble. Instead, she did as Valafar told her, willing herself not to imagine his efforts ending in failure. Trying not to think of what terrible thing might happen to him if he succeeded.

Valafar bent low over Soren's body and smoothed the dark brown hair from his face. Sooty lashes curled against her love's waxen cheek, lace on ivory. The prince placed one palm on Soren's forehead, the other on his chest. Softly, he began a strange chant in a foreign tongue Harley had never heard before.

Luc and Aldric scooted close, watching with intensity, their eyes red and swollen, as hers must be. Zen laid a reassuring hand on Luc's arm, but he appeared wretched with worry, like everyone else.

The air around Soren's body began to glow, then shimmer

with a zillion sparkly lights. Like tiny blue fireflies they danced, skimming his face and limbs. She watched, mesmerized, as they lit, cleaning the blood everywhere they touched, until he appeared whole again.

This done, Valafar paused, swaying a bit.

"Your strength is nearly drained and that wasn't the difficult part," Arron fretted. "Rest a moment."

"I can't. His spirit is still here for now. If I wait, the window of opportunity will be lost."

Renewing his efforts, the prince began another chant. This one rose, swelling in the atmosphere. His voice grew louder and thunder clapped, causing Harley to start. The wind picked up suddenly, whipping at them all. Valafar's black hair blew wildly around his shoulders and into his face and his wings fluttered, but he didn't seem to notice. Hands braced on Soren's body, he stopped the chant and threw back his head.

Lightning crackled, flashed. The storm unleashed its fury, the noise deafening. A blue bolt streaked from above, rocketing through Valafar and into Soren. The prince convulsed with violent force, every muscle straining, his teeth white against the darkness of his face. The blast almost made Harley lose her hold on Soren, but she clung to him out of sheer terror.

The tumult raged until Harley's arms went numb. She couldn't hold on to him a second longer.

Then the storm abated as swiftly as it had descended. Valafar fell backward, and Arron caught him against his chest.

"I have you, brother. Rest. By the gods, what have you done to yourself?" Arron sighed unhappily.

Harley studied Soren, icy dread snaking up her spine. "He's not b-breathing."

Valafar's features were drawn, his voice thin. "I have one last task, beautiful. Have patience. Arron, help me up."

He couldn't sit up without Arron's assistance, and Harley felt terrible. The prince had risked his entire future to help them, but was stubbornly determined to perform the deed just the same. She had a sneaking suspicion not many were foolish enough to stand in his way.

Kneeling over the man Harley loved, Valafar bowed his head. "Soren Fontaine, you are released from the curse of eternal darkness. I bind you once more into your vampire form, and gift you with this second chance. Use it wisely. Live," he whispered.

With that, the prince pressed his lips to Soren's. Harley thought the gesture a kiss at first. Valafar, however, blew a tiny puff of air into Soren's mouth and sat up.

Soren's chest heaved once. Twice. Then he gasped and began to breathe. Harley could've fainted with joy. Her fingers sought the pulse in his neck and found the plodding, steady rhythm. Maybe a bit weak, but she didn't have much experience with medical stuff.

"It is done," Valafar announced. Exhaustion had carved grooves around his sensual mouth, and he studied Soren with a peculiar hesitation that alarmed Harley. She tugged at his coat sleeve.

"What's wrong? Why isn't he waking up?"

"I won't lie to you. He resisted me, Harley. Bringing him back proved more difficult than wrestling a dragon."

"But why?" *Stunned* didn't begin to describe how she felt. This could *not* be happening.

"He believes he's unworthy of your love. His heart is broken and he doesn't want to live."

Not now, after all they'd been through. She shook him. "Soren, honey, that's not true! Listen to me, please. Don't give up on me! Valafar, what can I do?"

His face softened in sympathy. "Love him—that's all. You're the only one who can reach him now. I can do nothing more."

"Will he remember everything that's happened?"

"I *could* take the horrible memories and wipe them from his mind and yours, but I won't. A man must learn from his mistakes. If Soren doesn't face his and accept your forgiveness, he will never heal. If I intervened, he wouldn't remember all that has transpired, but his deep sense of failure would eat at him like a cancer until the end of time. Worse, he'd never know why. Do you understand?"

"Yes. That makes perfect sense, but it won't be easy."

"Perhaps impossible. He could still die without ever waking, Harley. All I did was to open the door. He must walk through it. Soren must choose."

"Thank you so much."

Soren's brothers took his hands, and Aldric spoke to him, the depth of his love catching his voice. "Don't be stupid, bro. Come back to her. She's one hell of a woman, and for some reason, she fell for an idiot. Don't give up now. Remember our parents' love. Seize what they had." He squeezed Soren's hand, then let go, looking at Val. "Luc and I will help clean up here, then go back to the mansion on our own. Please send them home."

Harley swallowed back more tears. "I'm ready."

Reluctantly, she let Valafar ease Soren to the floor. She lay next to the man she loved, clutching his hand, willing him to hang on.

Valafar pushed to his feet and stood over them. He held an arm out, palm up. "Sleep."

Her last impression was of a tall, gallant demigod, black hair tumbling into his eyes and to his shoulders, black wings glorious behind him. Blowing into his palm.

And blue stardust that carried her into sweet dreams of a tall, beautiful vampire with eyes like amber gold.

Valafar stood wearily in the middle of the gore. Leila and her demons, dead. He'd been fair and just and helped Aldric to rid the Coalition of a pestilence in the bargain. Maybe that would cut him some slack with the Terrible Twelve. His lips twisted. *Yeah, right.*

With a snap of his fingers, the carnage vanished as though it had never been.

"Hey, I said we'd help with that," Aldric said with a frown.

"Got it covered."

Gods, in his entire existence, he'd never been so empty. This cut much deeper than exhaustion. No, this was something more, and he took comfort in the truth. The endless days, winding down like a worn, forgotten timepiece. Numbered and finite.

At long last.

Aware of his brother and of Luc, Aldric, and Zen watching him anxiously, Valafar tried to straighten to his full height. Failed.

"Leila may be dead, but I'll find your son, Arron. Before I draw my last breath, I'll bring him home to you. I swear it." Now, if only he could endure against the impending war long enough to keep his promise.

And descend it would, the entire universe out to destroy him and bring his enemies down around his ears. The grim expressions on the faces of his companions told him they knew it, too.

"Your last breath? What kind of crazy talk is that?" Arron frowned.

"Let's get the hell out of here," Val said, ignoring him. Fatigue weighed his limbs, and he hated his weakness.

He took one shaky step, two, before his knees buckled. His friends rushed to his side as darkness swirled, beckoning with the promise of oblivion.

Yes, the vultures would arrive soon to feast on his flesh, pick him clean until nothing remained to mark his passage from this brutal world. No sons to carry on his legacy, no mate to weep for him.

Let them come.

16

*H*arley woke by degrees.

Tangled sheets. Rain thrumming against a window.

Cracking one eye open, she observed her surroundings. A gorgeous room. *What on earth?* Groggy, she sat up and searched for a clue. It didn't take long to find.

Next to her, Soren lay sleeping, looking like a dark angel. Valafar had sent them home as promised, and they were in his bedroom. Now it was up to Soren to wake. Determined, she reached out and shook a bare shoulder.

"Soren," she called. She stroked his hair, trying to think of a way to reach him. "Oh, honey. Don't you know how much I love you? I don't blame you for what happened with Leila. It's in the past."

He didn't stir. But she wasn't quitting.

"Soren, please wake up! I'm not giving up until you come back to me. Do you hear? Forgive yourself; let it go." She cupped his face in both hands and did the only thing that came to mind.

Leaning forward, she kissed him, touched his soft lips with hers. Gentle, urging. Willing him to hear what words could never say. To let her love flow into him and to understand that it would last forever. To allow that love to heal him.

To love her forever.

Spoken with a simple kiss.

A kiss . . . and a miracle. His mouth responded, his body arching into hers, seeking refuge. Warmth. His arms encircled her, strong hands splayed on her back. Shudders began to rack him, jerking his shoulders.

He was awake, crying.

Breaking the kiss, she pulled back and looked into his handsome face, so dear to her. So desolate. A man who'd been through hell and truly believed he'd lost everything.

"Let me go," he whispered hoarsely. "I don't deserve you."

"Forget it! Ain't gonna happen, vampire."

Her caustic response seemed to penetrate his sorrow a little, and he opened his eyes. He paused, searching her face as if trying to see into her heart, a flicker of hope sparking. But still painfully hesitant, unsure.

Terrible guilt laced his throaty rasp. "I betrayed you and I almost killed you. What if the beast in me comes back someday, like some sort of infection? I can't take that risk."

"I promise you, it won't. You were freed when you sacrificed yourself for the good of everyone you love. Valafar said so before he gave you this second chance. Besides, what difference would it make if you did have some weird lingering effect from all of this? The vampire I fell in love with is no coward. Is that what you are?"

"No! I want you safe and happy. But you don't deserve—"

"Stuff that, Soren Fontaine!" she shouted. Wild to reach him, she grabbed a handful of his hair in both fists and yanked him up with all her strength. Sitting nose to nose in the big bed, she launched into a tirade.

"I sat by and let Valafar break some cosmic law in order to bring you back to me, and now he's in deep shit with twelve pissed-off gods and some enemies who can't wait to barbecue him! What about *you?* Do you have the balls to fight for us? Are you the never-say-die vampire I thought I knew, or a wuss? Before you answer, think about whether you can stomach the idea of me mating some-one else, like Val. Joining with him, sharing his bed, having his fifteen children—"

"Not a fucking chance," he growled.

He kissed her hard and deep. They melted into each other, one heartbeat, one soul. She rejoiced in his mouth moving on hers, his tongue, hands, stroking. Her breasts crushed into his broad chest. This man, claiming her as his. Chasing away the shadows.

Alive and *hers.*

"I love you so damned much," he breathed. "Thank you for saving me."

She hugged him close, smiling into his wet hair. "I love you, too. Believe me, vamp, the pleasure is all mine."

"But what about the Council? My brothers and I used our swords, even though it was forbidden."

A voice interrupted from the doorway. "Under the circum-stances, and with Valafar returning to the helm, they decided to let it slide," Aldric said.

Soren smiled at his older brother. "Thank you, bro. For everything."

He shrugged. "I didn't do much except arrive with backup at

the right time. I'm just glad I healed from the ambush in time to get to you."

"What about Luc? What was this about being rescued by a Valkyrie?"

Luc appeared in the doorway next to his older brother. "Yeah, some badass chick saved my bacon after I got attacked by that werewolf Leila sent after me. She made me well and brought me back here."

"Where you promptly got captured by Leila's goons," Aldric said dryly. "Good going."

"Bite me, asshole."

Soren laughed, and it felt good to Harley to be a part of his family again, no terrible beast choking him with darkness. Damned good. "By the way," she said, "it will be nice to finally get to know you both under pleasant circumstances."

"You, too," Luc replied, smiling.

"Same here." Aldric nodded. "Make our brother happy— that's all we ask. Just like we know he will you."

"No worries there." She snuggled into her mate's side. "I plan to make him very happy every single day."

Luc elbowed his oldest brother. "Come on. Let's leave these lovebirds alone."

The pair left, closing the door behind them.

"I love you, Harley," Soren breathed into her hair. "Join with me in an official mating ceremony here at the resort. We'll invite all our friends and have a naughty celebration."

"Ohh, I think that's a big yes." She giggled, imagining the party.

He laid his forehead on hers. "You mean it? You'll be my mate, even though I've been more trouble than any vampire is worth?"

She gave a dramatic sigh, as if reconsidering. "Well, now that you mention it—vampires, demons, and *my* vamp being a distant cousin to a demigod? I don't know . . ."

"Never mind. I'll take that as a yes!"

She threw her arms around his neck. "Damned straight."

Soren paused in his work inside the pavilion and swiped a gloved hand over his brow, wiping away the sweat. Good thing vampires really didn't burst into flame. The end of summer in the South, and the sweltering heat at midmorning, was already enough to suffocate him after no more than five minutes outside. Not that he minded.

He paused to check out his handiwork in the covered area where their joining ceremony would take place. Flowers, vines, and all sorts of shit a female would love graced the rows and the pretty archway where they'd stand and exchange the words. "Not too bad, huh?" he asked himself.

Ten more pots of flowers to arrange. He threw himself into the task with relish, taking care of them one by one until his back ached, every muscle complaining. Sweet Virgin, it felt wonderful.

This done, he walked out into the sunshine. Lifted his face, enjoying the blaze on his skin. The marvelous sensation wasn't something he'd ever take for granted again. He strode to the corral where they kept the horses, bracing his arms on the fence, and just watched their mares for a very long while. There were two new colts, hugged against their mothers as if attached by Velcro. His heart couldn't swell any bigger or it would burst.

Now, if only they could have a baby. But he and Helena had never been successful.

Slender arms looped around his neck. "Enjoying yourself?"

"I am now." Harley pressed against him, laying her cheek on his back. "I'm all sweaty, baby."

"Mmm. Don't care." She snuggled closer.

"Good." He turned and took her in his arms, just holding her, counting his blessings. Next weekend, he and Harley would be quietly joined here. Okay, not so quietly, with his brothers and all their friends there to take part in what would no doubt end up being a naughty good time. Valafar, Arron, and Zen would come for sure.

"Hey, I was thinking about the baby roses. Why don't we put them over by the—"

"Shh. I don't want to talk. Not about flowers." He ground his hips to emphasize his point. Her hand came between them to cup the hard bulge in his jeans. She tilted her face to his, glossy auburn hair dusting the shoulders of her pink T-shirt.

"I see." She giggled, tracing the white block letters on his black T-shirt. He looked down at his chest, his grin spreading.

His shirt read, I'M SO GOOD IN BED, I SCREAM MY OWN NAME.

"Good to know some things never change, vampire," she drawled, waggling her brows. "Are you sure you can prove such a manly claim? I'm betting you're all tired out from all this manual labor you've done since we've been home."

He pressed his lips to hers, loving her mouth, soft and wet. "*Home.* Say it again."

"Home."

He cupped her delicate face, scooping his fingers through her hair. He kissed her breathless, until the need scored him like fire. The burning desire of a vampire for the woman who would soon be his wife as well as his mate. There was still darkness in his touch, but only the delicious kind that brought them endless pleasure. No evil ever again.

"Let's go inside," he managed.

Their fingers linked, he led her inside, where they made it as far as the living room. His brothers were nowhere in sight. Trisha and Jordy rounded the corner, chatting together, but quickly changed direction with knowing smiles. He and Harley each peeled off the other's clothing, unhurried. Drinking in this moment of reawakening.

Naked, he stilled before the hearth, thrilling to her touch, letting her explore at will. His face, chest, stomach. Between his legs. Telling her without speaking that he belonged to her and only her, for always.

He began his own journey, skimming her breasts, her hips. When he could wait no more, he sank to the rug, tugging her with him. He laid her gently on her back, covering her lush body with his, and pushed inside.

They moved together as one, their coupling a tender rebirth. Pulsing deep within this woman, he rejoiced in her love. The dance increased in tempo until he stiffened and shuddered with a hoarse cry, flowing into her, the river to the sea, giving all of himself. If he could, he'd give her more than his heart, his life, but he didn't know how. The only gift he had was to turn her, which he'd do after the joining, if she wanted. She clung to him in answer, accepting him. An ageless meshing of souls.

Afterward, he lay with Harley half sprawled across him, head pillowed on his chest. He stroked her smooth back, thinking that life didn't get any better. Practically humming with satisfaction, he enjoyed the featherlight touch of her fingers tracing lazy circles on his hip.

Soren tensed. She was examining the crescent birthmark.

"Harley, did Valafar say whether my mark could get me into more trouble?"

Now that Leila is dead. He'd never speak her name again, but a part of her, the awful lessons he'd learned at her hands, his betrayal of Harley, would go with him into eternity.

"Goodness, you're a worrywart!" She rolled her eyes and gave him an impish grin. "Thanks to Valafar, Arron, Zen, Aldric, and Luc, not to mention you, we have an entire immortal branch of our family. When you turn me, that's another one. I think our kid will be in good hands, too."

"Worrywart? I'm just trying to look out for—" His heart did a funny little tap dance. "What did you say?"

She kissed his cheek. "Congratulations, Daddy Soren."

"W-what?" The breath left his lungs. "But I didn't think I could have children!"

"Surprise! You managed just fine."

"When?" He felt shell-shocked and so damned happy.

"In our gazebo. Whoopsy-daisy," she sang. "Will you still love me when I'm as fat as an ogre?"

Tears blurred his vision, and he had difficulty finding his voice. "I'll love you when you're the size of my great-aunt Bertha."

"You don't *have* a great-aunt Bertha."

"Sounded good, though." He made a great show of thinking of something else, then pronounced, "I'll love you when you're as big as Val."

"Gosh, you're sooo poetic, I could just swoon," she griped, sticking out her tongue.

Choking back a laugh, he looked into her beautiful face, smoothed back her hair, and cleared his throat. "You, my darling, have made me the happiest, luckiest vampire alive."

She arched a brow, pursing her kissable lips. "Better."

"I died in your arms, my precious angel," he whispered. "And I took my final breath with your sweet face easing the pain of loss in my heart. The next time I leave this world, it will be forever. When I do, it will be glorious, because I'll fly away knowing that I'm a better male . . . all for having known your love."

"Oh, Soren." Plump little drops of wetness plopped to his chest. Her eyes shone, brilliant as diamond-studded emeralds. "Now, *that* was pretty damned poetic."

"I thought so." He swallowed the lump in his throat. "All this mushy talk is making this simple vampire a little jumpy. I'm a man of action, baby."

"Suppose you put your money where your mouth is, then?"

"Be glad to." He grinned.

Soren rolled, pinning her underneath him, delighting in her happy squeal. Determined to show this woman how much he loved her, would always cherish her. Which he did. Again and again.

Later, with Harley snuggled fast asleep in his arms, he fantasized about a child with wispy auburn curls and eyes the color of emeralds. Or a dark-headed one with eyes of amber, and a cocky, devil-may-care grin.

Of milky, unblemished, baby-soft skin.

Save for the magical mark of a crescent moon.

Turn the page for an exciting preview of

Desire
After Dark

Coming from New American Library

in August 2012

*K*assandra's day started pleasantly enough.

A good, hard fucking followed by breakfast in bed would put her in the right frame of mind to face the rest of the day—and to temporarily forget the never-ending demands of her sisters.

Hard-as-nails Valkyrie bitches, every last one, which she had no problem calling them to their pretty faces. With love.

"Taryn!"

The young man eased smoothly into her bedroom from the hallway, where he'd no doubt been anticipating her waking up and calling on him. Kass's personal body slave lived to serve her, which frequently included pounding his big cock into her pussy until she screamed the palace down.

Valkyries had a very healthy sex drive. Kass and her sisters were no exception.

Taryn's attentiveness, not to mention the eager member jutting proudly from between his thighs, brought a smile to her lips. The man did love his position. So to speak.

"Yes, mistress?"

She took a moment to appreciate his beauty. The slave stood patiently with his feet spread shoulder-width apart, hands clasped behind his back. His body was long and muscled from his daily fitness regimen, so different from the starved whore she'd taken in four years ago. Straight hair as black as a raven's wing spilled just to his collarbone, framing a face saved from being too pretty by the scar running from his left temple across his cheek, stopping an inch from the corner of his mouth.

A crazy john's attempt to filet the gorgeous young man, the last mistake the slimy bastard had ever made.

That went a long way in explaining the devotion shining from his soulful brown eyes. The man didn't give a damn that his mistress was a tough, heartless warrior. To him, she was a goddess, and he told her so on a daily basis. They shared a bond of sexual passion and an odd friendship for a rent boy—turned-slave and his mistress.

"Has my armor been cleaned?" she asked. "You know how I hate blood stains."

"This morning, mistress."

"And my sword?"

"Polished to a shine, of course."

She gave a humph of satisfaction. "Then come here, pet," she said, stretching like a lazy cat. "Give me a proper wake-up call."

"My pleasure, as always."

Watching him stride for the bed completely naked, wearing that hungry look on his face, had yet to get old. Maybe that was because she'd lived for about two thousand years and had only known him for a fraction of that time, but she'd enjoy his delectable body while the shine was still on the penny.

He climbed onto the bed and stalked her on all fours, a half smile on his full lips. She spread her legs, inviting him in. He knew what she liked and was glad to give it. Settling between her thighs, he combed his fingers through the dusky patch of curls and then parted the delicate folds to better reach the nub waiting there.

His tongue flicked out, tasting, and she buried a hand in his silky hair, urging him to feast. He didn't disappoint. After teasing the little clit for another minute, sending delightful shocks through her womb, he began to nibble. First the tender nub and then downward, to lave her slit. A few more swipes and she tugged at his head.

"Up here now," she said hoarsely. "I need you."

His smoldering eyes met hers. "As you wish."

Crawling up, he moved over her, placing the head of his cock at her entrance. He pushed into her heat ever so slowly, causing her to shudder with pleasure. When he was fully seated his hips began to pump, sliding deep, then retreating. Then repeating the process again. And again. If there was anything in eternity to compare with a man's hard body claiming hers, she couldn't name it.

The heat built, that wonderful crescendo that swelled in time to their music, carrying her higher. Her nails raked his back, just a bit of pain to remind him who was truly in charge. He shivered and groaned in response, hips snapping furiously now. Plunging into her welcoming channel with relish.

"Oh! Gods, yes!" she shouted.

"Can't stop, mistress!"

"Come for me!"

She didn't have to repeat the order. His big body went as taut as a bow string and he buried himself fully, shouting his ecstasy. His release filled her, and she followed him over the edge, clinging to him, riding the waves. When at last they were satiated, he placed his customary kiss on her cheek, a chaste ritual considering the intimacy they shared daily. But only a Valkyrie's mate was allowed the deep, mouth-to-mouth kiss of forever love.

A love her fierce kind had little hope of ever finding.

Withdrawing from her, Taryn stretched out at her side. "Why the frown, mistress? Weren't you pleased?"

"Oh, hush, you." She slapped playfully at his muscular arm. "You were fabulous, as always. I guess I'm just a little . . . I don't know how to describe it, really."

"Bored?"

She thought about that. "No, not exactly. There's always plenty to do, what with the never-ending politics and backstabbing among the gods."

"Hmm. Sad?" he said softly, tracing her cheek.

Startled, she met his gaze. "Me? I seem sad to you?"

"Yes, mistress. If you don't mind my saying so, you've sort of been in a funk lately." He paused uncertainly.

"Go on, Taryn."

"Well, I overheard your sisters talking about you. Not in a bad way," he hastened to add. "They're worried. They think you need a new challenge to bring the smile back to your lovely face."

"What kind of challenge?" Knowing her sisters, it would be sure to piss her off.

"They were discussing how long it's been since a worthy male warrior has been brought to Valhalla to appease the gods. The general consensus was that you should escort the next one."

Her brow furrowed. "That's not much of a challenge at all. What are they up to?" she mused aloud.

"I don't know, but from their laughter, there did seem to be more to it that I didn't catch," he said darkly. "I don't like it."

She had to smile. "Loyal Taryn. What would I do without you?" Kissing his forehead, she scooted from the bed. "They live to annoy me, and each other, so I'm positive it's nothing to worry about. What's the harm in taking a fallen warrior to serve the gods? It's an honor for the male, and a task I've done thousands of times. It'll be fine."

"I'm sure you're right, mistress." But he didn't sound enthusiastic.

"Get cleaned up and see if you can help in the gardens today," she said, waving her hand in dismissal. "And stop fretting."

"Yes, mistress." With a sigh, he headed for the door.

Turning, she padded into the master bath and paused in indecision. Normally she'd start her day—after Taryn's expert attentions—with a nice long soak in the huge marble tub, up to her chin in bubbles, but a sense of disquiet crept into her bones. This was a new feeling, totally different from the malaise that had plagued her lately.

There was suddenly a shift in the atmosphere. A heaviness, like black clouds gathering before a storm. The tempest was coming, but she wouldn't be able to move from its path, nor could she run. Not that a Valkyrie would run from any threat, but this was an unknown. Something bigger than herself, and for once she was afraid.

Laughing nervously, she turned on the water in the shower, letting it heat. Then she jumped in and took care of washing quickly when she would rather have lingered. And avoided the storm.

But avoidance wasn't in her nature, no matter the threat. The quicker she got on with her day, the quicker the problem would be revealed. She doubted that it would be half as scary as her fanciful imagination was making it out to be.

After drying her long hair, she fixed it in a braid that hung down her back. In the bedroom, she found laid out on the bed her black pants, short-sleeved black T-shirt, and boots. Beside those was her silver breastplate, a lightweight, deceptively strong piece of armor enchanted so that no weapon could breach it. And beside that, her belt and sword in its scabbard.

It appeared someone else sensed that today wouldn't be a lazy one for Kass.

She pulled on her pants, socks, and boots. Then her shirt. The belt with the sword came next, the armor last. She had dressed this way more times than she could count. The process came easily.

Glancing in the mirror, she was satisfied that she represented her kind well. Tall, though not as tall as her two eldest sisters, and strong. Not much was capable of defeating a Valkyrie.

She didn't care to meet an exception. Not today.

Striding into the corridor, she set out to find someone to tell her what the hell was going on. Her search ended in the dining room, where five beautiful women were chatting animatedly and munching on the usual breakfast fare of muffins, Danish, bacon, eggs, and toast. One by one, her sisters noted her arrival and conversation ground to a halt.

Serena, the eldest, arched an eyebrow at Kass's battle dress. "My, you're awfully sharp this morning."

"Aren't I supposed to be?" Placing a hand on the hilt of her sword, she scowled in annoyance. "This is how I always look when I fight—or when I escort a warrior to Valhalla."

The five hellions exchanged glances around the table.

Millicent said grumpily, "That slave of yours tells you everything. Someone needs to take him in hand."

"Touch a hair on Taryn's head and I'll scalp yours," Kass promised. "And strangle you with it."

"Anyway, it is your turn to escort a worthy warrior," Serena said, interceding before the argument could get warmed up. "Besides, the trip will do you a world of good."

Kass advanced into the room. "I smell five rats. Since when do you all sit around worrying over what's good for me or what isn't?" Silence. "What do you know that I don't?"

Serena stood and patted her arm. "Nothing, dearest, other than the name of the male and his location. His name is Luc Fontaine and he'll meet his end very soon—this morning, in fact. Odin wants him badly. Something about being cheated out of getting the warrior hundreds of years ago, and now he'll have his due. Will you escort Lord Fontaine?"

"*Lord?* He's vampire?" Kass asked in confusion.

"That's right."

"But . . . Odin doesn't take vampires! At least he never has before." She puzzled over that one. The temperamental god had never believed vampires worthy of his hallowed halls. Why this one? Then she shrugged. "I'll take him."

"You give your word as a Valkyrie?"

A chill of dread seeped into her spine, though she couldn't say why. What difference could this simple task make? What game was her sister playing? To refuse would blight her name, and another sister would be assigned to the task anyway.

"I give my word."

And if she broke it, the consequences didn't bear thinking about.

So she'd follow through. It was that simple.

Lifting his chin, Luc Fontaine inhaled as his horse walked at a sedate pace.

He loved riding. Always had, even as a young boy in the late seventeenth century, years before he and his brothers had reached full vampire maturity. He probably should've stuck around the mansion, what with his eldest brother Aldric gone on business and the middle one, Soren, under the thumb of that skanky voo-doo witch he'd brought home. Leila Doucet. Just thinking her name made his skin crawl. There was something seriously wrong with that female.

But the lure of a relaxing ride, of getting away from their plea-sure resort for a bit, had called to him. He had to laugh a little at the idea. What sane vampire actually looked forward to escaping from a constant feast of all the sex and blood he wanted? What was this restless longing in his soul, this urge to look for some-thing he couldn't name?

He shook his head at his own oddity. Whatever. He wouldn't be gone long.

The pungent aroma of the forest flooded his senses. Earth, pine, water—and animal. Warm, pulsing blood. Normally the scent would call to him, make his fangs itch, but something was off. The birds had stopped singing. Nothing moved.

Except a telltale footstep, not quite muffled in the under-growth. A creature walked here. Something very close . . . and fucking large. He drew his mount to a halt. Listened.

He felt a shift in the air. More footsteps crunched in the fallen leaves behind his shoulder. Coming closer. Shit. What the hell was it? The horse quivered, straining at the bit, eager to be gone. Probably a good idea.

"All right, boy. Let's go." He lifted the reins.

The staggering blow caught him square in the chest, sending him flying from the saddle as the horse squealed in fright. He landed hard on his back and lay stunned for a moment, wondering what had happened, listening to the pounding hooves of his mount fade away.

He rolled painfully to his hands and knees, then stilled, heart in his throat. Right in front of his hands were two paws the size of footballs. Slowly, his eyes crept upward, taking in the furred, enormous shape of the thing towering over him.

More than nine feet tall, it stood erect on two strong hind legs. The broad torso expanded into a thick chest and arms with claws like rapiers on the end of its fingers.

And its face.

Yellow, narrowed wide-set eyes glowed down on him with malice. Dark fur surrounded the face and the long black muzzle, which was full of teeth as long as steak knives.

A werewolf. Not a shifter changed into his full wolf, but a werewolf in half-form, which was on average three feet taller than a man and a third again as broad. The deadliest creature on two legs.

"Should've gone for the horse," it growled. "But you'll fill my belly well enough, vampire."

Luc's brain short-circuited. On his knees, he froze, mouth open, unable to utter a sound. The werewolf bent, grabbed him firmly by the arms, and lifted him clear off the ground. Rational thought fled Luc. He stared at the muzzle of the beast in mute terror, shaking his head. Fetid breath fanned inches from his face, the beast's canines gleaming in the darkness.

Mentally he reached out, his silent cry slicing through time and distance.

No! Oh, gods, help me—

The wolf's huge jaws clamped down where his neck and shoulder met, crushing bone and muscle. The thing shook him like a rag doll. A warm rush of blood splattered his clothing and face, and he was slammed to the ground. On his back, he could only gape in stark horror as the beast crouched over him, lowering its great head to feast on his flesh.

Sharp teeth and claws ripped into his throat and chest, and suddenly his brain shut down. Blessedly, he felt nothing more. A strange quiet enveloped him, and he floated outside himself, disembodied, no longer a part of the pain. Oblivion was the only defense left to a man being eaten alive.

Before the darkness took him, he saw an angel. Over the wolf's shoulder, the woman appeared from nowhere. She was tall and strong, with thick hair the color of dark honey pulled back into a braid. A great sword was gripped in one hand, and with a fierce expression on her angular face, she swung at the beast while emitting a harsh battle cry, sending the beast's head flying.

She moved to squat beside Luc, and she stared at him with something like awe. "Easy, Luc. You're going to be all right." A soft hand stroked his brow.

But it was too late for him. He didn't even have the voice to whisper his thanks to her.

Aldric. Soren. I'm so sorry.

Blackness closed over his head, and he knew nothing more.

No! Oh, gods, help me—

The man's terrified cry exploded in Kassandra's brain, taking her breath away. Stumbling, she put out a hand and steadied herself against a tree. Got her bearings.

She'd traveled south, teleporting to a wooded area on a resort located on the outer edge of New Orleans. She'd known she was getting close, had sensed someone else nearby. But she'd expected to find the male dead already, not to arrive as the poor bastard was being attacked and meeting his prophesied end.

Before she thought it through, she raced toward the sounds of a struggle, dodging brush and fallen limbs. As she reached a small clearing, the sight ahead filled her with horror. The biggest werewolf she'd ever seen was crouched over his victim, claws and teeth shredding skin. Ripping at the man, shaking him as though he weighed nothing. Was nothing but food.

It wasn't her fight. She had a job to do. Yet for some reason, her vision was awash in red—the crimson of rage. The beast was merely doing what it must to survive, but all that mattered to her was the man pinned to the ground, limbs flailing helplessly against one so much stronger.

Suffering a hideous death.

A loud war cry erupted from the depths of her soul, and before she considered the consequences, she launched herself across the space separating her from the target. The werewolf never saw the blade coming as she swung it over her head, cutting downward in a graceful arc. Its head went flying and the big body slumped to the side. Kicking it aside, she dropped her sword, crouched over the vampire—and gasped.

By the gods above, he was beautiful. An angel. A shiny cap of shaggy blond hair fell around a face that belonged on a cover model. Big blue eyes stared up at her in shock as he struggled to breathe. Beneath the blood and the stench of death, his sweet, natural scent called to her. Imprinted on her senses as no other man's smell ever had.

"Easy, Luc. You're going to be all right." Stroking his brow, she watched as his eyes fluttered closed. Desperation squeezed her heart. Shit—what was she going to do?

Indeed, very little could defeat a Valkyrie. Except finding the one special man she'd searched for these past two millennia.

And learning she was sworn to deliver that man—her mate—to his gilded prison upon his death.